LINE OF DECEIT

STEWART ROBBINS

Editing, design, typesetting and publishing by UK Book Publishing

www.ukbookpublishing.com

ISBN: 978-1-915338-84-6

Cover photo: Photo by Samuel Regan-Asante on Unsplash

LINE OF DECEIT

Chapter One

PC Winchester collar number 71630, was a six foot, stocky person with pale skin that went with most ginger people; he has been a full time police officer for three years now.

His ambition is to become, one day, a detective. PC Winchester worked out of Old Bow Street Nick, a local beat officer.

PC Winchester started off as a police Special in Essex for six years, waited for the recruitment to reopen for the Metropolitan police, applied and got in.

In his past he had been a fire officer for 17 years, finished his time as a fire investigation station officer. Single man, no family. The first day after training was June 2001. He passed his probation period very quickly due to his time as a Special. He would often team up with another officer, Reggie, old timer, 18 years he's been on the job. PC Reggie was a 5'8" man, average build little pot belly, jet back hair. Very laid back, almost horizontal.

PC Winchester felt very privileged to be working out of this old, antiquated station, it was brimming with history and old stories, pictures on the walls of back in the day, old officers looking timeless.

Due to a shortage of officers all over the capital, PC Winchester was temporarily transferred to another station to help out for four months – the government had cut numbers and not recruited, the bad guys had more than doubled and the police had lost ten thousand officers. Gang crime was on the increase, so was burglary.

What seemed to happen when the American TV shows started trends around gangs and other stuff, it seemed a few months later the UK was seeing a re-enactment on the streets.

He was placed at Notting Hill Gate police station. Winchester lived in Epping, Essex, so the good thing for him was this is a free train journey door to door on the Central line. Getting the first train out in the morning on early shift about 5:00am.

PC Winchester's first early shift at the new station was a Monday morning on a cold winter November morning 05:00 sitting on the train. On this train were sat three other people, and two cleaners were working their way along the train carriage cleaning. They had cloths and small spray bottles the size of a one-pint milk bottle. He thought to himself how strange they had different colour labels on each bottle. Just before them was a cleaner dressed in a London Underground uniform with a bin bag, picking up papers and old tins etc, but the other two just stayed in the carriage.

PC Winchester just asked one of the cleaners, "What sort of stuff do you use to clean the handle that hangs from the ceiling?"

This thin, very pale man, short black hair, black boiler suit on and plastic-looking black gloves, looked hard back at him and quietly spoke: "Just household detergents. We use this one with a red tag to clean the upright handles and the blue tag for the drop handles."

This was not suspicious to Winchester as he had never been on the train this time of the morning and it was the first train out as well. The other cleaner looked very uneasy; they spoke to each other and got off the train as the driver said we are now departing. "This is an Epping to Ealing Broadway train."

PC Winchester thought to himself that they had only got this carriage done as they walked off the train – unless others were on the train as well and they just had one carriage each to do.

The Central line cuts right through London – starts at the affluent area of Epping, not stereotyping at all; this is the opinion of PC Winchester and his observations. Working its way along picking up office people, bank and other blue collar workers, then it gets to Leytonstone, builders and cleaners get on; at Stratford you get the British rail passengers coming in from the suburbs getting on, then you reach Mile End interchange station for the Metropolitan and District lines again mixing all sorts of demographics, then the train moves along to Liverpool Street. It seems more people get off than on at this stage of their journey, office workers and a large amount of construction workers due to some of the major building projects in the area. From this point on the train starts to empty, for shops and offices.

This is also true from the other end of the Central line, West Ruislip, cutting through working class areas and some not so affluent areas. PC Winchester was well known for his attention to detail, which frustrated his colleagues and senior officers. PC Winchester, if not in uniform, would not look like your typical police officer. He did not hold himself like a person with authority. In fact, he was an unassuming man. Thinning red hair with an athletic body, just under six foot. Very pale, almost ghostly-like apart from his millions of freckles, deep voice. Very distinct manner when he spoke. He would always pause for a second before he would answer you, almost to the point you want to fill the air space yourself. Made people who did not know him unsure. He would look directly into your eyes when he spoke to you; it was like he was rummaging around in your head.

The shift pattern PC Winchester was on was: one week seven days early 0600 till 1800 then day off, back to 1800 to 0600 lates and four days off. His everyday partner PC Reggie, a veteran, was the right person to help and guide PC Winchester. Reggie had been there done it before, what he did not know about real policing was not worth knowing. The rest of the shift, this week in the mornings, PC Winchester did not see the two people cleaning again, but he saw the other cleaners with the bin bags working through the train.

A few weeks later when he was on his first early shift again, he was sitting at Epping station waiting for the train to move off. As always, the two people with bin bags with LU jumpers on, but two other cleaners on his carriage dressed like the other cleaners he had seen before, this time they seemed to have four bottles of cleaning stuff spraying the handles and supporting poles. PC Winchester looked at them and did not say a word, he just watched. The first cleaner, a female, she looked very wrong for a cleaner. Sorry if this is stereotypical but her hair was very well groomed, her eyebrows were very well trimmed and lined, her face was half covered with a medical grade mask for protection against cleaning products, she spoke very softly to the other person and it sounded like a private school voice. She had yellow and green tags on her all-white spray bottles, but the other two bottles seemed to have no tagging, just numbers; they all had a little trigger spray attachment on them; they were also colour coded. It seemed very methodical the way they both went through the carriage.

The driver announced over the train speakers: "This is a Central line train to West Ruislip, doors are closing." They both got off but what Winchester did see through the carriage inter-joining doors of the carriage was two others in the next carriage getting off too. They walked across the platform to another waiting train that was going to be the second train out of this station in 15 minutes. PC Winchester's inquisitive mind was beginning to play tricks in his head. 'Why would they not just rush through the train? They did not look to me like cleaners, most cleaners I've seen and dealt with often just have cheap working clothes, they looked like they were dealing with a chemical spill.' He could just not shake off this feeling something was not right, it was being done with the train operator's agreement or they would be picked up on CCTV. They did not look like terrorists as they would be picked up very quickly by the transport police and they would be all over it. It was bugging Winchester all day. 'What's going on?' he thought. 'I have got to get to the bottom of this.' But for the next few early shifts they were not on the train at all; in fact, that got him thinking more – 'did I spook them when I said something?'. Winchester spoke to Reggie who said, "Your imagination is getting the best of you. You want to be a detective so much, you are inventing your own cases."

Reggie had a big smile on his face. It was a strange day; they both were on foot patrol when they got a call to a sudden death at Mile End station. It was about 09:00 in the morning. The paramedics were already at the station, they saw the cars outside, transport police were there. Winchester and Reggie were just helping out, so they would be able to contact the next of kin. The paramedics said, "We think he had a heart attack." He was on the platform covered over as the trains were not allowed to stop and went right past slowly. You could see all the people standing looking out the windows trying to see what was going on.

"Heart attack?" Reggie said with a questioning tone. "He looked about 30 years old."

"Just what we thought," one of the paramedics said, "bit young, but the people who helped him off the train said he was clutching his chest. Looked very clammy and grey."

Winchester and Reggie put the report in their notebooks and asked what hospital would he be going to – "Whitechapel".

They looked for some ID on him, name was Norman Storm, he was married with two kids, worked in the city for a fund management company. They passed this information on to Epping police station to give the family the news. But they had no one at this time to go and see the family. This was not good as his company would be possibly ringing his home soon to see why he was not at work. The desk sergeant called them both up on the radio point to point – "Could you both go to the home address and speak to the families. Now please."

Winchester and Reggie looked at each other, and rolled their eyes back knowing what was going to happen – stood on the platform waiting for an Epping train, not knowing what the situation of the family is, young children would possibly be involved as he was a youngish man. They both got on the train heading back down to Epping. It was about a 25-minute walk to the house from the station. The road it was in seemed to have properties with gates, large houses set well back off the road. They arrived at two large dark oak gates, 112 the number, only one way in and out. Victorian brick house with two tall chimneys. On one of the gate pillars was an intercom. Winchester pushed it, and a female voice came over the intercom: "Hello, can I help you?"

"Yes, I am PC Winchester with PC Reggie from the Metropolitan police. Can we come in?"

The woman's voice changed to a quivering "yes ok".

The gate gave a little crack sound as it started to open very slowly. Both the officers walked through, the main front door of the house was about 25 metres away from the gate. A very slight blonde woman in her 20s was standing looking very apprehensive as they both walked towards her. PC Reggie took off his helmet as did Winchester.

"Can we come in?"

"Oh yes, what's going on, what's happened?"

"Can we confirm your name?"

"Mrs Kate Storm."

"Can we go to the main room?"

She nervously walked in-front of them knowing bad news would be coming. Then a man appeared in a track suit. "Hello darling, what's going on?"

She said, "I don't know."

"Hello officers, how can we help?"

"Sorry, sir," Winchester said, "what's your name?"

"Oliver Storm. Why?"

"Do you know Norman Storm?"

"Yes," Oliver said, "it was my father, he died ten years ago."

Winchester and Reggie had a good picture in their minds what the person looked like – delivering bad news is really hard on everybody and officers alike.

"Would you excuse me for a few minutes?" Winchester said as he walked out into the hallway, leaving Reggie with the silence. Winchester spoke to HQ on this identification mix up. He was told to hold on, a point to point will be coming. Just as soon as the operator completed that sentence his radio sounded with no caller ID.

The voice said, "Hi this is DCI Max Walters, serious crime team New Scotland Yard."

"Yes, Gov."

"Is this PC Winchester?"

"Yes, Gov."

"What I need you to do now is to speak to the people you are with and say this is a terrible misunderstanding and Oscar Foxtrot now please."

The two people in the main reception room looked very unsure as to what was going on. Winchester looked at Reggie and said to them all, "That was our control, there's been a terrible mix up. On behalf of the Metropolitan Police, we are very sorry."

Oliver just looked very red and angry. "What the fucking hell has been going on? Me and my wife have been having all sorts of thoughts going through our minds, what bloody stress would you have put my wife through if I was not here. I am not bloody happy."

PC Winchester and PC Reggie just looked at them and said, "All we can say is we are very sorry."

"Is that it, sorry? Get out of our house please, now."

As soon as they exited the house, Reggie said, "What was that all about..."

"Some DCI called me up and said 'just get out of the house and leave it'."

"Oh, that's great, make us look like a bunch of Nuts."

As they walked along talking, the radio point to point call came through from the sergeant. "Sorry, lads, for the mess up, apparently wrong ID was given. See you both back at station, the DI wants to talk with you."

Winchester said to Reggie, "They have already made the complaint about us, not our fault."

Reggie said, "There was no mix up on the ID."

"Why do you say that?"

"I took the information off the driving licence."

"That's right, you did."

They both got back to the Nick. "The DI is in interview room 5 waiting for you."

"Oh. Sergeant, can we have cup of tea first?"

"Yes they have one in there for you."

"Oh really?" This must be bad. Winchester and Reggie looked at each other with worried eyes.

They both went up to the third floor, which housed all the officers and professional standards. You only normally went up there for rollickings or rollickings – plods avoided this floor. As they both walked down the corridor towards the DI's office, the DI popped his head round the door and said, "Come on, lads, tea is getting cold."

This now really made them both extremely nervous. They walked into this big office, with a light oak desk with a round matching table for meetings, six chairs, his big leather throne chair behind his desk. Low level coffee table with four brown cloth seats.

"Sit down, lads. So you are Winchester, yes, and you must be Reggie, a veteran officer? This is not a rollicking, it's a discussion around what happened today. You see the person's house you went to was a protected person; this cannot leave this room. He was and still is very high up in the government research and he has been targeted before from animal rights groups. You would not have known this because he is in the Essex police area."

Winchester said, "Well we got a call to help out at the Mile End station, heart attack of a person. Reggie looked for any ID, he found his wallet with his driver's licence and his name. His bank cards also had his name on them. No pictures, his paper licence was very new looking. Transport police said they would not be doing the welfare call on the family and Sergeant asked the Essex police but they did not get back to him. This was going to come out on the news maybe, so we went along to deliver the news. Then we find out it was not him."

Reggie said, "We did everything by the book, sir."

"Yes, you did, officers, yes you did. Well, we have now handed it to MI5. This is a security matter now. Do you have any questions both of you?"

Winchester said, "Just one, sir, yes."

The DI looked hard at him.

"Why did the dead man have a dead person's ID?"

For a second the DI looked taken aback. "If I knew that, officer, I would be the Chief constable by now with that sort of insight. Thank you for coming. Lads, take the biscuits down to the Sergeant, they will only go to waste."

Reggie said, "What was all that about?"

"Don't know!"

"How bizarre, don't you think?"

Winchester said, "Better report for statements to be done to the Sergeant, he will be pissed off if we don't do the MG11 statements."

Winchester and Reggie walked into the Sergeants' room. Two other divisional sergeants were also in this office.

"HELLO SARGE, we been given these biscuits for this office." Before they hit the desk they were all gone, a big pack of digestives. "We will complete the statements on today from our notebooks."

"NO, lads, that is not required on this occasion."

Both the officers looked at each other. "Really?"

"Yes and give me your notebooks." Reggie and Winchester handed them over. The Sergeant got out a black marker pen and put black lines through the relevant pages so you could not read the words – this is not a done thing, even if you cross something out you still must be able to read what was written down. Then the Sergeant signed and dated the books. "Right, go to admin and get your new notebooks. Take them and hand them over; they will be kept as always, just in case you need something from them, okay." This is so off the wall.

They both got two new notebooks.

"Reggie, I don't like this you know how important our books are."

Reggie said, "They said we can come back any time if we need anything from the book."

"Yes I know, but something is not right."

Reggie shook his head. "You see too many conspiracies behind every door. It was probably a covert operation and we stumbled on it with our size 10 boots."

"Speak for yourself," Winchester said, "I am size 11 and six foot two and I have a big willy too." They both started to laugh.

They were both on late shift for the next five days, starting on a Thursday this time, so fight night Friday and Saturday outside bars and pubs were the nights taken up. Crew up with others in the vans waiting for the call to fights, then go and help other officers. A lot of the specials would do most of the fight nights. Winchester and Reggie were picked up outside the Bow station; other police officers were from Ilford, Romford and Stratford nicks. They had all been briefed by the Sergeants in the vans; in this van Sergeant Stiff, Barking nick sergeant. The reason for such a big turnout was the end of term, July, this is when the young lads and girls have the night out celebrating end of the school for them and Saturday was always busy with people off their heads on a warm night. Heat and alcohol do not work well together. Our call sign was VG11. Stands for Van Guard.

Six of the officers on board were trained for rioting and carried shields and everything, the rest of them were cannon fodder. Sitting around for the first few hours was the norm, nothing to write home about, they did a few traffic stops. Especially if it was a high-end car just to have a look inside really.

"Reggie, what's the procedure to get some information from our old notebooks?"

"Just go to admin, they will let you photocopy the pages you need but if you need it for court they will give it to you sign for it and return later. Why?"

"You know I nicked that drunk driver a few months back, his case has come up and I have to give evidence on why I stopped him."

The evening for both of them was quiet for a change – just one person nicked and that was to get an officer his first arrest, so he could caution someone under pressure. Some of the new recruits say the wrong things on the first one, they often start with the American one, you have the right to remain silent. Or the person you are nicking has been nicked many times before and they can smell out a new officer. They say, "It's ok, mate, I know it inside out." Get back to the Nick and the custody sergeant said did you caution the accused. With the knowing look of 'I know what is coming', and before the officer can say anything, the well-versed guy will say "no, he didn't". This is when the Sergeant will look down his nose at you. "Better do it now then" – as he knows you will not make the same mistake again because if you did you would get a roasting you would not believe.

PC Winchester was due in court Tuesday 02:30 in afternoon hearing time; this was at a magistrates court. Tuesday was when Winchester and Reggie's early shift would start. At 05:00 Winchester was sitting on the first train out of the platform, sitting waiting for the train to leave. The cleaner was coming through the train cleaning up paper with his gloved hands.

Winchester said, "Your other people cleaning the handles not doing anything today?"

The middle-aged man looked at him and said, "I am the only cleaner at this station. I do all the trains, me and the girl on the other train over there."

Winchester could see a girl in her 20s walking through the train with bin liner, picking up stuff. "So, who are the others I see sometimes cleaning up?"

"Oh, the boffins, no they're not cleaning, they are scientists, they make sure that the trains are checked for bugs – we had them in a few years ago. We had passengers complaining about rashes and itching, turns out the seats had been infested with some sort of bug. Most probably from some of the homeless that sleep on the seats. I must get on as the train leaves soon."

"Oh," Winchester called out, "how often they do that then?"

"I think once a month." The cleaner hopped on to the next carriage.

In Winchester's mind that still did not sit right. 'Maybe they were jumpy when I spoke to them because if it got out about bugs in the cloth seats the public would be a little upset. Oh well,' Winchester thought to himself.

Today Winchester would have to stay at the police station to help on the front desk as he would be going to court for the hearing and admin opens up at 0900 to get his notebook, as he has to read everything from his book in court. Reggie was out with the response team doing warrants, the Sergeant did the morning briefing: six still in custody, six warrants this morning, they have over the past few months had six people jump on the tracks on the underground. Transport police are asking for our help in speaking to relatives, because they have not had this cluster of people doing this before in the history of the underground. Starting next week, Winchester and Reggie, you are both dealing with this – "Yes SARGE".

Reggie nudged Winchester and whispered, "your first detective job" with a grin on his face.

"Winchester, you are at court today, so he is helping front desk. Be safe, lads, now 'Oscar foxtrot'. Sorry, lads, forgot to say this: we have a new chief inspector and he is walking the beat today. You know that means changes is coming again very soon."

Everyone just rolled their eyes to the heavens. This happens all the time, the waste of money. The station gets a good system running then a new Government, then we change again. Winchester went to the front desk. The desk was manned by police staff now, not police officers. But sometimes when someone was on light duties you are behind the desk or with the custody Sergeant. That's not good getting anal searches and cleaning up sick, or just getting into a fight with drunks. Or if you get court so you don't get tied up in a job behind front desk.

The new CI, Karen Austin, she was an Essex officer, took the job in the Met. Hard person was the rumour. Said it as it was. Did not tolerate fools, the word went round. Not very tall, say 5' 6", black short hair and teeth so white and filled her mouth Jaws would have been proud to own them.

Winchester sat next to Jeff. This man had issues, if a cold was going around he would get it. If smallpox was in the country, he would get it. Tell you what, if you saw him getting on a plane, don't get on with him. At this time, he was suffering from a cold sore. Winchester could see it from 50 feet away in the back office; it was massive on his lip, also pink eye. The front desk was just two tables put together, glass full height screen like a bank. Seating area for people to report stuff.

The first person through the door was a young lad walked up, looked about 18 years old, baseball cap on, grey tracksuit and white trainers, said, "I got a 7-day producer from some Cop. Here's my stuff, insurance and licence; I can't find my MOT." He looked at Jeff and said, "Fuck me, man, that looks bad, you sucked something to give you that, man?"

Winchester did not know whether to laugh or keep looking forward.

Jeff said in a dead pan voice, "It's a cold sore."

"Mate, get it sorted, bro, it's a monster," and walked out.

The next person in line was Malcom. A frequent flyer. Always keeps an eye out on everything, he was a one man community watch. "Hello officer, I'd like to report a man and woman having sex in a car out in their driveway."

"When was this?"

"Last night, it was about 1230 am. I was walking Norman my dog, I could see this car in a drive all fogged up so I went to see what was wrong with the car. They were having sex; it went on for some time, at least an hour and 10 minutes, I timed it."

Winchester had to ask: "Is it outside your house?" – "no" – "Is it close to your house?" – "no, it's about three roads away, I always walk my dog late at night; my dog don't like walking when other people are around, he is nervous."

"How did you know this went on for more than an hour?"

"I kept my eye on them."

Winchester looked at Jeff, Jeff looked at Winchester. Winchester said, "So you timed them and kept an eye on them?"

Dead straight face, Malcolm said, "Yes, that's right."

"Well, sir, you see it's on their land, ie drive, and it's dark; there's not much we could do about it, to be honest."

"Well I could have been school kids going to school."

Winchester said, "I don't think school operates at them sort of times, sir. If they had been doing that in the day by all means let us know, sir."

His voice was very flat and monotoned and grated in your head.

"Oh, sir, be careful because if they see you looking in the car on their drive, it could turn very nasty. We could be arresting you for trespassing."

He was a small man, very slight.

Winchester said to Jeff, "I've got to go to Admin to get my old notebook for court today."

Jeff nodded. Admin was two floors up. He went up, walked in, saw the person he had given the book to a few weeks ago. "Hi, I am PC Winchester, I need to get my old notebook for court today."

"Okay, fill out the paperwork for me to get it, I'll need your name and collar number plus the dates reasons you need it."

Winchester gave Megan, who was the head of admin, the information form completed. She was gone for about 15 minutes, then came back sort of red-faced. "Sorry your notebook is gone."

Winchester said, "Sorry? It's gone?"

"Yes, two notebooks are gone; a PC Reggie and yours."

"I need it, I will have to let the inspector know about this."

Megan said this not ever happened in the ten years I have been running this department and I know where they were as I placed them in the correct location myself."

Winchester was a bit taken aback. "Okay," Winchester said, "I will also have to let my Sergeant know. Going to court without the notebook was a bit of a wing-it sort of thing – 'they will see I have not got it'.

Winchester called his Sergeant.

"You will have to tell the Prosecutors when you get to court."

Winchester headed off to the court early and spoke to the prosecutor who would be dealing with it. He looked at Winchester with a frown. "It can't be helped. Let me speak to the defence lawyer." He walked off to the other end of the court where the lawyers seem to congregate, sorting out deals before they go into the courtroom. He was about five minutes, then came back and said, "We have dropped the case, you can go."

"NO, that cannot be right." Winchester's eyes fixed on the drink-driver sitting at the other end of the waiting area in his suit, head down looking at the floor.

"What is not right is your notebook's missing, you will have to explain that to the Clerk of the court and that will not go down very well. This was a prolific drink drive case against this young thug, he knew he was going down for it."

He said things to Winchester at the time that incriminated himself because he was a little drunk, this led the police to a garage full of stolen goods, but now he was saying he knew the garage that had this stuff in was someone else's and he was giving me a tip-off.

PC Winchester watched as his lawyer told him what had been agreed.

"Yes!" the little shit shouted out and looked at PC Winchester with a grin.

On his face, the only thing that PC Winchester knew was that this skid mark on society was going to keep going till he was caught. Believe you me, as he was walking down to the front of the court to leave, two detectives from Croydon arrested him for burglary. PC Winchester went over to them and said, "Thank god, I thought he'd got away with it today."

"Well, it was your Sergeant called us, we knew he was in court today and most probably would get time; we would have gone to the prison and charge him when he was coming out in about six months. We was told about a lost notebook."

The accused looked very dejected and the grin was gone from his face. They had him down for five burglaries and one assault leading to the loss of one eye on an 80-year-old man in his home. Good five years, one can only hope.

Winchester went back to station, on his way he point to point with Reggie: "Hello mate," Reggie said, "how long did he get?"

"They had to throw out the case, but luckily the lads at Croydon got him."

"Why?"

"Because our notebooks are missing."

"What?"

"Yep, they are both missing. See you back at the NICK."

"I am on my way back," Reggie said. "We have nicked a fail to appear on a warrant, so will be in the custody area."

As Winchester was heading back, his radio was sounding for a point to point but strangely no caller ID – this would be only someone in the Rat team, they got called this because they were the officers who investigated other officers, but Winchester's view was they were good to have, because of the days of the 70s and 80s.

CHAPTER ONE

"Hello, this is Inspector 'Holiday' E10 division. This is about your missing notebooks, we have been tasked with tracking them down. Can you come to my office after shift, I will be in the interview room 4 and I have also contacted Officer Reggie; he will also be meeting me at the same time. See you then." They were based some place in central London.

Winchester was on the bus heading back to station, when this man who looked in his 50s, slight of build, jumped up and started shouting at this young woman in her 20s, calling her a slag and a tart.

Winchester stood looking at him to see if he would notice a police officer was sitting on the bus – no, he was focused on swearing at her.

Winchester said, "Sir, can you calm down."

"Fuck you, pig!"

"That is so out of date," PC Winchester said in a deep voice.

Winchester had started to move towards him when he pulled out a knife.

"Step back, pig, or I will change your face."

Having no appointments on him, nothing, not even cuffs. Why we travel to court with nothing, it was silly. We have a bloody uniform on – anyone can see.

Winchester looked at him directly into his eyes, the bus driver looked in his mirror as he was coming to a set of lights. Winchester was holding on to the handrail firmly and other passengers were getting very, very upset. The driver slammed on the brakes, and as he did the man fell backwards and Winchester moved forward, went for the hand with the knife; it was a risky move. The driver had also set off his silent alarm in the cab so police would have been mobilised. Winchester headbutted the man right on the nose – this was the best option that would incapacitate him with his vision. The bus driver opened the doors as people filed quickly off. Members of the public offered to help but PC Winchester said, "No, it's ok, thanks."

Winchester had this idiot now face down, one arm really pushed hard up his back, the bone had gone crack. The elbow was dislocated, the male was screaming in pain calling him all the names under the sun. Winchester could hear the response units coming, a welcome sound as three cars and a van pulled up. Officers piled through the doors like the cavalry – thank god, Winchester thought, longest six minutes of his life to date. The knife was bagged, the suspect was bounced off the bus into the van and gone. Officers were very concerned about Winchester when they saw blood on his shirt.

"I think it was when I headbutted him." Winchester was told to sit down till the ambulance crew saw him.

"I am good," he said.

An inspector from Mile End station got on the bus. "Winchester, you ok, son?"

He nodded.

"We've been looking for that prick for months, he's wanted on five accounts of sex attacks that we know of."

Winchester was still shaken, his hands were trembling as the adrenaline pumped through his body.

"I know you took him down, son, but can we have the collar, do good for our figures?"

"Yes, Gov."

"Good. I will let your inspector know how helpful you are. PC Willo–" an officer standing at the door of the bus– "take PC Winchester back to his station for me, would you?"

"Yes, Sir."

"Thanks."

When he got back to the station the Sergeant just said, "What is it with you, lad, trouble just follows you?"

"Yes, it seems to, SARGE."

"You did a good thing giving Inspector the nicking. He had a grin on his face. Not sure Chief Inspector Aston will be happy about that, though." He winked at Winchester. "Four more hours to end of shift. Reggie and you, can you go and give some inspiration to some scouts, they have some badges they need when they are dealing with the community. They need to know what to look out for, when they visit people's homes and Care homes. A few words about crime would help, it's an easy end to the day, show yourselves on community work and the control will only call you up for urgent assistance."

Reggie said, "I still can't believe our books have been misplaced, not so bad for me, my book was new anyway... nothing that would be needed in court, that is. One good thing when the Sergeant carries out his notebook inspections, I will not get my ears bent, this time all up to date so there is a positive."

But it would just not go away, it kept getting into Winchester's head – why our books, why? Even the admin manager said it's the first time she has ever known it to happen. Well the Sergeant did not seem too fussed.

Winchester said, "Don't we have a meeting with some person from the Rat team?"

The Sergeant said, "Not now as Inspector Aston hit the roof them contacting you directly; watch this space, lads, off you go."

Chapter Two

It had been a busy few weeks on shifts due to the demonstrations about something or other. Winchester said to Reggie, "I think this month we've dealt with, No to war, No to poverty, No to newspapers invading people's privacy."

"Oh yes."

"NO to NO demonstration."

Reggie laughed. "We have a few days off now, what you doing?" Reggie said to Winchester.

Winchester look puzzled as he looked down the corridor of the police station that led to the mess room. "I know that face from somewhere."

Reggie looked behind him. "Sorry, mate, have not got a clue what you are on about."

"I know," Winchester said loudly, "on the platform, when we was at that male body, Mile End, remember the one we had to go to Epping?"

"Yes, I remember the body."

"Well, yes he was standing with the transport police officers. Why is he here?"

Reggie said, "They are always here. Remember we have about six jumpers a year on that bloody platform."

"Yes, you're right, it's my imagination getting the better of me since our books went missing."

Reggie said, "You still on about them bloody notebooks!"

A few weeks went by and Winchester was back on his early shift, this time when he was sitting on the train he saw the same two people doing the same thing as before, but this time when they saw Winchester they spoke to each other and got off the train and walked down the platform and got on another carriage. Winchester was intrigued. Winchester got up and also walked down and got on the train a carriage back so he could see them through the adjoining carriage's dirty window.

It was fascinating to watch them – they were very methodical about what they did. The tall, thin man with like a dark factory work coat sort of a trench coat, had three plastic bottles with spray attachments, each one this time with a big black marking, Q7, Q9, QK 2; the other person was short and slimmer, very pale face, had the same bottles; and they both had latex gloves on. Each time they did the handrail they had this little dark brown notebook; they wrote something in it. What Winchester could make out was the Q9 was used on the standing pole handrails, Q7 was on the overhead handles, but QK2 seem to be sprayed on the disabled reserved seats by the doors. Winchester thought to himself it must be to keep them disinfected.

The two men went through the carriage very quickly, got off the train and seemed to write down something they looked at on the side of the carriage; Winchester was sure it was the carriage number. This was really odd behaviour.

When Winchester got to the station, he pulled Reggie aside. "Guess what I saw today?" Winchester went into explaining what he had seen.

Reggie looked at Winchester. "You know what, mate, you have a very vivid mind. They are bloody cleaners""

Winchester said, "Should I take this to CI Aston?"

"What, and get sent to look after lost property for a few days?!"

"Maybe you are right. But Reggie, when they saw me they got off the train and moved to another carriage."

"If you kept looking at me, I would get off and move away from you as well," Reggie said with a grin on his face. "I would think you are the local nutter that speaks to everyone, you know what I mean, no eye contact sort of person."

Over the next few mornings Winchester kept his notes on what they both were doing on the early morning trains. The same two people every time. But on the last day of his early shift, on the carriage Winchester always sat on, were two men dressed in very posh suits, not the sort of suits you see this time of the morning. They looked military types, shoes polished so you could see your face in them, short back and sides haircuts. Both of them six-footers, well built too. They both sat opposite Winchester. You could see Winchester was either a police officer or security guard. But this time of the morning most likely a police officer.

They both looked at Winchester, said, "Morning, it's a cold morning."

Winchester said, "Yes, it is," as he was looking for the cleaning people again.

"Looking for something, mate?" one of them said.

Winchester said, "No, not really," waiting for the train to move off. No cleaning people on the train today, Winchester thought to himself.

Winchester looked at the two men and thought to himself they are off someplace in the city, they looked like MI5 sorts.

Winchester got to the police station and swiped his ID card through the police staff entrance, only to catch a glimpse of the two men on the train walking to the lift, heading up to the top floor. I knew it, Winchester thought, they are MI5 boys.

In the briefing room Reggie and Winchester and the rest of the shift were getting the day's works assignments with the Sergeant, when CI Aston walked in.

"Morning, ma'am, what can we do for you, ma'am?" the Sergeant said.

"I need to speak to PC Winchester and PC Reggie in my office after the morning briefing."

When she left the Sergeant said, "What have you two been bloody up to"

They both shrugged their shoulders.

They both went upstairs to CI Aston's office again. "Come in, both of you. The deputy chief constable has given me a new project and for some reason they want you two to do it."

"Us two, Reggie said, "why?"

"I don't ask the questions, I just do the job like you will."

"Yes, ma'am."

"As of today you both are on NPT, neighbourhood patrol team. So this will be from 0900 till 1900, four days on two days off. You will work with two others and the Sergeant will be Alan Busterball, 25 years in the job, old school. I don't know how you both got this easy job – it's for the long-term lads wanting to have an easy life and cuff off work. But you both got it, words from upstairs. Your last shift today with your team, but I am still your CI – got it?"

They both nodded. Reggie was happy, big smile on his face. He knew if he was not with Winchester he would not've got this job as it was for the long-term coppers, seen as the retirement run in but not very good for your career. Winchester did not want this.

"Reggie, when I saw them two suits this morning heading upstairs and now we have got this easy job, I think this is something to do with what is going on – the books missing and the person found on the platform and this morning they sat opposite me on the train."

Reggie looked at Winchester and said, "Mate, no more getting up at silly o'clock, four days on two off, what is there not to like?! I am really happy."

Winchester knew that Reggie did not put in for this before because he and Winchester really got on well and Reggie had had some wrong partnerships before. Reggie was once going to leave the job, but after a few weeks with Winchester got his mojo back.

Reggie said, "Let's get breakfast at the old greasy spoon." This was a café called the cop shop café, all the police from miles around come to it for lunchtime, breakfast and lates. It stayed open 24 hours. It was a supergrass who had started it, believe it or not, saw it as full-time protection. Officers night and day using it and he was a good cook too. Often you would see the SO19, crime squad and dogs team in the café as the dogs were allowed in. It was funny once a load of drunk thugs came in, it was late, say 1 am, they were noisy till they sat down and saw that every table had a police officer at it, they went from 10 decibels to 1... They were so drunk they did not even see the big German Shepherd looking at them, licking his lips. Word did get round, no one really came in, only police. It had about 40 seats and pictures of old criminals on the wall like the Kray twins, and old police stations, a few other bits including some signed pictures from cop shows, like The Sweeney and The Bill. Also, it was a safe place: three great big bollards out the front, so no one could drive into the place, good CCTV and parking out the back that was floodlit. It's been known to be a place the informants could come to and give information and feel safe. They could come in through the back to a small area out of sight in the back. You never got any senior officers come here at all, only detective sergeants. Armed response team would come in all tooled up as always. This was the new canteen as most stations had lost their ones, the café had officers from Stratford, Whitechapel, Bow, Docklands and vans from all over other divisions if they had a demonstration to deal with in the city later. The tea was free with any meals and the meals were really cheap. The shopkeepers along that stretch of road never had any trouble – Winchester wondered why, with tongue in cheek.

They both sat down to a full English breakfast. Put themselves on the estates beat today. The area was full of drug dealers, money lenders and hookers; it had been left by the councils and let the people who lived there to get on with it and now they needed to try and win it back. This was a fruitless situation – they could see them coming for miles away, then they just kept their heads down. The police had had to deal with three murders on the estate in the last three months due to drug wars. People turning up to A&E with broken bones because they could not pay the £20 loan back that was now £500 after 10 days being late... Drug ODs three to four a week, no mugging because no one had anything. Never walk too close to the high rise building or you will get covered in all sorts of things coming from the windows. Even a TV once landed on top of one of the police vans. Police also knew that this was an area of undocumented people who did not even speak English. Police officers just paid lip service and the gangs who run this estate did the same to the police. Two of the bosses, Lee Roy and Micky Byrne told their people "never upset the coppers, be good to them, don't give them reasons to come after us or you"... Officers saw a gang of lads they never said a bad word to the police. Officers asked them to disperse, they did and as soon as they were gone they would come back as soon as the police moved on.

The fire brigade did not like coming on to the estate – they got half their kit nicked a good few times, even a ladder from the top of the engine once.

Winchester could not shake off this feeling that they had been moved for some reason – was it because of the body and something to do with the notebooks? It did cross his mind for a second. Was it because what he saw on the train, the people doing their thing that was so strange. No, he thought to himself, that one Winchester dismissed, that was right out of left field, the strange cleaners. Why have they both got this easy job, even the Sergeant commented, "Are you two in a lodge or something, or kissing someone's ring?"

After a few months of the NPT, things started to work. The people living on the main estate started to see the police were not leaving, a new satellite police station opened on the estate from 0900 till 1900, seven days a week and it was managed by six PCSOs. Winchester and Reggie would not operate from this place because this was okayed by the community liaison inspector – because PCSOs did not have the power of arrest they were seen as no threat, all sorts of people would just talk to them with so much intelligence on gangs and drugs and just talking about their day-to-day worries about what was going on. Council started to clean up as well; they put in a rapid response team for repairs, cleaning up rubbish and graffiti removal.

Reggie and Winchester were on a call to a person who'd collapsed at Liverpool Street station, it was off their beat but as every other officer was dealing with yet another demonstration, everywhere was short. I think this demo was to stop demonstrations from clogging up the roads. Or was it the climate people blocking up the road, creating loads of pollution? Winchester got the whole climate worries, but every time the government saw it as 'let's put up costs and taxes', that just upset everyone.

Winchester and Reggie were in the patrol car. As they pulled up outside the station there were two ambulances and a British transport police van and a body on the floor covered up and it was just outside the rail station; in fact, city police were closer than them. Reggie walked over to the paramedics, everyone just nodded at each other.

"What do we have here, lads?" Reggie asked.

"Young male, say 28 years old, looks like a massive heart attack, member of the public tried CPR but we got here say within eight minutes of call, we tried everything, nothing.

Winchester said to the transport officers, "We can take this if you like."

They did not need another reason to go; they were off.

It was outside the station. Anyway. The private ambulance was called and the doctor had just turned up to confirm death. Winchester walked over to the young man who had tried to carry out CPR. "Can I ask you a few questions?"

The young man was shaking and having a fag.

"What's your name first of all for the notebook?"

"Windy Miller."

Winchester looked at him hard. "Windy Miller?"

"Yes, I know, my mum named me. It's been the bane of my life."

"Date of birth?"

"10th May 1980."

"So you are about 21?"

"Yes, home address, Stock yard. Farm Epping."

"Can you tell me what happened?"

"Yes. I've known Steve Walnut, we work together for Quite Pharmaceuticals. He was fine when he got on the train at Epping, we was talking about football and the weekend ahead, then as we got to Liverpool Street station Steve said he felt like his chest was tight, he looked a little grey. As we walked out of the station here he just grabbed his chest, went down and smashed his head on the floor with a thud. I looked at him, he was not breathing so I started CPR, I am a life guard in the summer at the seaside."

"Do you know his home address?"

"Yes, it's 100 yards from my place. I know his mum and dad, my sister goes out with him, what am I going to say to them?"

"Nothing yet, sir," Winchester said, "leave it to us please. We will need to confirm his identity before we do anything. Do you have the phone number and address of your sister?"

"Yes I do – she lives at home with me and Mum and Dad."

Winchester could see this young man was very shaken. He asked the paramedic to have a look at him. Inspector Aston arrived at the scene, looking stern as always. "Can we get this cleaned up please and ensure we gather what we need. Is this suspicious or just what it looks like?" She walked past everyone to the doctor just looking at the body. "What do you think, Doc, heart attack?"

The doctor grunted. "I cannot be sure, but not foul play my first impression."

"Ok then, let the private ambulance service take the body. Have we confirmed his name and information?"

Reggie said, "We got his wallet, it has his new photo driver's licence. His address is on it."

Winchester also said, "Ma'am, this is his friend, they work together and his sister is the deceased's girlfriend."

"He is 28 years old, looking at his licence," Reggie said.

Aston said, "You and Reggie head off to the person's house before this gets out, take the friend with you."

Winchester got in the car with Reggie and Windy Miller. Winchester looked in the mirror of the car. He was starting to reverse to turn round when he saw the same two people that were cleaning the train, standing looking at what was going on, he was sure of it. He pulled up and went to get out of the car and Reggie said, "What you doing?"

Winchester said as he was half way out of the car, "Wait a minute, just seen someone." But as he got fully out of the car, they were gone. Winchester scanned the area but could not see them; hundreds of people were just mingling around.

Reggie said looking baffled as Winchester got back in the car, "What was all that about?"

"Nothing, speak to you later about it."

They all headed over to Epping through the morning traffic. Winchester could see in the rear view mirror the young lad was starting to understand what had just occurred. He nudged Reggie, gave him the eyes as if to say 'Look at the lad'.

Reggie started up a conversation. "Windy" – "my friends call me W" – "how long you known Steven?"

"All our lives, we have lived next door to each other always, we went to school and university, Cambridge, we both studied chemistry, we work for the big pharmaceutical company Quite, they are world leaders in their field; we both worked in the city office, promotions worldwide. My sister also works for the company, she is the head of biotechnology and monitoring the spread of viruses in the world.

Winchester's mind was still buzzing with questions, was he seeing things, or did they just look like the people on the trains. How could they be them? Plus, most of the time he could only see the top of their faces on the train as they wore face masks. His brain was hurting him. They got to the house; it was a big house: eight bedrooms, swimming pool. Both officers knew this because Windy did not stop talking about the house his friend lived in.

A man appeared from behind the wall, holding a pitchfork. "Can I help, officers?" When he saw Windy in the back the face on him changed from a smile to being very worried.

Reggie and Winchester got out of the car and asked his name. He kept looking directly at Windy in the back...

Winchester said, "Sir, are you Mr Walnut?"

"Yes, in fact, Lord Walnut. Why what's happened?"

"It's your son, sir, we need to speak with you."

"Tell me what's happened, now please," as his eye looked right into Reggie's soul.

Reggie said, "Is this your son's driver's licence?"

"Yes, yes, tell me what is bloody going on."

"I am afraid to tell you your son Steven collapsed and died this morning on his way to work."

"My god, my god!"

Winchester said, "Shall we go into the house?"

"Yes, yes. What am I going to say to LIV, his mum?" As they walked towards the house the door opened and a woman in her 50s, blonde and slight of build rushed out to greet us. "What's going on?"

Windy was walking behind, the father was in shock. "It's Steven, he's dead."

She stopped dead still as if someone had stunned her and she fainted to the ground. Her husband managed to half catch her. As they all were round trying to get LIV to her feet, a Range Rover pulled into the drive – it was the sister, she'd been riding. She pulled up, jumped out of the car in her horse riding clothes. She saw Windy and rushed over. "What's happening, Mum, Dad?" She was very, very confused.

Winchester said, "We must get inside and speak about this inside."

They all managed to get into the library at the front of the house, and the housekeeper came through.

Winchester explained everything to the family. "Your son Steven will be at Whitechapel hospital. We are so sorry for your loss, we really are."

Windy started to tell them what had happened and what he did. Windy's mum and dad came to the open front door too.

It was time to leave. Winchester and Reggie were just feeling sorry for the family as a young man with his life in-front of him gone in seconds. His father said he had just done a medical. He was thinking of doing the London marathon.

Winchester said to the father, "Your son was in pharmaceuticals?"

"Yes he works for my company, we are the leading company in the UK, Quite, the name of the company I am one of the founders."

"Just a question: did you know a Oliver Storm?"

"Yes, he is a board member of our company, his son was a friend of my son's too, why, what's that got to do with my son?"

"Nothing," Winchester commented. The father looked at Winchester with inquisitive eyes. Winchester and Reggie felt that there was nothing left they could do right now but leave the family to come to terms with this very sad situation.

Winchester said to Reggie, "Can you drive back, I got a lot on my mind right now, I can't seem to shake off the feeling. Something is not right here, two young males seemingly fit just died of heart attacks."

Reggie said, "Do you know how many people died every year in London from heart attacks?"

"No."

"Well, must be hundreds."

"I saw them well dressed military types from the train the other morning at the incident, I am sure of it, really sure of it."

On the way back they both got a call from the inspector asking again to come to the office at the end of shift. "What now?" Reggie said.

"Aston is a real stickler for paperwork them teeth she got, I been told if you can't see them you are in real trouble."

Both of them went right up to the second floor to Chief Inspector Aston's office and this time two well-dressed men were sitting in her office.

"Come in, this is PC Winchester and PC Reggie, this is two officers from special operations, New Scotland Yard."

They never said or offered their names, though this was not unusual, for the security services, as they were known as spooks. All ex-military types...

"They have some questions about the male you attended at Liverpool Street station today, did you see anything suspicious or not?"

"Right... yes," Winchester said. "It seemed the same as the young man at Mile End station."

"What do you mean?" one of the spooks said as he lent forward as he became very interested.

Reggie piped up and said, "Two well, fit young men died of suspicious heart attacks."

One of the spooks said, "Nothing suspicious about that, young and old people die every day from just that."

"But they both seemingly worked for the pharmaceutical companies."

Now they both seemed to lean forward. "What company?"

"Quiet is the name, I do believe."

The two men looked at each other and said, "It's nothing, just a coincidence, but we will look into it, thank you for your information; good police work."

'A bit patronising,' Reggie and Winchester thought.

The inspector seemed to get a nod from one of the suits and she said, "Thanks, you're both off shift now."

Reggie and Winchester took the hint, just got up and left. But before Winchester could say a word, Reggie said, "What the bloody hell was that about? In all the years I have been in this job, I've never seen so many suits or even spoken to them." He looked at Winchester and said, "You may have something, mate, this is beginning to look and feel odd."

Winchester always drove to the station and parked up and got on the train. As a police officer the cost of the parking was ok because of the free travel. He got to his car at Epping and a note was on the windscreen, under the window washers, but it had rained and it was unreadable – he could only read 'I will contact you soon', the rest was mush; it also could be on the wrong car – it has been known that hookers leave notes on cars for business.

Winchester got booked in for duty in the morning and Reggie was already dressed and ready to head off to the café, for the bacon roll and tea, waiting for Winchester, when CI Aston saw them both.

"Morning," she said.

Both officers looked at her – what's coming now, what we done, must be alright as we can see her teeth from 20 feet away, they were very white this morning.

"Both of you doing ok NPT?"

"Yes, ma'am."

"Good, good" and she walked into the Sergeant's office.

"Let's get out of here, mate we are going to get collared for something."

They both went to the café; it was very busy today, in fact two full vans of the ball buster lads were in; they had on the old dark blue boiler suits ready to kick down some doors. Winchester got a call over the radio to point to point from the Sergeant. "Just a heads-up, lads, there will be a big raid on the estate this morning. Can you stay off the estate till it's over, can you both do response and patrol this morning?"

Winchester was the response driver as Reggie had never wanted to do the response drivers' course, everyone should do it in the Met at some stage, but Reggie had managed to duck it.

"The search team are on channel 17, keep off the estate till the raid team are finished. The thing is the NPT will have to clean up the fallout from this big project."

It's a good thing what was going down, but to be honest this was a show for the government people; it was election year.

Any way they will see the vans coming from a mile away, the drugs and the weapons will be down the bin shoots, just stand at the bottom of the flats in the bin store and wait for the drugs and the guns and knives clunk their way down. Only the people still asleep may get caught.

Winchester and Reggie patrolled around. Reggie kept his radio on the NPT station so he could hear what was unravelling on the estate. Eight arrests at the moment, all for possession of drugs, no dealers then, sounds like the cannabis lot. They were still on cloud nine. They got an urgent attendance call to Stratford station, person taken ill possibly fatal. Winchester put on the blues and two tones, they got there before the ambulance and anyone else. A woman in a black coat was on her knees carrying out CPR on a young man say in his 30s. As Reggie got close the woman in her 40s said, "I am a nurse, do you have a defibrillator in your car?"

"No, we don't," Winchester said, "but there is one in the station ticket office." As he ran off into the station ticket area, the station manager was just coming out with it in his hand, and Winchester took it and ran over to the nurse. It was an idiot-proof one that spoke to you. They could hear in the distance the ambulance coming, the nurse set it up and got him back; he was unconscious but now breathing. The ambulance crew arrived, spoke to the nurse and they were off like bats out of hell. The nurse looked at Winchester and Reggie and said, "It was lucky I was behind him, he was just walking along, he just went down face first on to the concrete."

Reggie took the nurse's details and he was smiling at her and to be fair she was smiling at him; it was a cool moment. Her name was Helen, she was a trauma nurse at Royal London. Winchester went back to the car and left them two talking for half an hour. The male had been taken to Whitechapel hospital. They knew he would be at the hospital being dealt with for a few hours so they would need to get his details for the report and his information. Reggie came back with this smile on his face that was so big it distorted his whole head.

"You alright?" Winchester said.

"Yes, I got a date tomorrow with Helen after work."

"Bloody hell, mate, she seems a nice woman."

Reggie lost his wife three years ago, well he sort of did, she did not die or he lost her some place, he just tells everyone that – she ran off with her boss to Australia. He knew it was OZ because she drew all their money out and left a note saying 'sorry I took all the money from the joint account, needed it for the flight to the other side of the world' and her boss was from Australia; she was saying Fuck you, basically.

"Good for you, mate, good for you, about bloody time," Winchester said. "Don't do a joint bank account again, though."

Reggie looked at him with daggers. "Not funny, mate, not funny."

Winchester said, "Well, mate, everyone in this station will never have a joint bank account after what happened to you, you told everyone day after day after day, I think even the Commissioner even changed his bank account."

Reggie's face changed back to a grin. "You're right, I did go on a bit, didn't I!"

Chapter Three

Winchester and Reggie pulled up outside A&E, London Hospital. As Winchester walked inside the front entrance, he saw the two paramedics and they exchanged nods as he walked to the reception, asked about the person brought in from Stratford rail station, possible heart attack.

"Sorry, we have no record of anyone coming in."

Winchester said, "I just saw the paramedics who picked him up, the receptionist said they may have not booked him in here yet, they take them through the other doors; if you head through the doors to the trauma area they will help you."

Reggie went in and Winchester said he would go and speak to the paramedics, but they had gone. Winchester could have kicked himself – he would normally take the paramedic's name and the ambulance registration. On his way back in, Reggie came out saying, "They never brought him here, no one come in through these doors..."

"What's going on?" Winchester said. They walked over to another ambulance crew and asked about the other crew.

One of the paramedics said, "Oh that's Pam and Tom, do you need them?"

Reggie said, "Yes, can you call them?"

"Well, they are still on site, round the back restocking up. Winchester and Reggie drove round the back, about six ambulances with back doors open, all getting cleaned or stocked up. The paramedic called Pam saw Winchester wave at him.

"Hello, officers, we got to stop meeting like this."

Tom emerged from the back of the ambulance as well.

"Can you help us?" Reggie said. "We need the location of the male you picked up at Stratford." "Another ambulance took him from us when we got here, private hospital in Cambridge. Some times it happens, they had all the documentation, it's a hand over, the male was stable. Talking."

"Did you get his name?"

"Yes, hang on." Pam looked at her ECG information. "Yes, it was Nile Storm, DOB 10/12 1978, 23 years old."

"Did he say anything?"

"He was heading to work, felt a bit off, got off the train to get some air and after that he can't remember."

"Did he say anything about what he did?" Winchester asked.

"No, he had oxygen mask on and I was monitoring him."

"Thanks for your help."

"Any time," Pam said as she looked at Winchester.

"Hello," Reggie said, "she likes you."

"Mmmm–" as Winchester got back in the car. "You know what, Reggie, this is getting more and more intriguing every day."

Control came over the radio: "Can you attend an RTC on the A13, motorbike and lorry."

"Oh, this is not going to be a good outcome," Reggie commented.

It was a nothing job – the lorry driver had rolled forward and hit the bike up the back. The two of them had got into a heated debate in the middle lane of the A13 close to the Blackwall Tunnel. Hand bags. Reggie just got them to exchange information and Oscar foxtrot. Winchester's head was hurting with the situations that were going on, but he could not say anything because it's wild and you could not substantiate anything, the inspector would move him to dog poo watch.

End of shift and Winchester was heading home and Reggie was looking forward to seeing Helen for the first date tonight.

Winchester said, "Have a great evening, mate, let me know how it goes, see you in a few days." They were both on the four days off now.

"Yep, will do, mate."

Winchester got back to his car and another note was on it; this time it had not rained.

'Can you meet me tomorrow morning at Epping station first train out I will be sitting on the last carriage, Jennie.'

Winchester was taken back. 'This is very odd, I never seen anyone called Jennie sitting on the train with me before, but I will get up early and get on the train.' All night this letter was running round in Winchester's mind and he was also meant to be off for the few days.

He got up at 0400, had a shower, left for the station. It was a wet morning and very cool wind. The station was quiet – the car park had about four cars in it, room for about 60 more cars. The lights were shining down on the wet floor. Winchester was looking around to see if he could see anyone remotely looking like a woman. Winchester got on the train and saw the LU cleaners with the bin liners cleaning up. As he sat down, a female about 5'4", short blonde hair, slim build came and sat right next to Winchester.

"I am Jennie."

She was good looking as well. She had a soft voice. "Sorry for the cloak and dagger, I am also a police officer in the Met, I am based at the Yard, I am in the intelligence division. I have made contact with you because you, I think, have seen what I have seen."

Winchester never said a word, then he said, "Do you have your warrant card on you?"

Jennie got it out of her back pocket. You could see she had on the black police trousers, black shoes well polished and the white shirt underneath her black puffer jacket. Winchester thought for a moment – what have I seen that you think I have seen. The cleaners that are not cleaners, the people that don't fit, the odd deaths of young people for no real reason, the hushing up of what the people have died of.

"I have been authorised to speak to you from the head of my department. We are covert but in plain sight. If you want me to fill you in on everything then come with me to the Yard and meet with my CO and we will explain, then it will be up to you."

"Ok," Winchester said, "nothing to do today anyway and Reggie's got a date and they are both going to play tennis indoors at the David Lloyd centre, that would be Reggie's thing."

Winchester did not say much on the way to the yard and Jennie was also very quiet, not much to say really, they both thought. Winchester did think Jennie was very nice looking. Jennie didn't think the same – she thought he was an uptight, strange person, who didn't engage in small talk. As they both went into the Yard through the staff entrance, Winchester was sure he spotted one of the spooks that was on the train walking in the front entrance. Winchester thought to himself, 'I am so confused but right now I will go with the flow.' Once inside the building, both showed their warrant cards to the security guard as they passed through the entry tubes, to the main lifts, and got in the lift to the top floor.

They both walked into a conference room, long beech table, 30 chairs round it, six TV monitors along the back wall all off beech panels around the walls, the window overlooking the street on one side only. Jennie walked over to a small cabinet that had two silver pots of tea and coffee on.

"Tea or coffee, Winchester?"

"Coffee with one and white thanks."

"Sit down, Winchester."

"Never been here before, it is something else!"

Jennie said, "This is Gold commander's room when they have incidents."

As they both sat down, three men and one very well dressed female walked into the room, and just said, "Morning, Jennie,

Winchester." They also grabbed a coffee, and sat down.

The head of them was one of the males Winchester had spoken to on the train. He spoke, "I am thinking you must be wondering what is going on, well, my name is William, I am the head of counter intelligence with MI5 and the others with me is Jacob, hello, Jennie you met, Shelly, Jerry and finally Justin. Winchester, we have called you in because you have been causing us a bit of a headache. We are carrying out a surveillance operation and you are spooking the people we are watching."

Winchester said very quickly, "The cleaners on the train?"

A few of them looked at each other. "No, not sure what's that about, the Storm family they are being investigated for activities they should not be doing. What we want to ask you is, when you went to their house, did you see anyone that looked out of place?"

"No, not really, only it seemed when I spoke to them about the dead male in London that seemed to have the grandfather's ID, they seemed very distressed. I put it down to they thought it was their son."

"No, you see we think the grandfather, a Mr Norman Storm, is not dead, he is wanted in connection with drug trafficking, we are not talking about your common cocaine or them sort of drugs, but importing your off-the-shelf drugs from other countries that are very cheap, and re-boxing them to get past the rules. We are talking a billion pound operation. We was informed by the Indian authorities Mr Storm was killed by a tiger and was dragged off while he was out hunting them."

Winchester just said, "Got his comeuppance then."

"Yes, we thought that, but we have confirmation this was not the case – the blood found was Norman Storm's and a body was found, but it was cremated before we could get the UK government to get hold of the body. We think he is here, their company is also a government-backed company, no need to tell you this is secret restricted information."

Winchester looked right at William and could see he was not telling him everything. Winchester said, "Why are you speaking to me? Well you live in Epping and looking at you records you was a fire officer in that county for a good few years and an Essex police officer too."

"Yes."

"Well you have more information or access to information than we could ever get in a short period of time."

"Not sure I get what you are trying to say."

"This family is well known in the area and you live in the area, you know some of the PCSOs, do you not? You know some of the Retained fire fighters whom live and work in the area. All we want you to do for us is keep your ear to the ground."

Winchester was really baffled now, he knew nothing of what they were trying to say.

William said, "Jennie will be your point of contact and will keep us apprised, if we get nothing that's okay."

Everyone just stood up and started to file out of the room. On their way out, they all shook Winchester's hand but didn't say much, just a nod.

"Finish your coffee, Jennie will take you to the restaurant to get you some breakfast."

Winchester said to Jennie, "I don't have a foggiest what that was all about – can you explain it to me please, because I thought this was about the train cleaners or the two people's deaths."

Jennie said, "Let's speak later, I will call you and sort out another meeting once I have been debriefed on today, because I am also at a loss." Jennie had a puzzled look on her face as if to say she had no idea what just happened.

Winchester felt like it was a fishing interview for information.

Winchester went home feeling a little frustrated about the whole day, on reflection a waste of a day. Winchester lived pretty much in the centre of Epping in an old converted manor, it was now six two-bedroom apartments with grounds. He was lucky to have got this place – it used to be his mother's, he had inherited it, a bit extravagant for a PC. In one of the other apartments lived a GP, lawyers husband and wife, city banker and his mum's old friend Lady Robbins. The other seemed to be someone from overseas that only used it from time to time.

Winchester knew the lads at the retained fire station just up the road from his fire service days. It was a nice day, so Winchester walked up to see if anyone was at the fire station. Looks like they had just come back from a shout. Winchester just walked in through the open bay door, the fire fighters were washing and cleaning down the fire appliance. The sub officer called out as he saw Winchester walking through the bay door. "It's the fire officer who went to the dark side," he called out with a big smile on his face.

"Hello, Sub, you ok still alive then?" Winchester said. "You are older than this station, any chance of tea?"

SUBO just walked into the mess room that was just off the rear of the appliance bay followed by Winchester and put the kettle on. "Can't keep away from the service then, mate! Any regrets?"

Winchester said, "Well, I miss the shouts not the politics."

SUBO just laughed and said, "That's funny, you have gone into the police and that has more paperwork than this job I bet. Come to my office, I got the better biscuits in my drawer. So what is this visit for? Want to become a retained fire fighter? Good job, we are on 550 call a year."

"No thanks," Winchester said, "but I know you know everyone in the area... my god the forest is younger than you."

"Yep, I think I do, lots of new money in the area now, yuppies and hedge fund people from the city."

"Do you know the Storm family?"

"Yes, I know them, they are big in pharmaceuticals, they have a factory in Harlow and one in Cambridge. I think from what I can gather they also own a chain of pharmacies all over the city, nothing in Essex. Mind you, I have been told they are up for a bit of cash; aren't we all?"

Winchester said, "No, you know they do stuff under the table?"

"Oh yes, they own Poll-Cat cleaning, we saw them once at a big chemical spill on a job on the M25."

Winchester's conversation got cut short as the printer went off and the bell went down; they had a shout on the M11 car fire. Off they went, and Winchester walked off back down the high street.

Winchester went into a baker's to get a roll and a tea to take away. While he was waiting he noticed a car he had seen parked down his road, close to his apartment, was right across the road with two males in it; it was a two year old Ford Fiesta, black; he made a mental note of the registration. Got his tea and roll, walked off towards the park to sit and eat it, hoping not to get jumped on by all the pigeons that seem to follow everyone from the baker's with some hope of getting a crumb.

As he sat in the park he saw the car again, this time no one was in it but it had moved. Winchester's mind was working overtime – 'I am seeing things, I think I am being watched, but why and what for?'.

No one was in the park apart from two old ladies feeding the ducks.

"Hello," a female voice behind him suddenly said.

Winchester turned round as his teeth sunk into his roll. It was Jennie. Winchester said with food in his mouth, "What you doing here?"

"I went to your place I wanted to catch up with you. You're not home obviously, so I decided to walk into town and I saw you sitting here," Jennie said. "Look, I am just going to walk over the road and get a tea, I will be back soon and now a crusty roll with bacon."

Winchester just said, "You mean bacon roll?"

Jennie looked at him with a sarcastic look and walked off.

Winchester thought what the hell is Jennie doing here, and also: Jennie is attractive. She had a black trouser suit on with a short black jacket and black high heels on. No handbag, just a large purse, matt black leather. Winchester watched Jennie as she walked back towards him, he knew she must have had a boyfriend or husband.

Jennie sat next to him on the wooden park bench that had a name of a past love on etched into the back of the bench; it had faded away from rain and the few years it had been donated to this spot. Winchester noticed Jennie just took little bits as he was taking big bites, as you do after years of gulping down food when you are working in any of the emergency services, you are trying to eat it before a shout or a call.

Jennie said, "Winchester, I need to understand what you have been observing on the underground trains in the mornings."

Winchester explained in great detail; Jennie was listening with real intent. She had turned her body towards him, fascinated with his imagination. At the end of the 15 minutes of information Winchester had given Jennie, she said, "Wow, and you observed this when going to work! So let me ask you what do you think they are doing?"

Winchester said, "I really don't know."

"What makes you think it's wrong?"

"Nothing, but it is not sitting right with me. I know what the transport unions are like – they look after their members and I could not see them letting an independent company just randomly doing what these guys are doing."

Jennie said, "How do you know they don't?"

"Well the union rep on this station said to me that he has not got a clue who they are, he was going to look into it."

"How do you know the union rep?"

"He is the station ticket office manager, he is always on the station in the morning. I got to know him over the last few months, but when I went to the station the other day, they said he had been off sick with an illness, also they don't think he will be back on early shifts for a long time due to his illness."

"What was his illness?" Jennie asked.

"Don't know."

Winchester said, "I thought at the meeting this was what we was all discussing, but instead we spoke about the two people that me and Reggie had to deal with."

"Yes it was and that is why I am speaking to you off the books.

"I think you have stumbled onto something with what is going on, so does my bosses, but we have to be fearful, this is embedded in the home office and a very senior level. We do not understand what is going on, but we know you did ruffle someone's feathers, as you and your partner were shifted to the NPTs, that gave us a red flag, why you was moved we are still trying to figure it out. Was it because the Storm family who are really in bed with the government, the fake driving licence for such a well known dead person being used by another person, but both work for the same company?

"I have been authorised to give you this information. As of next week you will be back on shift, but this will upset your partner Reggie, we hear he was really happy to be with the NPT."

"Yes," Winchester said.

"We could leave him there but that is up to you."

Winchester said, "I will speak with him, you know I will tell him everything."

Jennie knew if she said no, Winchester would anyway. She nodded. Jennie said, "After we have sorted this mess out and we get to the bottom of it, you want to take me out on a real date?"

Winchester looked at her. "Eeerr yes, I would."

"Good you have no girlfriends and you're single, that's good, just like me."

Winchester said, "What no girlfriend?"

Jennie said, with a dead pan face, "What do you think?" Jennie stood up and put out her hand with her M15 card in it.

"Intelligence manager, you have a card."

"Yes, do you not have one? That is my direct line number on the back. Is my personal number. Speak soon, have a nice day," she said as she walked off.

Winchester headed off to see if Reggie was home and speak with him. He was seeing his new girlfriend, but she had just left. He was besotted with her, they were good for each other. Reggie opened the door of his apartment with a little surprised look on his face. "Come in, mate, glad to see you on my day off. What has happened?"

"I have to speak to you about something."

Reggie made the tea and still had not got dressed yet; he had on a tartan dressing gown, his dark hairy bow legs sticking out, black toe nails from when he dropped a paving stone on his foot, trying to help a dog that had got stuck between a pallet of paving stones.

Winchester explained the meetings he had had over the past few days. Reggie was looking at him with confusion on his face but then the penny seemed to drop. "This is about the bloody Storm family... Is that why we got the NPT duty?"

"Yes, it was someone upstairs from the Home Office got us on this, Reggie."

"I want out as I have a few friends in the job who have had their noses put out of joint because we got it, they are even giving me the cold shoulder."

"Well that's good because Jennie told me we are going back to shift as of next week but you could stay."

"No, mate," Reggie said. "In a few years maybe, but I am not on the retirement run yet."

Reggie added, "Do they believe you?"

"Not sure, we'll see, but I will have to look at the situation again."

"I was going to pop in tomorrow, speak to CI Aston, she needs to know what is going on."

"No. She will get that from the senior management. Leave it be." Winchester left after drinking his tea, heading off home for the rest of the day.

It was a very wet Monday morning and Winchester on his day off was informed that he and Reggie were back on the normal beat looking after the usual suspects, the homeless, drug addicts and just generally everyday problems, but their start times had changed from early say 0630 to 0930 and finish at 1930 – a ten-hour shift – then the following week back on nights, then back to the 0630 start. This was because of the changes that were coming, they were going to move everyone to three shifts soon, early, lates and nights. This was about getting more out of everyone and trying to do away with less overtime, but you get shift allowance twice – someone thought this was cost saving.

Winchester and Reggie had the first thing to do list, the shop owners calling the police to move on the homeless from the doorways and the drug addicts leaving needles lying around and some of them still high in doorways and in rubbish skips for shelter. Winchester and Reggie kept respectful communication when dealing with anyone, but for the life of them, both thought this like a third world problem and it should not be happening in the UK with all the money sloshing around. Police officers dealing with this time after time, it's like a revolving door doing the same old thing every shift.

Winchester was asked over the radio to point to point CI Aston. Winchester called back, and Aston said, "When you are back for changeover this morning, can you both come and see me?"

"Yes ma'am."

Luckily this morning they both had one of the patrol cars, when they went round for the inspection before taking it as you should, the log book was not complete and someone there must have nicked it in the night and been sick in the back, called up the Sergeant – his response: "You want the car or walk in the rain, clean it up first."

"Great."

"Just wash it out with a jet washer, the seat's covered in black plastic sheeting." Also they had kerbed it. Reggie just noted it in the log book so they never got the blame.

Winchester and Reggie both knew something was up, seeing the Chief inspector again in such a short period of time. At the end of shift they both went to her office. Winchester and Reggie stood outside the open door of the CI – she was not in her office; then from nowhere walked in the deputy chief constable with the CI. A feeling of dread come over both of the officers – what have we done to deserve this.

"Hello Winchester and Reggie, last time I saw you was at the passing out parade for the new cadets, that was over a year ago. Good turn out that day I thought," said the DCC. "Now come into the office, I need to talk with you all about a situation that has been brought to my attention. The Chief constable has had a complaint about the way you both handled the Storm family situation; your CI has explained everything to me, but why I am talking to you about it for is I want your version in your words, as we are not letting the Essex police give us a kick up the backside when they did not do the work on their own patch."

"To be fair, sir," Winchester said, "they did express to us they would do it, but as all their units were tied up at a major incident at Stansted airport it would take some time, because it was at the station it would be news and a friend was also present, he would have called ahead."

"This is a very prominent family and have influence, he had been asked to send an apology."

Reggie said, "Sir, we did our job correctly and with decorum."

Reggie also piped up again, "I hope this is not going on our records, sir."

"No, it's not."

DCC said, "Okay, I have what I need, off you go, lads."

As Winchester and Reggie went down to the changing room, Winchester said to Reggie, "Something is fishy, mate and I can't put my finger on it. We are back on earlies tomorrow, see you in the morning."

Winchester kept turning over in his mind, something's not right. He got home and found a note poked through his letter box with a phone number on it: please call. He did and as soon as he called and heard the voice on the phone, he knew it was Jennie.

"Can I come round?"

"Yes," Winchester said. "How long?" He still had some pants hanging up in the living room and stuff in the sink, also it could do with a quick Hoover.

"An hour," she said.

"I need to get some milk."

Jennie said, "I will pick some up on my way."

Winchester was like a tornado and then he jumped into the shower, brushed his teeth. Why, what is she coming to see me for...

She was dead on an hour, she was wearing a royal blue dress and blue shoes, hair up in a bun, she had a long neck – seemed to go on forever.

She had milk and a bottle of wine with her. She walked past Winchester and he could smell her perfume – it was not too heavy, just light enough to make him want to get to know that smell more.

Winchester said, "Coffee or tea?"

"Tea please, and I have come round for three reasons."

"What are they then?"

"One, I am a football nut. I really follow Chelsea and the game is on tonight and I did hear you say to your partner Reggie that you have Sky Sports. I also need to talk to you about the Storm family situation."

Winchester said, "What was the third one then?"

"I am hungry."

Winchester said, "You are out of luck on the last one: I have got pork pies, tomatoes, pickles, cream crackers, cheese and marmite. Or I could order an Indian takeaway?"

"My god," she said, "you are so 1970s – next you will be telling me you have tea leaves not bags."

"How did you know that?"

Jennie just burst out laughing.

Winchester didn't know what to say about how she looked, so he said, "Don't take this the wrong way," so he covers all bases, "you look great, love the dress."

"Good," Jennie said, "I wondered when you was going to notice me or say something."

Football was on the TV; they both watched it but Winchester's mind was on the situation with the DCC and now Jennie was here too. Chelsea lost and Jennie almost kicked the TV through the wall as she was a big Chelsea fan.

"Open the wine, then," Jennie said, "let's get down to talking about business about the Storm family. Did you get a visit from the DCC today?"

"Yes, how did you know?"

"The Storm family have connections in the government, we in the security services don't like that, makes things clouded."

"What do you think this is all about, Jennie?" asked Winchester.

"I really don't know, I am at a loss."

Winchester was beginning to feel this was no coincidence: Jennie is here right now, feels like she was interrogating him to see what he knew; Winchester just played dumb.

Winchester asked a question to Jennie: "You want my theory, it's to do with prescription medication in some way, we cannot put our fingers on it, we have been tracking them for years but the connection is being blocked by another agency. They have connections to the USA that makes life even more of a problem; as always the American government closes the door on us every time."

Winchester started to understand in his own mind that because he had put together information very quickly in his mind that he was of interest to the security services. What they think he knows is really unsure at this time, he has never been paid so much attention in his whole life.

Jennie had polished off the whole bottle of wine as Winchester only had one glass. Jennie said to Winchester, "Open another bottle, let's make it a night."

Jennie seemed really relaxed and was quite talkative about her life. She went to Oxford University and was a professor in biological infectious disease. She had joined MI5 six years ago – she was recruited at the university. She has been to most of the world, boyfriend was a major in the Royal Marines, broke up a year ago as he slept with her sister and now is marrying her. Winchester thought ouch that must've hurt. Jennie had a dog, Doberman called Rambo, two years old, she lives with her mother and father in Buckinghamshire, very wealthy people.

Jennie said to Winchester, "I have never opened up to anyone like this for years, sorry to let you have all my thoughts. So tell me about you, Winchester?"

"Well, not much to say, started life with a father in the Royal Navy, he was a captain, Mum passed away when I was young, only ever been out with two women, both run off with other men, single, always wanted to be a police officer and want to progress up the ranks become an inspector in six years and also do firearms."

Jennie said, "My first encounter with firearms was in the job, it's one of our training if you are operational."

Winchester, knowing she was a little merry and flirting a lot, said, "Where does your real interest in me come from?"

She looked at him right in his eyes. "I was asked to look into the situation around the Storm family and because you and your partner Reggie had two encounters with them it heightened our interest. Our operatives at the second incident overheard you talking to your partner about your interest in incidents being linked and Reggie said to you your imagination was running wild.

"My report on you was nothing to worry about and I felt you would not mess up our long term investment in this investigation. When I saw you in the park sitting on the bench, you made me feel interested in you as a person."

Winchester said, "You are an attractive woman and I like you but–"

Jennie looked at him with apprehension.

"I thought to myself, why would someone like you be interested in a plain PC like me."

She said, "I will stop you right there. I am a woman first and an agent second, and if I see someone I like I say so and like you. Do you want to kiss me or have I got to instigate that too?"

Winchester went red in the face but before he could say anything she gave him a right smacker kiss on his lips, still holding her glass of wine – good balance. Winchester really liked it and reciprocated. She grabbed his hand and put her glass down and started to pull him towards the bedroom. Winchester stopped and pulled her back to the sofa. "No, not like this, you have had a few drinks. When I make love to you I would like to be totally clear headed and no regrets in the morning."

Jennie looked at Winchester with a confused look – she always got her own way. "Why, don't you find me attractive?"

"Yes, I bloody do but I hope you understand."

Jennie said, "Can we just lay on the sofa and watch the TV, I'd like that."

Jennie fell asleep, laying her head on his chest. Winchester left her on the sofa, put a pillow underneath her head and a blanket over her.

Winchester was on earlies in the morning, up at 0430. He crept around as Jennie was snoring and well out for the count. He knew she was not going to steal anything, so he went to work, leaving her asleep. He left a note with a spare key, saying 'I have left a spare toothbrush out for you and the white towels you can use. Also the door has to be double locked so keep the keys till I see you again'.

Winchester was on the first train out. It was strange again, the two people were back but this time they saw him and stopped what they were doing and got off the train and walked over the platform to the other train. Winchester had a tissue in his bag so he walked up to the upright handle and rubbed it up and down then smelt it, as he had seen them doing something to it; it smelt chemical but not bleach. Winchester then rubbed his hand up and down the pole; it was a little oily as well.

Winchester got to work, but for some reason started to sneeze and his head was light, like a cold was coming over him very quickly.

"Bloody hell," Reggie said when he saw Winchester. "You ok, mate, you look poorly, mate, your eyes are blood shot."

Winchester said, "I been sneezing for about an hour." Winchester thought to himself, I was fine this morning, I got a bloody headache now.

Winchester said to Reggie, "When we are out I need to stop at a chemist. Get some stuff for this bloody cold."

Reggie, after sitting in the car with him also started to feel a bit sick and said, "You've give me it now."

Winchester all day felt sick and then when they got back to the station some other officers were sneezing and with some sort of cold. The Sergeant called out to Winchester, "Look what you brought to this station, half everyone and me are feeling off. Go home, Winchester, don't come in till you feel better.

"I am fine, Sergeant." Winchester was trying to think of any other people whom he'd been round to get this cold but the only person was Jennie. When he got home a note had been left on his kitchen worktop: 'I am so sorry but I used the last of your hair shampoo and drunk your last bit of milk and cornflakes.' Big smiley faces on the paper. 'Bit of a hangover but I am fine XXX Jennie' – she kept hold of the keys. Winchester was not that bothered because he thought she was the last person was going to break into his apartment. Winchester was feeling really unwell by this stage – he had no temperature, did not feel sick, just weak, a head cold clogged-up feeling. Jennie called him at his apartment which he was surprised at, as he did not remember giving her his number. She did explain she had called her phone from Winchester's and that gave her the number; she explained she still had the keys and would it be alright to come over tonight.

"I have this head cold so I am taking some medication, try and sleep it off, so can we make it another night? Oh, by the way, you feeling ok not cold or anything?"

"No," she said, "why?"

"Well, you are the only person I have been in close contact with over the last few days."

"Well, did you not get on the train, that is always full of germs. Mind you," she said, "the cleaners you been talking about, they must keep the place clean."

The chemist had given Winchester some stuff that cost the earth. Then Winchester's mind went in a different direction – 'what if they were the people spreading the germs on the train? I did smell the stuff they used and put it on a bit of tissue. No, that is too far-fetched, they would be terrorists of some sort. Why not? You get some groups like animal rights and save the planet who have resorted to direct action'. Winchester thought, 'no this would be a massive scandal for everyone, the implications and ramifications would be unthinkable'. It's the medication making him go nuts and thinking of this outlandish thoughts.

In the morning, Winchester felt a bit better but the thought of going to work, feeling crap, was not what he wanted to do; however, crime and letting down his colleagues who would have to pick up the slack was not right. This morning no one was on the train at all, the cleaners were not there either, but Winchester's mind was on his head cold, not anything else.

Winchester walked into the changing room of the station only to be met by Reggie looking really pale and sniffy.

"Thanks, mate," Reggie said, "I feel like crap this morning, so do half the shift, that is about 15 officers. We are down this morning by five off with that cold you brought in, even the Sergeant thinks it's you."

"Shit," Winchester said, "had the Sergeant..."

"No, lucky you, no self-respecting germs would ever penetrate the Sergeant's skin, would not stand a chance against the rhino skin."

Winchester and Reggie went to the morning briefing ready to go all out, all you could see in the room were officers with tissues.

Sergeant said, "You sad looking bunch, we need you all out in the fresh air today. Right, three response teams this morning and no vans, we have five warrants to do and three persons of interest, they are wanted in connection with a shooting of a scrapyard owner in Barking. SO19 are guarding him at the London hospital on our patch, it's gang on gang, on your notes you will have the photos and the hangouts of the individuals. Don't approach them, let the Control know asap. We are short of manpower this shift because of this horrible cold going around, thanks to Winchester–" they all looked at Winchester with the look of 'thanks, mate', but they all knew that it was not his fault, it was just banter.

"Winchester and Reggie, sorry, lads, have another one for you at Liverpool Street station, inside this time, male fell on the tracks at the underground tube stop, did not get run over but was dead on the arrival of the ambulance team. They need help with the information and statements, transport police also have a team on site at this time. Can you both work with them, get the information and get it to our control."

Winchester and Reggie walked to the station and got on the underground to Liverpool Street.

They found the Central line platform and could see the train was half in and half out of the platform, the body was still on the track as the fire service was just about to get him off the tracks; they had to wait till confirmation the people were off the train and then all the power was shut down while they worked between the tracks. The doctor was on the side of the platform and the private ambulance lads were there as well. The two trans sport officers came over and introduced themselves.

"Hi, I'm PC Nutcracker and the PC Fishermen, he is a probationer, first fatality."

Reggie introduced them both. "Do you have any information on the individual?"

"No, we are waiting for their team to bring him up."

Nutcracker asked, "Is it alright if I get Fishermen to carry out the ID search on the person, he needs this for his log book if you get my drift?"

They both nodded 'of course'. The male who looked in his late 40s was very well dressed in a tailormade suit, briefcase was also on the track as well. They got the body to the platform and before anyone could do anything the doctor had to confirm time of death and record he was actually dead. The fire service lads said they were off now.

"Okay, lads, thanks," Winchester said.

The private ambulance lads were standing like a pair of vultures in that movie Jungle Book. Very smart dark grey suits, polished shoes and black ties. Fishermen started to search the body and found the wallet and his ID driving licence. Professor William Harrison-Smith OBE. He had a Westminster office address and security pass to the House of Commons – this is an automatic call to the OIC and a commander will be dispatched. Winchester called up point to point with the Sergeant as this must be kept off the main radio traffic, as other officers could be standing by members of the public with radios on. The Sergeant then called Chief inspector Aston who contacted New Scotland Yard – this will be now the intelligence services-run situation or incident.

Within ten minutes of Winchester's call, six plainclothes officers and one assistant chief officer were at the station. The two waiting private ambulance lads were told to Oscar Foxtrot, they would no longer be needed; they both shrugged their shoulders and walked off with their kit, a body bag and trolley. The inspector from what Reggie and Winchester assumed was the security services, did not speak to either of them; instead he directed his comments to the plainclothes officers to "get our information" and sent them on their way. The two transport officers were called up on their radios; they said "we are off now, we been dispatched to another incident"; everyone nodded at each other and went off.

Winchester and Reggie were having a conversation with the plainclothes officer.

"Lads," he said, "can I ask you a few questions about what you found and what you saw when you got here."

Reggie said, "Nothing really, the two transport officers were working with the fire lads, got him up on the platform and the doctor declared the male as dead."

"Ok that's you both can go now, we will deal with this."

"What about the CCTV on the platform?"

"We are on that," said this very military type officer, short back and sides hair cut, his shoes very polished; in fact they all did, it's the way they all stood, very upright from years of military service.

"Come on," Reggie said, "let's get out of here.

Winchester said to Reggie as they left the station entrance, "Don't you think we have seen too many military types over the last few months? They are like buses, you get none for ages then you get four in one go!"

They both nodded and agreed with a chuckle, "Let's get down to the greasy spoon, I really could murder a bacon roll and a strong tea."

Reggie booked off on the radio for breakfast. You always know what sort of café it is, when two police officers walk in the Illegal DVDs and the other stuff that is up for sale just comes off the tables. Reggie ordered two rolls and two teas. They both sat in the window seats. This was a good place to sit, you could see the local small-time crooks do an about turn once they saw who was sitting in the window.

Winchester said to Reggie, "Something is not adding up to me; they are all connected, I know they are."

Reggie said, "What are you on about?"

"Don't you see, this is not a coincidence. I just think something is wrong and we are right in the middle of it."

Reggie said, "You are off your head, you must have been dropped on your head when you was born, you see conspiracies everywhere."

Winchester said, "Let's look at this as a whole, from when I saw the people on the train and then the mix-up on the identification of the death of a member of the Storm family. We was both not well for a few days after I looked at the stuff they seem to put on the handrails on the train. Seeing security Services all the time and then Jennie, I am telling you this is connected in some way."

Reggie booked them available on his radio again and right away they were called to attend a suspicious person around a supermarket, shoplifter, they both thought it's going to be the usual suspects, but when they pulled up outside they were greeted by a very agitated manager of the store, and standing next to him was Tim but not so dim security guard. Tim wanted to be a police officer always, but because he had dyslexia he kept failing the written test; however, things were changing in the Police and he had applied for Essex police. Winchester had informed him that in Essex they were one of the first to accept dyslexia, too many really good people that would make great officers missed out, so did the public...

"Anyway what's the problem?"

The store manager said, "I am Rodger, we have a man in the store room and he is asleep and when we asked him to move he said, he would detonate his hand grenade."

Reggie said, "What did he look like?"

"He had ginger hair matted, old smelly clothes."

"That's old Captain Chris Burt. He was a captain in the Royal Engineers, lost it after his mate got killed in the Gulf War. Army and his family have tried everything to help him out; this is real mental health, not some of the claims of some of the people we deal with day-to-day."

Reggie got on the radio and called in to stop all the other units as the manager had called in a bomb threat. Winchester walked in with Reggie and Tim the security guard, who was saying, "I told that tube he was a harmless homeless person; but some good news – I have my entry exams next month for Essex, thanks, lads."

"Come on, Chris me old mate, let's get you out of here. Fancy tea and a bacon sandwich?"

The store had a canteen in it. Winchester spoke to Tom the Sergeant over the radio who also was ex-Military. "Give him a good meal, lads, get him few bits to eat and drink; I'll get a van round sorted, give him a night in the cells."

Chris did stink big time but they both thought, if they put him in the car it will smell all day, so Winchester asked the security guard, "Do you have showers here?"

"Yes we do, just out the back for the staff."

"Could you get us permission to let him shower, will stay and sort it."

Out the front also was the clothes donation container. Reggie walked out to the main shopping area to got some shower gel. Chris never spoke, ever; he never drank or took drugs, he was just an empty shell of a man, though if someone threatened him he would say something. Once a few youths thought it would be fun to piss over him when he was asleep in a shop doorway – worst mistake they ever made. We saw the CCTV, he jumped up and took out all three of them before they could do up their flies. They never reported it because they were too embarrassed. All he wants to do is forget in his own way. Two hours later he was showered and dry with some odd-looking clothes on, but warm and with a new pair of army boots someone had thrown away too.

His old clothes were thrown into the rubbish bin, he'd eaten two breakfasts and drank four cups of tea; and a bag full of food that would be ok for the streets for a few days. Reggie booked them both available.

The Sergeant called up on a point to point to Reggie: "We have person trying to jump off a bridge over the Blackwall Tunnel approach. If he does it will be a right pain. I am going home to the in-laws tonight, can't be late, so get him off that bloody bridge and nick the blighter."

Reggie said, "You're all heart, SARGE."

They could hear all the cars beeping their horns as they went past him. He was a middle aged male, did not look like he was just trying to get attention; he was over the top of the handrail. On the ledge 30 feet above the main tunnel approaches; no one was going to stop, they were all 'got places to go', if he jumped the whole place would grind to a halt and he would most definitely be mashed up on the front of a lorry or a car, but he most definitely would have been run over by then – white van man, they will not stop for anyone. Cars were dispatched to close off the road back at the approach; till then Winchester and Reggie would have to speak to him from a distance, but what did not help was the amount of drivers, mostly builders' vans, shouting out as they went past: "jump, hurry up, mate, jump".

Winchester managed to get close enough to speak to him without the traffic noise drowning out what was being communicated to him. "What's your name?"

"Go away," the man shouted, "I have nothing to live for."

"What's your name? My name is Winchester and my colleague is Reggie."

He was about 5 10" slim build, shaven head and suit and shirt.

Reggie then said to him, "Mate, you know it is never too late to put things right in your life, we can get you help. What's your name? I did not catch it."

The cars and all the traffic had stopped now, the other police units had stopped them. Winchester and Reggie was now not alone – two other officers on motorcycles had also arrived, Winchester and Reggie indicated to the two bike officers they were going to turn their radios down very low so the person they were dealing with did not hear the radio traffic; this allowed them to report direct back to the operational inspector, Silver commander.

With all the traffic stopped it was quite enough to speak to the jumper. He said his name was Justin, he worked as a dealer in the city. His wife had left him for his best friend. Winchester and Reggie were not trained in this situation; the detective inspector who was trained was on his way and point to point. Winchester took the call as Reggie kept asking about the person's family.

The inspector said, "I am ten minutes out, but do not focus on his mistakes, talk about positive things, don't focus on the reason he is there. Keep it generally open questions."

Reggie managed to get the man to open up, talk about his job, nothing to do with the situation. Winchester could hear Reggie asking, "What can we do to help, I am sorry you find yourself in this situation, can we contact anyone for you?"

Then the jumper seemed to stop looking only down to the road below, he looked across at Reggie, as if someone had switched the light on. "She flipping left me for that twat of a friend of mine. I'm not going to jump or kill myself, I am going to start over and show them."

Reggie helped him over the handrails back onto the main road as the cars and lorries that were stuck just seemed to burst past beeping.

The inspector turned up and said he would speak to the man and let the ambulance crew take him to hospital for evaluation. "Good work, lads."

It was going to be one of those days, you just knew it. Reggie said to Winchester, "Yep, we got a call to a male hanging from a rope in a warehouse. Ambulance been requested."

Winchester said, "These are often a very poor outcome."

The factory warehouse was called SBS building supplies, been around for years, quiet part of BOW. When Reggie drove through the gate, they were met by two males, looking very uneasy. "Quick," one of them shouted, and ran off through the lorry-sized opening into the warehouse itself. As Reggie and Winchester rounded the corner, they saw two men trying to hold their work colleague's legs, trying to keep the rope from killing the person. Reggie could see the male was grey and his eyes were bulging, lips were blue too.

Reggie ran out, got in the car and drove round; he pulled up right close to the two men, then he said, "Winchester, jump up on the bonnet, grab his legs"

Winchester did so, and as he did Reggie said to the other two, "Need to cut the rope now, right now."

Then one of then jumped into the fork lift with an empty pallet on it. Reggie jumped on using the Stanley knife given to him from one of the warehouse lads, cut the rope, got him to the floor, took the rope off his neck and started CPR. The ambulance and another unit turned up. The ambulance crew managed to get his heart started. The ambulance paramedics asked how long was he without air.

"Not sure. When we got here," Winchester said, "he was already blue."

One of the lads from the warehouse said, "It could only have been minutes as he was having tea with us then we come out, saw him swinging."

"Ok, we may have a chance." The paramedic asked one more question. "Did he jump from a height? If he did we are looking at recapitulation of the neck and spine."

"Not sure."

They put a neck collar on him, he was still breathing very shallow; the ambulance crew took him off as fast as possible. Reggie went along in the ambulance; Winchester had to keep the possible crime scene secure until the SOCO lads got to the incident. Winchester put tape round the area and stood guard, taking notes from employees; he could not take statements yet till he had help. They have CCTV in the warehouse – this was good news, it should show what went on. After two hours and Reggie also confirming the person was stable but not out of the woods yet, two crime scene technicians came over. Winchester took three statements from the managers and forklift driver who had found him. The CCTV showed him just walking up to the high shelving racks, tying the rope on the low beam and stepping off the racking. He did not fall far, just swung out about six feet off the floor. Winchester bagged the CCTV disc and updated the incident log with control, then headed off to pick up Reggie at the hospital.

They had both just pulled up for tea and a doughnut, when Control came over the radio and requested an urgent call back point to point with DCI Aston. "We have another death at a station close to our patch, can you both attend now, take the information, looks like heart attack, transport police and paramedics are at the scene, Mile End station."

On arrival the doctor was just walking out of the station. Winchester and Reggie recognised him from before. "Hi Doc, confirmation of death?"

"Yes, not sure the cause of death, that's the coroner's job. Shame, he looks to me in his late thirties no age at all."

Winchester said, "What is it about this train line, it must be stressing everyone out so much they are having heart attacks."

Reggie looked at him with a grin on his face and shook his head. "Mate, you see conspiracies behind every event. Come on, let's get down to the platform."

Two transport officers were standing talking next to the covered body, as well as one paramedic writing in his notebook and two private ambulance lads waiting to take the body to the morgue. The two transport police officers looked up said, "We got his wallet, his name is James Will-Snatch, has a pass as well, works for Feel-good pharmaceuticals."

Winchester looked at Reggie with questioning eyes. Reggie just looked at the person on the ground knowing what Winchester would be thinking right now.

Winchester said to the two transport police officers, "How many people this age you get dropping dead on stations in a year?"

Ted, the older looking officer, just said, "Last year I think I attended about six to seven, over the network, that's not including the jumpers. It's getting worse."

"What about on this line, the Central line?"

"We pay no attention to it, only jumpers they seem to do most on the Northern line. Ok, lads, we leave it to you, we have football fans arriving later for a WEST HAM home game so we got to go for the briefing."

Reggie looked at the deceased's home address; it was Chigwell, Essex but that's a Metropolitan police area.

Winchester called it in to Control, response back was it has and will be dealt with by the local station to deliver the bad news. Reggie gave the all-clear to the waiting private ambulance lads to take the body. Reggie bagged up the belongings and took them so he could put it in the property office back at the NICK; it was the end of a long shift.

Chapter Four

I t was very early Saturday morning, it was like a monsoon as Winchester got to Epping station to catch the first train out of the station. The floors of the train were a little slippery as the rain just drove across the platform horizontally through the open doors. Winchester shook his umbrella off and sat down only to see one of the strange cleaners working on this carriage – never seen this one before; he had the same stuff on, three bottles with him as well now as three different colour cleaning cloths. As the train driver announced "we are leaving, mind the doors", the cleaner, who was a big man, bit of a fatty, slipped on the floor, fell back, hit his head on the window seat at the end of the carriage, landing on his bottles, which just exploded under the pressure of his body weight, made a shed load of yellow mist and he was on the floor unconscious. Winchester quickly jumped up, pulled the emergency lever – the train had not started to move yet so the door just opened up again. Winchester could see blood coming from the back of his head. The driver sounded the whistle from his cab and the station staff came from out behind the ticket office door. Winchester said, "Call an ambulance, tell them he is unconscious and breathing, but head injury."

At this juncture four other people, three males, one female, with the same clothes on or protective equipment appeared. One of them just said, "We will take it from here. George, you ok?"

George Winch said, "An ambulance has been called."

The male who was trying to talk to George did not take any notice of Winchester. This really irritated Winchester. "What's your name, Sir? I am PC Winchester."

The other three people just seemed to walk away at that point. "I'm his manager, he is my responsibility."

Winchester snapped back now all the station staff were on the carriage and the ambulance lads had arrived in the car park. Winchester asked his name.

"Jerry."

"Jerry who?"

Jerry Byrne." Jerry was kinda like a boffin, spoke very carefully and calculating. The paramedics walked on to the carriage. "So we meet again." Winchester recognised the paramedics from the hospital a few weeks ago. "What have we here?"

Winchester explained, "He's got to go to the hospital, he is out cold."

"What is that smell?"

Winchester said, "It's whatever was in that bottle, it stinks, Jerry."

"What's in that bottle?"

"Cleaning stuff, nothing to worry about."

Jerry said, "I will pick up all his stuff and take it back to the office."

Winchester said, "okay", then Jerry was gone.

After the paramedics removed the man, Winchester saw on the floor a black notebook; it clearly belonged to the person who had been injured. He put it in his pocket. Winchester was late for roll call, and the Sergeant gave him the look – you are late.

"Winchester, stay back after roll call," the Sergeant said.

Winchester knew he was going to get a hairdryer moment; everyone had gone.

"Why are you late, lad and it better be good?"

Winchester explained.

"Alright, don't make it a habit."

Winchester met Reggie in the locker room.

"What happened this morning? Not like you to be late, overslept did we?"

"No," and then he proceeded to explain. As Winchester put his hand into his pocket he felt the notebook he had picked up. He thought I will read it later then log it in, but he noticed it had three different colour tags sticking slightly out; he opened it up but before he could start to read it they got a call to a public order situation at a bus stop on the Mile End road.

Reggie and Winchester arrived on blue lights to find two drunks with kilts on, shouting happy words to all the people going by. "It's the blues brothers, Jimmy." He lifted his Strongbow can. "Cheers, lads."

Reggie said, "You need to move on and keep the noise down."

"Yes, mate, we are having fun. We missed the bus, the rest of the lads are heading back to Scotland. We got tee get a train."

"Get in the car, lads, will take you to King's Cross station."

"Thanks pal." Both the men staggered and fell into the back seats of the patrol car.

The two lads sang all the way to the station.

Winchester said, "Let's get coffee if we have time, I. need to look at this notebook. I am not feeling too good, got a headache and stuffy."

Reggie said, "Your eyes are looking a little red, you got a cold, mate? You must have got wet this morning."

They both sat outside the mobile burger van with tea and bacon rolls, Reggie asked what the notebook was.

"It was the one from the man on the train who slipped over."

"Aren't you meant to hand that in?"

"I will, just having a peek."

On opening the book Winchester saw a list of medical names and what looked like viruses. With colours next to each name

Yellow 12321 Nasopharyngitis   Central line carriage. 1 3 5 6

Red. 65478. Rhinovirus   Central line carriage 2 4 6 7

Green 99807 Pneumonia's   Central line carriage 1 and 7 only

Black 66677 Allergic rhinitis   central line carriage 1 2 3 4 5 6 7.

Then on the back of the book were the station names, Epping Central line 1st 2nd 3rd 5am.

District line Upminster, July to September, yellow only.

The book was just full of numbers and dates, Winchester could not decode it.

Reggie just looked at it and said, "That is above my head, it looks like what he has to do every time."

They both got back to the station and Winchester went straight to the photocopier and copied a few of the pages of the book before he logged it in, as he had a feeling this book was going to go missing very quickly. He knew this book was some sort of key to what was going on.

Reggie said it was just a book, just like what a train spotter would have. People have notebooks and I know he thinks Winchester is a little away with the fairies.

They were both sitting at the desks doing the end-of-shift paperwork when the Sergeant walked in the room. He could see Winchester and Reggie at the far end of the room, heads down, trying to finish.

"Lads, need you to come with me to see the DCI. What have you both been up to? You will be the death of me, my wife will kill me if I am late again tonight, got the brother and his wife over for dinner, so off you go now and see her."

Winchester looked at Reggie. "I told you we would get dragged up again because of the book."

They both stood outside the DCI's office. She was on the phone, they could hear her say, "Yes, sir, yes, sir, I will deal with it, of course, sir, thank you, sir." And the phone went down with a bang. Winchester and Reggie looked at each other. "Come in, you two."

Both of them walked through the door. Before they could close the door, the DCI just said, "When you dealt with that heart attack this morning, did you pick up anything that was his?"

"Yes, ma'am, we found a little notebook but they had already taken him to hospital so I booked it in the property room a few hours ago."

She looked at them with fixed staring eyes; she said, "Winchester, knowing you as I do, you must've looked inside it."

"Yes, ma'am, all it was, numbers and locations, that is all."

"Okay, well sign it out now and take it to the front desk, leave it for a person from his company to pick it up tonight. You can go now." The DCI was not impressed with someone, but it was not Winchester or Reggie. Calling someone sir would be like the Chief or the assistant Chief.

Jennie was coming round to see Winchester tonight – he would share with her the notebook information, see what she makes of it. He really liked Jennie even though she was technically a spy.

Chapter Five

Jennie arrived at Winchester's flat, wearing an all-in-one trouser suit, black, she looked fabulous, Winchester thought; low heels, hair was up revealing her neck. She had a sports bag with her as well so Winchester thought she was going someplace later.

"I bought some wine," Jennie said. "What we eating tonight?"

"I have done us a salmon mixed salad with new potatoes."

"Sounds great," she said.

Winchester said, "You going to the GYM later?"

"What makes you say that?" Jennie said.

"Your gym bag with you?"

"If I was going to the gym I would have left it in the car, Sherlock." Winchester got the point. "It's my overnight bag."

She walked up to Winchester who had in one hand a knife, in the other a tea towel. She kissed him and said, "I am going to have a shower then I am going to come back for dinner," with a big smile on her face.

Winchester was lost for words.

The next morning Winchester was in bed looking at Jennie lying next to him, wondering how to tell her she was fantastic last night but her snoring was unbelievable – the doors and windows were rattling. Such a sexy woman could make such a noise. Winchester made them some tea. As she woke up, the first thing she said was "did I snore last night?" – yes – "was I loud?" – yes – "do you want to sleep with me again?" – "well, sleeping with you will be a problem if I don't get ear plugs, but if you are asking would I make love to you again, yes, oh yes".

Jennie smiled and said, "Well I can tell you now then, you can't cook, you must be the worst in the world." She laughed.

As they lay talking, Winchester explained to Jennie about the book. She seemed very interested. "But you have not got the notebook now then?"

"No, but I took some copies of it."

Jennie said, "You make a good spy. Let's see what you have but first, let's have some more fun."

As Jennie sat up in bed reading the information on the photocopied sheets from the notebook, she become very thoughtful as she lay her head back, looking at the ceiling. "This is very, very interesting. I am going to give you some confidential information that you must not repeat."

Winchester looked at Jennie with anticipation.

"Well," Jennie said to Winchester.

"Well what?"

"You will not repeat?"

"No of course not, who do you take me for?"

"Well you're telling me everything thing in bed, it's called pillow talk." Jennie grinned.

Winchester kissed her very softly on the lips and said, "I promise."

"We carried out an investigation about five years ago about the very thing you are talking about; we got shut down very quickly by the dark boys."

Winchester looked puzzled. "Who the bloody hell is the dark boys?"

Jennie said every country has them, USA are the CIA, Chinese have mystery of state security, Russia has FSK and so on, but they all have a Dark arts sort of branch that the governments all know they exist but do not know what they do. They are all self-funding as well, they keep what they get from shutting down things. Win-win for all, but no real accountability. We got told what was a going on was sanctioned by the government.

"So, Winchester, be very careful."

"I will."

Jennie also said, "You have come of interest to my head of department."

"Why?"

"Because of your mind and the way it works; in a few years I would say you may be poached. I must go to work. I will be gone for a month," Jennie said. "I will call you. We are over in the USA with homeland security services in the States agreeing the next visit to the UK by the president."

Winchester was on the early shift again this week, and winter nights were drawing in, the cold rain and winds walking to the station were going to be back. Winchester did not mind the getting up and walking, but when it was cold rain, the day was just a poor start.

Winchester was a little late for the train and as he jumped on he saw two new faces this time; they were dressed in LU cleaning company uniforms. Winchester nodded to them, "morning, lads".

They both looked up from what they were doing and nodded back. Winchester looked at them and he thought they were not cleaners —as long as I got a hole in my backside, they just looked too clean cut. The way they both spoke to each other, he was trying to say to himself stop stereotyping as he was trained not to. Cleaners are on five pounds an hour; one had a watch on that looked 200 pounds of anyone's money. This time they were cleaning the seats only, spraying them with something.

Winchester stood up and walked towards them both. "HI, lads, what's that you are using on the seats?"

"It's a bacterial cleaner, everyone who sits on the seats forget all others that sit on it, building workers, drunks, office workers, homeless sleep on them sometimes, also think about the bodily fluids, and people passing wind all the time... if you thought about it, you would never sit on them again."

The driver announced "this train is departing", and they both jumped off, but as Winchester started to walk back to his seat, he was thinking what they had said about what was in and on the train seats which made him wonder. He kicked something on the floor; it was a small spray bottle with IGI – the cleaners must have left it. He picked it up. It was a clear bottle with a small number on it. He could just make out the writing, it said Pneumococcal. Winchester thought never heard of that before, he put it in his bag and put it in his locker at the station and never said a word. He knew later when he was doing his paperwork he would look it up on the internet.

Today Winchester and Reggie were on traffic stops, seat belts, no tax, no insurance. This was going to be a fun day, knowing the abuse they would get – it is unbelievable, from 'you are wasting public money', 'I am colour blind it wasn't red light I went through', 'haven't you not got better things to do like getting real criminals off the streets first', 'I can't put on my seat belt I am busting for a pee and it's hurting me'. It's a government drive, we get them every so often. For a few weeks it gets all the newspapers going, then the police have to spend the next few months trying to get everything back to some normality.

Winchester spotted a car with four youths in it, BMW 7 series. The driver did not look old enough to own one of them; it was a year old according to the plate. None of them had a seat belt on anyway. Winchester pulled them over. "What you want, Plod?"

Great, Winchester thought, this car stinks of cannabis. Winchester looked at Reggie, as the driver who was about 12 years old in appearance and had a toilet mouth, started saying, "Why you pulled me over, man?"

"Because you are not wearing a seatbelt."

"Fuck off, man, do you know who I am?"

"No," Winchester said, "but I am about to find out very soon."

"Can you turn off the engine and give me the keys, sir," Reggie said.

"No," the driver said, "it's my car", clearly out of his mind on drugs. "My dad told me all coppers are bastards."

"Yes we are, so give me the keys or I will show you what sort of bastard I am." Reggie was getting inpatient. "Get out of the car now, sir."

Winchester noticed that none of the others were saying anything, just looked totally away with the fairies. "All of you, one at a time, out of the car."

Then all of a sudden the car shot off for about 20 feet right into a lamppost. Winchester and Reggie now had a van full of eight other officers for back up, officers turned up and everyone in the car were all dragged out of the car, they were all laid on the ground and cuffed, loaded in the van and taken to Mile End nick. Reggie and Winchester had to wait for the police recovery lorry for the BMW, and while waiting they carried out a search of the vehicle. They needed evidence bags as well before they removed anything; the crime scene team sent a car with bags and records search book. Winchester found six small bags of cannabis in the back seat, and nine credit cards with different names on them, plus one hand gun plastic toy real lookalike. The car was insured and he was the driver; he was 18 years old, nine points already on his licence, PNC came back as father was a known gangster in the West End. When Winchester and Reggie got to Mile End nick, they were told detectives have taken over the situation. "Thanks, off you go," the Sergeant said, "sorry, lads."

Winchester looked at Reggie with the feeling of disappointment but acceptance. "Get yourself tea out back, lads, leave 20p in the jug."

Back out on the streets to continue seat belt and other stops, just did nine tickets each for the day, got back to station, only to see CI Aston looking really fed up, walking past to see the Sergeants about some problem with turf wars with the City of London police.

Apparently one of our officers arrested someone on their patch without informing them, they do get a little twitchy.

Winchester arrived home. As he walked towards his front door number 13, on the floor was a box marked PC Winchester. Firstly, who would call him by that name in the flats and you would never order something with the word PC in front of it. It was a small bag with a letter sellotaped to the front. Winchester picked it up, took it inside and opened it first before the letter; it was a small memory stick wrapped in bubble wrap. Then opened the letter, this was handwritten to Winchester. It said: *dear PC Winchester, I am giving you a memory stick that has information on it that is top secret, you have come to my attention through observation, I will not explain now but see what is on the stick, the password is COBA 999. Regards a friend.*

Winchester had a standalone computer that did take a memory stick, but then Jennie knocked on the door with a bunch of flowers. Winchester started to laugh. "What are they?"

"To brighten up this man cave of a flat."

Winchester said, "That's not true, every time you come here it brightens up the place." She smiled as she kissed him on the lips.

He said, "I got this left outside of my door. What do you think it is?"

Jennie said, "How do I know, I just walked through the door."

Winchester started up the computer. While he waited for it to boot up, he and Jennie went to the kitchen to see what they could rummage together for food. Inside the fridge looked like the typical 1970s Male fridge: two pork pies, lemonade, butter, a few eggs, milk, cheese triangles, pickled onions. Jennie said, "Wow, this is not going to feed us. What you got in the cupboards?" – opened it up: cream crackers, white bread, tins of beans, spaghetti hoops, tinned tomatoes, marmite, Cornflakes. Oh yes, custard.

"My god," Jennie said, "I never seen such a time capsule from the 70s before."

"There is a chip shop down the road, let's get some."

They both went off to get them. Winchester ordered pie and chips. Jennie looked at him and said, "I knew that is what you would get." She ordered Rock (salmon), chips and mushy peas. Winchester said, "You cannot take the northerner out of you."

They got back to the flat and sat and ate. "What do you think is on the stick?"

"Not sure, but it's making me uneasy."

"Someone is watching you," Jennie said.

The stick fired up and it said:

'This is a training manual for Central line only. Safety section one briefing.

All operations must be kept top secret. All PPE must be worn but discreet.

Operations 1

From November till March, options 1 April to July option 2 August to November operation 3,4, 5.'

So far this looks nothing; the name of the company was on the screen, it was Dazary UK & International Global Industries plc.

Run by a billionaire Nikolai Dazary, took over from his father, a ruthless businessman. Little like a godfather of the manufacturing world of the medical drug market. This company has a reputation for not liking competition, but mind you, who does. Then the film of what to do, it was a makeshift train carriage with a commentary of what to do. You see the person wash with some yellow cloths the standing handrails at the end of each row of seats by the doors, then green cloths for the drop down handles, spray bottles one squirt per seat from one metre high. Only summer will this operation take place. A small little red-looking item that was magnetic, which was the size of a chicken egg, placed out of view between the interconnected doors of the carriage – this will omit a timed release, this will then flow through the carriage if the windows between the carriages are open, this will be in the summer only. We do not apply any of the chemicals to the last sections of the front or the rear of the train as they may affect the drivers.

Anyone looking at this would think it was a standard cleaning manual for the train. But this was delivered to Winchester with a short note: *I will let you know what this is about if you want, I will meet with you soon, I will contact you.*

Jennie said, "This is a woman who has left this."

"How do you know that?"

"Look at the writing, she is also left handed. It looks like we have a whistleblower," Jennie said. "I need to take this with me so I can show it to my team I work with. Don't download it, if it is what I think it is you could be in trouble if you do download it."

The following morning Jennie left about 6 am taking with her the memory stick. Winchester left for work, only to be called in to see the CI again. Winchester and Reggie got to the office; they could see that CI Aston was not in a good mood, you could not see her teeth – that meant she was pissed off. The whole division knew this.

"Come in, sit down."

As they walked in the door they saw a BTP officer sitting with a white mug of tea in his hand, fully uniformed up, looked like a Assistant Chief. "This is Jamie Mills, we have a small problem and both of you seem to be right in the middle of it again."

"What is your understanding of jurisdiction between British Transport Police and us the Metropolitan Police?"

Winchester said, "Not sure, Ma'am."

Reggie said, "BTP looks after all land and property that includes British transport, ie trains, stations, rail lines and sometimes just outside the station."

"Well, you are correct, so why have we dealt with three incidents on BTP ground and not handed it over to them?"

"Ma'am," Winchester said, "we are not sure what you are on about. Any time we have done anything BTP have cuffed it off to us. It was as easy as that."

The BTP AC just looked hard at Reggie and Winchester. Never said a word.

"Okay that will be all and in the future make sure we get the jurisdictions right and take the officer's name if they cuff off. Off you go."

"What was that all about?"

"They are right," Reggie said, "the incidents, two on the platform and the delivering bad news was their job not us, but it come through our control room."

"You know what I think," Winchester said.

Reggie rolled his eyes to the ceiling knowing what Winchester was going to say.

"I think it's because of what we have uncovered, or we are getting someone's attention."

"What do you mean?" Reggie said.

"Well I got this memory stick posted to me or left by hand anyway; it was some sort of instructions how to clean the inside of a train, throughout the year."

"Why would anyone want to send you or give you that?" Reggie enquired.

"How do I know?"

"I think someone is messing with your head. Come on we have a job to do today, we got the warrants to do later this morning, three failed to appear."

"Really?"

"Yes, I bet we know who they are before we get the paperwork, it's always the same twats yet the courts still let them walk the streets."

They picked up the paperwork from the Sergeant.

"Well," Reggie said, "I know where Chris Smalley will be, out washing his cars as always. It's Thursday, he will be doing the hospital vans. Let's nick him last as he is doing a good job, let's let the ambulances get cleaned first. I know baby face Western, he will be playing with his small banjo band in his mum's shed, I bet, let's get him first then swing by and pick up knuckles AKA Mike Newlands, copper top, 20 points on his license, 12 of them before he could drive on his scrambling bike." He was wanted in connection with beating up a motorist for knocking him off his bike. This was an interesting, easy day for them both, they got all three of them, they came quietly and they all got bailed to reappear.

Winchester was walking towards his building; he could see a woman standing outside the entrance door to the apartments. She looked a little uneasy, looking side to side then walking away from the door, then back as if she couldn't make up her mind. Winchester could just about see this going on; it was about 8 30 pm and the nights had started to draw in. His road that led to the flats was 500 yards long; once you turn into the road you could see Winchester's apartments, it used to be a big old manor house. She spotted Winchester and became more agitated. Winchester got to within ten feet and said, "Can I help you?"

"No," she replied and started to walk off, then stopped and turned round. "Are you Winchester?"

"Yes, that's right, who might you be?"

"I am Hellen. I left you the memory stick. Can we talk inside?"

"Yes, of course."

Hellen was about 5'8 tall, slim build, brunette, private school accent, all words calculated and pronounced.

She was very nervous; her hands were squeezed together, fingers moving all the time; her eyes would not make direct contact.

"Would you like a drink of water or tea?"

"Oh yes please, I have been waiting for hours for you to come home."

"Yes, on that," Winchester said, "how did you get the memory stick to the outside of my door?"

"I saw your neighbour, I gave it to him. He said he would leave it outside your door," Hellen said. "You still have the stick?"

"Yes, it's at the station in my locker."

Winchester gave Hellen her tea, one sugar, white, in a china cup. "Sit down on the chair," Winchester said, "and take your jacket off, tell me about everything."

"I am a biological scientist, I work for a large organisation, in London, and I found out they were up to no good." Hellen said, "This is going to be hard to believe. The government knows what they do and it's sanctioned, but what the government bodies don't know or if they do but turn a blind eye, is that my company is also carrying out assassinations and other private money making schemes."

Winchester's eyes opened really wide. "Can you prove this?"

"No, because if I could I would have gone to the papers, but I also know that I could be killed as well."

Winchester looked at Hellen hard. "Really?" he said. "We are in this world of people being killed over this situation, in this day and age, it's not the Cold War."

Hellen looked at him. "You really are missing the point here. If this got out, they would lose billions; people kill for much less."

Winchester thought for a moment. "It's true, people have been killed for a few hundred pounds."

Winchester then said, "Explain to me the history and how and when this is done."

Hellen said, "It goes back to when terrorist attacks started, we had to look at dirty bombs. The government approached the pharmaceutical companies to carry out experiments, like nerve agents. So what people like I did was to use the underground as a system of tracking, so we could not use a nerve agent, that would be silly, but something that would spread very quickly. This was of course Viral Rhinitis, the common cold. So we use two lines, the District and the Central lines first. We felt this would give us a wide spectrum of social spread, the demographics being London, because this would be the biggest impact for any terrorist organisation. Our company was the only one allowed to do this because our CEO Dazary had connections in the government.

"What it showed is that the spread was amazing, more than anyone could ever have suspected. Central line day one being zero say was Monday. Day three for incubation, day four we saw 500 thousand people going to chemists throughout Greater London, this was carried out in the summer so we did not get it mixed with the winter colds. Best results, we had a few hayfevers in this but in general we noted a big lift. Day 6 we noted 3.9 million visitors to the chemist. We in the world of drugs know everything that chemists do, everything is logged and recorded. This country is one of the best in the world at this from doctors to all healthcare. By day 10 we had 10.3 million people infected then it started to decrease over the next four weeks back to normal.

"This information was passed to all the government bodies and a COBRA meeting was held because of the results. This was all very top secret and rightly so, and counter systems have been put in place to suppress this. The government tasked our company with three-month monitoring for the next 10 years. This we have been doing. But greed has also become part of this. So drug companies were approached by our board and a secret agreement was made to make billions of pounds."

Winchester's jaw had dropped wide open. He was hanging on every word. "How did they do that?"

"So you see, you have already stumbled on it. I will put it to you in layman's terms. You produce as a company cough mixture, you sell on average a million units a year, if I said I could generate ten times that amount across the country, what would you say?"

"Yes."

"There are three entry points to our bodies, we work on cuts and abrasions, but skin absorption's very hard, airborne mouth, nose and eyes."

Winchester took a deep breath and looked very hard at Hellen. Winchester's mind was working overtime. "I get the making money bit, that is the world over – but killing people, why..."

Hellen seemed to stammer, before saying what she did. "From what I can gather, a family pharmacist in Epping was about to blow the whistle, not sure what his name was, but it was a small company in a very large pond.

"I am sure they targeted his business, I can't prove it but I know they killed his colleague with a heart attack drug. This would have had to be sprayed onto his skin directly, it's a short exposure time. It evaporates within seconds, it will go right into your skin. It was developed by the US Government in the 70s, Cold War."

Winchester said, "Why have you not even gone to the security services because they know about this."

"I think that I can't trust anyone."

"Why me?" Winchester said.

"I saw your name on a piece of confidential file, you are under surveillance, you've been noticed carrying out observations on the trains."

"Are they watching now?"

"No, it's only when you are on the train. I would not be here if you were."

"BTP must know this is going on under their noses."

"Yes, but they have been told to keep out of the way as this is government business. They are in the dark, they think it's the terrorist ongoing future planning the government is doing. We were told one of the inspectors at BTP asked a few to many questions and was made to retire. They've got stuff on everyone. We are talking multi-national companies with billions at stake."

Winchester said, "Right, let me get my head round this, explain to me what they do, how they do it."

"In the winter they are less active because colds and flu are around and humans just spread it naturally. But they still need to give it a push. It's not prescription drugs they want, it's over the counter stuff. It's more money, short turnaround, most people that use the underground are of working age, reasonably healthy, well this does not include obesity. So in the Winter months they may introduce a new strain of flu. This will affect say your eyes and taste, smell. From this people will buy eye drops, nose sprays and new other mild drugs that a company wants to sell. If you think about it, how come the new drugs are in the pharmacy front and centre. I give you, for instance, a drug company brought out a new inhaler for chesty coughs last year. Our company will agree with them on what they are going to release into the carriages, this will be tracked, easy systems. You go into a chemist and ask for something for a chesty cough, they will recommend this inhaler, this then is tracked because of the sale, as a request will come in for replacement for just sold. The company can predict the amount of spread with modelling from the history of the government trials. But you have to be really careful because as asthma sufferers could get caught up in this, if en masse they started going to the doctors it would flag up a problem and it would be investigated by the NHS – they are very good at track and tracing this sort of thing.

"So right," Hellen said, "you know when you saw the people on the train, they were the super spreading team. Did one of them sit by the window that adjoined the other carriage?"

"Yes, once."

"Well he will have an auto spray on him some place, designed to release every two minutes and the train moving will generate airflow throughout the carriage and everyone will breathe it in. So you infect the whole carriage in seconds. This will be repeated every day for one week, infecting about 20 million people plus. But you see not all people are the same, young people are more resistant to flu, so they go for more easy entry points, like hands. People don't wash their hands enough, they touch their face, pick noses, put makeup on, shake hands, humans make it so easy for them. It's a billion dollar industry.

"So the teams you will see, that is their jobs, they are not cleaning but spreading the bacteria on the trains and we as humans do the rest."

Winchester said, "Where did the assassinations come in?"

"Not too sure," Hellen said, "but it is known that the security services are sniffing around with the Americans, they do this all over the world you know, it's on the Metro in New York, but the London project is by far the most profitable, because of the NHS."

Winchester said they could spread anything.

"Yes, they could, but I only know of this situation within the organisation, I know of other groups doing other stuff," Hellen said. "I came to you because you are a police officer and you can research information others and I cannot."

"I think they suspect me already, I need to speak to someone about this," Winchester said.

"Yes," Hellen said, "but don't give me up please because if you do, I am sure I will disappear like a few others I know. Not sure if they've been transferred or just got rid of."

Winchester said, "I have a friend in the security services, she is trustworthy."

Hellen looked at him. "Did she suddenly appear when you started to see what was going on on the trains? Because if she did, they, as I said before, they know you have noticed something, now I have told you what is going on you are in their crosshairs.

"Because you are a police officer, they would not try anything, they will keep a close eye on you that is for sure. The good thing is at this time they obviously don't think you know much," Hellen said. "How they get away with all this, all the police services do not pass information between each other. BTP have some, City of London have more information and the Met, well they have bits all over the place. If someone looked at this as a whole, it would show a pattern. No joined up thinking and that is what the organisation rely on.

"Think about it, it's so hard to prove or be detected."

Winchester looked at his white wall in his apartment trying to think.

Hellen suddenly said, "I will need to go. I will contact you, but what I will do now we have spoken is give you this."

It was six pieces of A4 paper with names on it. "This is the list of suspected names of people that have died over the last ten years from mistakes."

"Mistakes?" Winchester said.

Hellen said, "Yes, they don't want people to die, it's counterproductive. Think about it, if they are dead their value is nil."

Winchester said, "So how will the mistakes be detectable?"

"Well," as Hellen sat back down. "In societies, you have the weak people. When I say this I am referring to their biological make up. To make it easy. You are a fit person, you don't smoke or drink heavily I am assuming, well a virus like a cold will say make you unwell for about 10 to 14 days. If you are a smoker or diabetic or suffer from respiratory problems, this could have catastrophic symptoms and effects. This list I give you is a direct link to when we used a summer cold testing on the District line, mostly in the areas of Barking and Dagenham. They kept an eye on three hospitals in the area. It was put down to pollution, poor standards of living and lack of interest from government bodies. Just like police, NHS hospitals do not share information very much, they all rely on word of mouth. I can tell you over the tests of ten years, 1800 people are on that list. But again you could never prove it, people with underlying illnesses, it's taken for granted they will possibly die from winter colds or pollution. It's within government expectations of common deaths."

Winchester said, "If they all died over 10 years, why did they keep trying the colds in the summer?"

"Summer is the low time in drugs over the counter, so hayfever and asthma, insect repellents, sunburn treatments do not make as much money. So, if you introduce a cold like virus they make billions of pounds over the school holiday season. I know of one team that works around aircraft coming back to the UK, not going out.

"Think about that: they land and are all infected, a week later they get a cold and blame the holiday. They have a spray called Musk cold. It smells great, so they would walk down the carriage or any place and you will smell this nice what you think is perfume, so you are smelling it and taking it in."

Winchester said, "What happens to the people spreading?"

"They have antibodies."

Winchester sat there in disbelief. "My brain hurts," he said. "This is like a web of coverups and defrauding I have never thought possible."

Hellen said, "Just be careful who you tell without evidence; also, keep stuff out of your place here. They will break in to find it. I will not contact you again unless I have anything else."

Winchester said, "How can I get hold of you?"

Hellen said, "You can't. I am off to the USA for a year, been transferred."

She said goodbye and "be careful". She was gone.

Winchester had to think about who he could bring in on this. Reggie, of course, and maybe CI Aston as she is above reproach. Winchester was thinking all night about what Hellen had said, but he could not understand about the assassinations on trains. She did not explain how and why, something he would have to work out himself.

Winchester remembered that Hellen had said they would break in, so when he left for work that morning he took some Sellotape, put it on the bottom of his front door so if anyone opened the door he would know.

Heading into work at 5 am, it was still dark, the rain was fine like a mist. He got on the first train out; his mind was all over the place, with this new information, everything was falling into place. Winchester saw the London Transport cleaners working their way through the train, they were most definitely cleaners, had the uniforms and they looked like they were cleaners; but one tall male with a trilby hat on, dark long coat got on the carriage, sat at the far end of the carriage away from Winchester. The rain outside had started to get heavier. The male looked very smart, seemed to look very stiff, he had a briefcase, he opened the window that joined the next carriage, it was raining but it was still the beginning of September so a little warm, but Winchester thought he has a coat on. Winchester caught himself looking at him too long, a little creepy. The train pulled out and as they moved up along the stations more and more workers got on, other police officers and office cleaners, builders, the carriage was say 60% full, no one standing. Winchester noticed the male started to do something in his briefcase. As they pulled into Mile End station, he stood up and walked down the carriage, passing two sets of doors then out the last door next to Winchester. Winchester got up and got off the train to see what he did: he walked across the platform and got on the waiting District line train that had just pulled in. He saw him go the end of that carriage and as it pulled out he opened the window again; this is one of the things they do, they spread it using the natural air flow through the train to dispense the virus. Winchester waited for the next train to get in; he had only one more stop. He put the information in his notebook. If Hellen was right, he would get some sort of illness in the next few days at best. Winchester got to the station and was having a mug of tea with the other officers before roll call.

Reggie said, "You are looking in deep thought."

Winchester said, "Mate you would not believe what I now know, we need to talk later."

In roll call the Sergeant was in a funny old mood, he was a little stressed. "First of all, everyone, I need to confirm with you all the following. Do you all understand BTP's jurisdictions?"

Some of the older officers nodded but a few of the younger ones said we had some inductions at training school but not that much.

"Well, right," said the Sergeant. "Any area that's transporting the public is the easy one, this is not including buses having problems on the roads, but the bus garage is BTP. All rail stations are BTP. If you get a call to assist you must let them take the lead, even if you are first on scene. Control room will liaise with BTP force control. Do not let them cuff it off to you. If in doubt contact me on the radio or any other Sergeant. Today we are on the lookout for a missing person, he is 75 years old, went shopping last night, has memory problems, he's 5'10, dark hair, black raincoat, trainers, brown trousers. Last seen leaving the supermarket on Bow Road 1830. Never gone missing before. One thing, lads he is ex job Sergeant city officer. Now be safe, off with you all, see you all safe and sound here later."

Reggie and Winchester were on the beat round the main trouble areas this morning, as the local councillors were unhappy with young yobs making noise and graffiti on walls. But as always, they shout a lot but think the police will sort it out, it's a community issue they need to sort; we as police officers can only try and catch them in the act, and how likely will that be as most of it's done at night. It was hard enough with all the knee jerk stuff we had to do when the government wanted to score brownie points. Knife crime is on the increase, young gangs black and white, stabbing each other. This carnage is so sad, it devastates families on both sides, even the person who stabs the other often never went out with the intention to kill someone.

A new team had been set up to combat this crime but just stopping people and searching them will not stop people carrying some knives, but it will really upset young black lads; they seem at this time to be most of the people being stabbed. Well people higher up the ladder have the job of sorting this out, we just take the crap on the ground.

Reggie and Winchester were walking along the main Bow Road. In front of them about 100 metres away, they saw two Asian young males get out of two cars, attacking each other with yellow steering wheel locks. Winchester started to run towards them shouting, "Police, Police, put them down."

Reggie got on the radio, calling up for back-up units. As Winchester got to within 30 metres, one of the lads jumped in his car, that was behind the person's car he was hitting with the crook lock, standing directly behind him was the other lad. The driver started to pull away when the lad at the back smashed with his crook lock the rear windscreen. The driver slammed on his brakes, put it in reverse, and drove at the lad behind who had no place to go. Winchester saw the lad get smashed against the other car at knee height. For a split second he was trapped between both cars. As the other car sped off, he collapsed to the ground, but as luck would have it, a traffic car saw the lad trying to speed off and rammed him and wedged him in his car and a lamppost. Winchester shouted as he got to the lad, "Call an ambulance." A fire truck was also coming up the road.

Winchester looked at this young lad on the road, he had to opened sheen fractures jeans all open he was screaming in pain. Winchester said stay still, no fuck off pig, I will kill him he disrespected my sister. A station officer from the LFB and three. Others come over with first aid kit they saw what was going on from the other side of the road they were doing hydrants testing. A doctors come out with a nurse from a GP practice across the road. Winchester said to Reggie this is a right mess, yes the Sergeant is on his way.

The other driver had been dragged through his driver's window and was on the floor with blood pouring down his head from being hit by the yellow crook locks, they were also coned off for the crime team. Then all hell let lose. Four unmarked cars turned up; they had guns, they were the covert antiterrorist team, they flashed in like the owners of the situation – we really never see them much. They grabbed the one on the floor and said to the two traffic officers, "We will take him." One of the traffic officers said, "Hang on, need a bit more than that, mate."

The senior looking person went over and grabbed the traffic officers, pulled him away from earshot, said something and then went back and said "let's go". They put the young lad in the car and took him off. The traffic officer was really hacked off. You could see that. The doctor was trying to treat the other one; he was losing a lot of blood. He would not shut up, kept saying, "I am going to kill him."

The ambulance arrived and they spoke to the doctor. The other two cars from the anti-terrorist team said, "we will follow the ambulance", and one of them got in it with him just as the Sergeant got to the scene. Reggie had noticed the old woman sitting in the car that had been rammed and the lad was smashed against, was sitting in the car with the look of shock. Shaking and tears running down her face. He sat next to her and tried to keep her calm. Her car was ok but had blood all over the front of it and a dent on the bumper. The fire lads cleaned it off. One of the firefighters said they could clean the road, but the Sergeant said no we have to leave it for the SOCO boys. "This lad is going to lose both legs," the doctor said. They were hanging on by just a few bits of muscle. The bones were shattered.

The traffic officers were tasked to take the old woman home and drive her car. Winchester was instructed by the Sergeant with Reggie to "get back to the station and complete your statements" as they had also witnessed what happened. The traffic officers had to also take a statement from the woman, but get her home first.

Winchester and Reggie went to the canteen to get a tea and try and sort out the statements of what they had seen. CI Aston and the DCI walked into the canteen looking around for someone.

Reggie said, "They are looking for us I bet."

Yep he was right. They spotted them but first went to get tea themselves. You could see CI Aston was ok, you could see her teeth and the DCI Stewart Robbins who was a grumpy git also had a smile on his face. "Well, well, well, what have you both been up to?" DCI Robbins said.

Both Reggie and Winchester looked puzzled. "Not sure, sir, what you are referring to."

"Well, you have both stopped on our ground a small terrorist cell. Operating in Bow."

"Oh you are talking about what happened today when we both saw the incident between the two Asian lads? That was not a terrorist situation, was it? Seemed to me," Winchester said, "it was a honour thing, one lad had been knocking off his sister without his family's permission. They got into it and trying to kill each other."

"The person on the floor, Hassan, is an undercover operative for the government and he said the person who did this to him had been arrested by the security team following him."

Winchester said, "So what do we need to do with our statements?"

"Well this is why we are here, your statements will be part of the terrorist cell investigation, because of the highly top secret situation, you both must get this dead right. We want this to be a situation that they believe what you said and were told so we can get the other person out of the terror cell. He will do time and will be put on remand. We are not sure if our man was made or not. So when you have completed your statements, take it to CI Aston. We need to make sure that the CPS are happy with every word in the witness statements we can get."

Winchester said, "We have the female witness in the car, she saw everything, it was right in front of her; also CCTV at the roundabout may help."

Winchester and Reggie finished their statements, took them to the CI and left them for her to go through. They both headed off to London hospital to take the statement from the middle aged female that had been taken ill when the traffic unit was taking her home.

Winchester said to Reggie, "Do you remember what she looked like?"

"Yes, she was the really vivid redhead."

The hospital reception desk was long with three people sitting behind, it had a protective glass screen for the staff, they all had name badges.

"Hello Molly, can you book me in on location?" Reggie said. He had been to this hospital so many times he knew all the reception staff.

She nodded. "You're both booked in."

They were directed up to the general ward. "Why is she in a ward, I did not think she was injured?"

"Neither did I," Winchester said.

They got to the general ward to be met by the staff nurse who looked very grumpy and fed up. "Can I help you two officers?"

"We are looking for a female that had been bought in after the RTA at Bow roundabout, by our team," Reggie said. "She is very ginger."

"Oh she has gone, the security services come and met with her about two hours ago and she went with them; she was okay."

"This is not good; we have not taken a statement from her; we are in real trouble now. The CI will be blowing bubbles out of her ears."

Winchester got on the radio and requested a point to point with the Sergeant. It took two seconds before his radio was making the distinct sound of the point to point on his radio. "Gov, the female has already left the hospital with the security services."

He did not say a word, just ended the call.

Both officers went to the staff hospital canteen; the food was okay here and it was cheap for service personnel.

"What a day so far. We need to get back to station and get the statements on the system or we will get another telling off."

"I must say," Reggie said to Winchester, "we have worked together for a year now and I have never in all the years on the job had so many bollockings." With a big grin Reggie added, "Well it's also good fun to see the brass get all hot under the collar."

Winchester said, "I will go and inform the CI about the redhead who has vanished. Did we get the reg number of the car? We can find her through that, I will look on PNC."

"Why you are getting chewed out?"

If looks could kill right now... as Winchester headed upstairs trying to think of an easy way of giving bad news and thank god they do not shoot the messenger anymore, but with CI Aston you could not tell.

Winchester knocked on the door.

"Come in."

"Ma'am, I have some bad news."

She was reading a file off the top of eight other files sitting on her desk; she had on black glasses. She kept the file in-front of her in both her hands and looked up over the top of her glasses, like a school teacher when you know you have done something wrong. "Yes, Winchester, what is the bad news?"

"We have lost the female at the hospital–" and before the CI could say a word Winchester added, "but we know her reg number of her car and PC Reggie is on PNC now looking up the home address."

Aston never said a word, just let Winchester ramble on about what had happened. Winchester had run out of words now and stopped talking. From behind the file she said, "Thank you, that will be all and close the door on your way out."

Winchester went back out the door like a bullet out of a gun, forgot to close the door, got halfway down the corridor and turned back, closed the CI's door very quickly. "Phew that was not too bad, I am getting out of earshot."

Reggie was sitting at one of the hot desks in the main room behind reception. "We must have taken down the reg number wrong."

"No we didn't, you got the same as me, we both could not have done that."

"It comes back as a bread van in Birmingham. Could this day get any better?" Reggie said.

"Yes, well the gov never went off as we thought she would."

"Wow that's a first. Is that good?"

"Not sure."

The Sergeant walked out of his office and caught sight of both of them. "Just the two I am after."

"Yes, SARGE?"

"Transport Police have just called in, they have another very dead person but he is just outside the station and they need us to attend."

"What station?"

"Mile End, take the VG 06, it's an old Ford transit people carrier from the SPG days; it's due for the scrap heap but it's all we have left outside."

Reggie and Winchester took some old bin bags from the cleaner's cupboard because the seats in the van were rank, sick, blood, food tea and coffee stains everywhere. Inside the windscreen had spit and snot; it was so bad.

They could see as they got close to Mile End station the ambulance and two British transport police cars, lights flashing, body on the floor was covered waiting for the doctor to pronounce.

"Hi lads, what we got here?"

"Young male in his late 20s, just walked out of the station and dropped dead right here. People saw him grab his chest, fall to the ground, a local nurse started CPR and called the ambulance, they got here and he was blue. Paramedic said he had kicked the bucket, they thought massive heart attack."

"Bit young," Winchester said.

"Yes, he is. Well, we hand it over to you, lads because if he would have gone over five feet back there we would have been in our jurisdiction."

Reggie said, "Did you drag him over here then?" with a smile, as the BTP lads walked away smiling as the got into their cars.

"Reggie, they bloody did you know, I bet they dragged him over here."

Winchester and Reggie spoke to a nurse on her way to work who had tried in vain to resuscitate him. She said, "He fell where he is right now."

Reggie had a look on his face: I was wrong.

The doctor turned up and confirmed what we all knew: he was dead. The private ambulance had arrived to take him off to the morgue. Reggie confirmed which hospital he was going to so they could take his information correctly to inform the family.

The doctor said he could not confirm the cause of death – "that's for the coroner to confirm, but from what I see, I think massive heart failure."

Winchester got out the young lad's wallet, his name was James Welty-Robbins. Home address was the Manor House, Dunmow, Essex, he is a pharmacist.

Reggie said to Winchester, "OMG that's going to get your conspiracy stuff going again, isn't it."

Winchester said, "We need to contact Essex police to deliver the bad news, we need to follow this to its conclusion as well, he works at the research centre here in London for the Government. I know the place just off Tottenham Court Road, it's a new research centre."

They confirmed with the control they were going to the offices of the dead person before confirming his information. Winchester and Reggie arrived at the building; it was an old Art Deco building, Shropshire House, fabulous-looking building. They went into main reception, and the security guard behind the desk asked, "What can I do for you, officers?"

"We want to speak to someone James Welty-Robbins works for or with."

Each side of the reception desk were a line of glass tubes, six to be correct. The security guard spoke to someone on the phone and then said, "You can go up to the second floor, someone will meet you from the lift."

Winchester and Reggie walked up to the tubes and they opened and then they walked in one side, which closed behind them then the front opened. They could see CCTV cameras in the tube. As they come out of the lift they were met by a woman in a white lab coat. "Hello, I am head of this department, how can I help you?"

"We need to inform you about James Welty-Robbins."

She stepped in before they could finish. "Professor."

Winchester looked at her and said, "It did not say that on his ID."

"No they don't, it's names only here, but he is a professor of biochemistry."

Reggie said, "Well, Miss Byrne, we need to get confirmation on his address and a description of him."

She looked puzzled. "Well I think you should ask him yourself. I will go get him."

Winchester and Reggie just looked at each other with confused expressions.

She was gone for two minutes and returned with a male, about 5'8, black hair, who asked, "Can I help you, officers?"

Winchester said, "Can you confirm you are James Welty-Robbins?"

"Yes, that's me, why, what's happened, is my wife okay?"

Reggie said, "Do you have somewhere we can talk privately, sir? And yes, your wife as far as we know is fine. You can call her if you like."

Winchester got on the radio very quickly as he knew that an Essex officer had been given the task to deliver the news after confirmation of ID.

Reggie said to James, "Someone has died and was carrying your ID and even has a driving licence. Would you know if anyone has been using your ID?"

"No, not at all."

Reggie said, "I think you best ring your wife, sir, as an officer has been tasked with informing her about your demise and the situation."

As he was ringing her, Winchester said, "This is getting weird."

Reggie nodded in agreement.

Winchester's radio went off on a point to point from CI Aston. "Both of you need to get back to station."

"Yes, ma'am, on our way." Both officers said, "We are sorry for the mix up," and left.

In the van heading back, Winchester was in deep thought. "This is getting silly now, this is the second person dead with someone's

ID. What are the chances of that?"

Reggie said, "I am right, you are a magnet for trouble."

Winchester and Reggie went right to the office of the CI, and knocked on the door, expecting yet another telling off over the location of the body – was it Met police or BTP?

"CID will take over the case now," the CI said as they walked through the door. "Can you confirm what hospital the body went to as they have no records of the body at any hospital at the moment."

"Ma'am, it went to London Hospital Whitechapel. That's what we was told."

"Get down there and find the missing dead person please."

As they walked out, Winchester said, "You know, mate, I was surprised how quick the old private ambulance was on site; I thought it was the BTP lads called it. No records of anybody coming in that fitted that description."

They drove to all the hospitals in the area that had a morgue. Called it in and had to go and see the head of CID. DCI Linda Dolan, she was from the old school of detective work: trust no one and everyone is guilty. She was a bit of a Columbo sort of detective. Tall woman with ginger hair and would take anyone on in a fight. She started at the bottom and worked her way up the real hard way, even becoming part of the Special Patrol Group; as a woman that is hard enough. Her brother is a fire officer in Essex and two other brothers are in the Army.

Winchester and Reggie went into the CID office; it was an office with paperwork everywhere, pictures of most of the wanted criminals, missing people of interest and most of all the bad list of thugs and gang leaders in the London area. All officers knew them by heart and sight. Twelve desks with a computer on every one and a brown phone, empty white mugs around on desks, two officers only on today, as they saw Winchester and Reggie walk through the door. "Hi, lads, got off on the wrong floor, did we?"

Reggie knew all of them as they had been with him as a probationers. Reggie had a lot of respect from all ranks, Reggie was happy being a police officer on the beat, he was happy with that and he was a qualified training officer. Over in the far corner of the office was another office; the door opened and a voice called out: "You two in here now please."

"Yes, ma'am."

"Close the door."

Her office was very tidy, everything in place, pictures on the wall were of her officers and the queen. Big oak desk with a meeting table for six people. "Sit down, want a tea, lads?"

"No thanks."

"Nonsense." She opened the door and called out to one of the detectives, "Three teas please, white."

"Yes, ma'am." Within two minutes the tea was on the table and the DCI was on the phone.

Reggie and Winchester just sat looking at each other. They knew DCI Dolan was on the phone to the Chief Constable as she pointed to the picture of him on the wall and pointed to the phone.

"Yes, sir," she said, "I will get on it right away." She put the phone down with a look that would kill. "Right, drink your tea, it's not poison. Want some sugar?" She placed the container on the table and both took sugar. "Now you are both wondering what you are here for?"

They both nodded.

"Well you see we have a missing person, or should we say body. Losing one body is embarrassing but two bodies is careless, don't you think? And I am getting it in the neck for this from that ivory tower in Victoria (New Scotland Yard). So we are going to talk through right down to the smallest details and see if we can make some logical sense from this whole debacle."

Winchester and Reggie went through everything and the DCI took notes, going back over and over them again, asking the same question. She said, "You are right what you say, the private ambulance is the key, no one has a record of it being requested, both us and BTP. I am going to request both of you to be part of my team on this, I will put my request into CI Aston. Report here tomorrow morning; we have a briefing at 0730 am."

"Yes, ma'am."

They both left, went back to the changing room and just said to each other "what just happened?"! Neither had a clue and were very confused.

Reggie said, "Can you imagine being investigated by the DCI, she would have you in knots, she is good."

Then a voice from the other side of the lockers said, "MI5 have tried to recruit her many times." It was one of the detectives. "If the gaffer has asked you to work with us, you must be alright, the governor doesn't tolerate fools."

That night Winchester had some homework to do. He was putting his own detection together over the weird things that were going on, on the trains. As he got home, he noticed the tape he had put on the bottom of the door was flapping around on the floor – someone had opened his door. Winchester was very quiet opening the door and the light was on in the living room. He grabbed from the hall a broom that was standing against the wall he'd left from the night before, but it was Jennie; she had set the small two-person dinner table and had cooked something for them both.

"Evening," she said.

Winchester remembered he had given her a key.

"Did you think I had forgotten you?" she said.

Winchester said, "I did a bit."

"Well, I am here now, and we have lots to talk about. Food first and some wine, fish and vegetables."

Winchester walked up to her and kissed her very softly on the lips and looked into her eyes and said, "Thank you so much, I missed you."

"Missed you too."

"So what's been going on with you, Jennie?"

"Oh,we have a new director of operations and she is a real task master. We are looking at the new terrorist regulations that have now come into play, we now can intercept conversations and act on international information from the USA – before, the cooperation between us was good but it has now been sanctioned by both governments."

Jennie asked, "What about you?"

Winchester told her all about his last few days.

"I know the DCI you are talking about, she's a really good Officer, but off the record she works both sides of the tracks."

"What do you mean?"

"She is MI6 and police, but keep this to yourself."

After the dishwasher was loaded that still had the last dishes in from the other day that had not been removed, they sat down to talk about what Winchester's thoughts were on the trains and all that he knows.

"One thing I have now found out was, you know the numbers in that book I could not work out? It's carriages, 92205 is a train carriage on the Central line. I was on the train the other morning and I saw the number above the door between carriages."

Jennie said, "Look, what I can say is this is really something you have got here, but not enough to take to anyone yet, get some more evidence."

Winchester said, "I really know I am thinking that the deaths are all linked. I have looked into this a bit. The two I have dealt with, both bodies have gone and they are not the people their ID shows."

Jennie looked at him. "Be careful, if you are right then big money is involved, they will not care who you are, they will ruin you. We in MI5 are not the only secret services, we have other covert black ops teams that operate throughout this country and the rest of the world. They could hurt you without raising suspicions, police rank affords you some protection. Take this to your DCI and run it past her."

"No," Winchester said, "I don't know her very well. As you said I do not have enough conclusive information yet."

When Winchester woke up in at 0730 am, Jennie had left for the airport. She was flying off to the States for a few weeks, some international homeland security conference. On the table was a card with a picture of a dog on it with a crash helmet on and goggles, saying 'see you soon' big kiss on it. 'X`.

Today was Winchester's first day off of his leave. He had a week off as Reggie also took the same leave and went away with his new girlfriend. Winchester wanted to make the most of his time thinking to understand what was really going on, on the tube lines. He set up on his sofa, got out the copy of the notebook he had found and the instruction DVD that Hellen had given him; it took some time to find it. He had forgotten what music DVD he had put it with so someone would not find it! It was with his Elton John album. Captain Fantastic. He was now ready to work on the notes, the training DVD.

When the introduction started it was clear this was for more than just underground trains; it was for planes and other confined spaces. It showed a typical LUG carriage, but what he did see was this number, 91323 above the door of the carriage, this was one of the missing links, in the notebook he had found and copied, Winchester and Hellen could not understand what the numbers were making reference to, but it was the carriage number, each underground train had its own distinct number. Now it makes sense. Winchester now had the link he needed, it seemed to open up in front of him, all the numbers at the end of each line was a reference to a carriage, or plane, even overland trains.

Looking at the DVD it made reference to time release capsules over two hours, they would be placed under the grilles at the back of the seats on the Central line. The DVD made reference to another training manual for other locations. It was now time to take this to the DCI, so he called and asked to speak to the DCI. She was a little taken aback to get a call from Winchester. He explained to her he had some information that would shock everyone to their very foundations.

She was intrigued. "Come in and see me, and bring everything you have. I will get the team together."

Winchester said, "Ma'am, maybe can we just look at it first as I don't want to look stupid."

"Ok, what I will do is bring in your CI Aston; we will meet you in the conference room on the 5th floor, we have the screen and DVD players, let's say 1300. Can you tell me what it's about, Winchester?"

"Not over the phone, ma'am."

Winchester had a shower, got dressed and was thinking, if I'm wrong this will make me a laughing stock for ever.

Winchester got to the station early to get some photocopies done and set up in the conference room. He felt a little nervous – the reputation of both the DI and the CI was formidable, they do not suffer fools lightly. He was thinking what was he doing, all this is based on his word, well most of it.

They both walked in with pads in hand and a mug of tea.

"Do you have a tea, Winchester?"

"No, ma'am."

"Well go get yourself one and bring back some digestive biscuits."

"Yes, ma'am." Winchester gave them each a copy of what he was going to talk about and then went to get his tea.

One of the Detectives saw Winchester. "What you doing in today?"

"I got a meeting."

"Oh, is it you they are meeting, with the DCI and the CI, good luck on that," as he walked away with a smile on his face.

Winchester got back to the room and the DCI and the CI were in deep discussion and looked up as Winchester walked back in the room. "Sit down, Winchester, let's talk about this, let's start from the very beginning."

"Well, it started about six months ago, I noticed on my way to work suspicious individuals doing some sort of cleaning on the train I was on at 0530, to me it looked very odd and I could not put my finger on it. But I also met the London Underground cleaners who seemed not to know much about them, they knew they were doing something, but was not sure, in fact they thought they were checking their work and reported them to the union; the union made some enquiries and they said they were checking the carriages for bacteria.

"They struck me as educated scientists sort of people."

The DCI said, "What did you base that on?"

"Well I heard them talking and it was about chemicals and stuff I had heard when I was at school in the science class.

"They were very systematic in what they were doing, they wrote everything, down and when I spoke to one of them, they looked very unsure what to say."

"Well, Winchester," CI Aston said, "would you not feel a little intimidated if someone like you walked up to you and asked a question you have never met before."

"Possibly, but they did get off the train and walked across the platform to the other train waiting. I don't know, as we are trained to look at suspicious behaviour, but it just struck me as odd and this happened twice a week, when I was on early shift. Then, Gov, when I saw the two MI5 agents on the train then in your office, it threw me a bit."

The CI said, "Yes I forgot about them two." The DCI seemed to sit up and started to take notice.

"Then the missing bodies..."

"Yes," the DCI said, "we are looking into them now, but they both died of heart failure and they were young and they both worked for pharmaceutical companies. Yet the private ambulance that took one of the bodies was not even registered or called by any police."

"Then I found a notebook left behind when this male cleaner collapsed on the train, and I went to help him and this was left on the floor. He worked for this large international pharmaceutical company, the book you will see is full of numbers, dates and locations and times. I have sussed out what they are all are now.

"First the numbers are of bacterial and viruses, all around the common cold, hayfever, sore throat and much more of your common illnesses. When I looked at the dates, they correspond to when we see them happen in everyday life."

DCI said, "So they could be testing for them?"

"Yes I thought that, but why were they spraying and wiping down different parts of the carriage that people would hold on to?

"Also, I had numbers that I could not fathom out till I was sitting on the train; the end numbers were carriage numbers. I started to get in my head they were spreading something, but they would have been jumped on by the BTP lads."

"So what has changed your mind that this is just not a conspiracy theory?"

"I got a visit from a woman in her 30s, she claimed she worked for them, she gave me a DVD, it's a training manual for all the staff. I have loaded it and it's ready to go."

"Let's see it then," Aston said.

They both watched it with stern faces. "You say you got this from an employee of the company as a training DVD?"

"Yes she was worried I would be found with it and said to be careful who I show it to."

The DCI said, "Winchester, can you go and get yourself a tea and stay in the mess room till we send for you."

"Yes, ma'am."

Winchester sat in the mess room for a few hours before one of the staff behind the counter in the mess said, "You are wanted back in the meeting room." As Winchester walked in there were 12 people in this room, one being the ACC, the Assistant Chief constable, other people all in suits he'd never seen before.

"Come in, Winchester, sit down; we have questions. All the people in this room are all police in some form or another. Are you sure that all the information you have gathered to date is correct as far as you know?" asked the ACC.

"Yes, sir, I believe so."

The ACC looked around the room and he said, "I will leave it in your hands and I will report back to the Chief Constable. Are you taking the lead on this, DCI Dolan?"

"Yes, Sir, I am."

"Good, keep me abreast of what is going on and you can pick your team but not too much overtime, money's tightening."

She grinned at him.

"Right, now the brass has gone I will do some introductions. Firstly, this is PC Winchester who bought this to our attention; this is CI Aston; to my left is my operations investigation team: Gary, Martin, Catherine and Tom. You have met the rest of the team before, but the head of CID BTP and his colleagues, this will be a joint investigation. Winchester, what we are going to talk about is classified and I am afraid you have to leave the room, but you will be kept informed by your Sergeant. We will take it from here, thank you for your help. Before you go, if anyone makes contact with you in regard to this matter then you must inform your Sergeant, is that clear?"

"Yes, ma'am."

Winchester left feeling a little dejected; he'd put all the pieces together and it had been taken away from him; that was his ego talking. But as he got home Hellen was standing outside his door, she looked very uneasy, she was pacing. She saw Winchester walking towards her and she started walking towards him then stopped, turned and walked off to the left and down the road. Winchester thought something was wrong so his instinct was to chase after her, but she may have seen someone or something. Winchester went in without even looking behind him or at where Hellen went. As Winchester walked through the front main entrance to the apartments, he looked back from where he had come from and a male in his 40s seemed to make a sudden turn to the left; it could be nothing. The good thing about the apartments was the ground floor had two entrances, one at the front, one at the back. Winchester walked right through, out the back, down the path and he knew where Hellen may go... he was right, she was heading back to the train station. He caught up with her and said, "Hello Hellen." She jumped, did not expect him to be next to her.

She said, "They are following you."

"How do you know?"

"Because I saw that man outside your place the night I left, he was sitting in his car."

"Could be a coincidence."

"He was following you the other day when I came to see you."

"You didn't see me the other day."

"I know, because I saw him following you; I went off home. Look, something is going on; they are spooked. I was meant to head off this week but all of us have been recalled. All activities have been stopped for the moment on the underground anyway. This happened once before and they had eliminated the problem they said. Winchester, you must understand, they are ruthless, we are talking billions of pounds. You have government people also involved..."

Winchester said, "I have handed it over now to the top people."

She looked stunned. "Did you mention me?"

"Yes. But not in name or description."

The look of panic came off her face. "I am here just to warn you they have you and your partner in their sights. If you feel ill all of a sudden, go to your doctor's, get treated right away."

"Why?"

"Because they will try and make you ill, keep you off work for a few months, but now you have handed it over they may just think you are a flat foot who was lucky to have stumbled over this. Your partner Reggie, tell him the same. Oh yes, they are doing a new way of testing the really bad stuff on humans, the homeless, they will go out, offer tea and food laced with new forms of bacteria. Then monitoring their progress, they don't care if they live or die – if they die they will claim the body and remove it for testing; most of the time the coroner will not even do a full investigation... they bank on that. Police don't care if a homeless person is found dead, as long as it's not murder, they just let the body be scooped up. They get a lot of information from the homeless. Because they are a living test for them. All they do is keep feeding them. Also, they come round on the pretence of being a doctor, saying they would give them a health check – they are doctors, but they're monitoring the bacteria homeless have been given."

Winchester said, "Don't they need blood?"

"Well, that is easy, they just say they will give them a small finger prick and take just a small drop. Job Done. To be frank, most of the time they do not even know it's been taken. Look, I am going away," she said to Winchester, "you will not see me again because we get moved around every six months so we don't get noticed, like you go to the same coffee shop or café, some bus or train people start to remember you."

Winchester said, "Where you going?"

"I am off to Glasgow; we have a new problem in this area, for the good, in fact: we are trying to understand the major drug addiction, we are looking at new synthetic drug replacements, that will work with the body not destroying it. It will be a way of slowly helping people off the drugs without massive problems. This is government-backed, but the public will never know about it, people would be very unhappy thinking the Government is possibly going to be drug dealers."

Winchester looked very, very confused.

Hellen looked at Winchester very hard. "Do you understand the gravity of the information you're now in possession of?"

"Yes of course, but who will ever believe me?"

"It's not who will believe you, no smoke without fire. Would you have believed me if I came to you with this story? Think hard before you answer."

"I am not sure, unless I saw it for myself."

Hellen left the apartment via the rear entrance downstairs, slipping away in the dark. Then Winchester's phone rang; it was the DCI Linda Dolan, AKA Miss Columbo, affectionately named by top brass. "I need you and Reggie to come in first thing in the morning at 0730 for a briefing."

"Okay."

Chapter Six

Reggie and Winchester headed up to the meeting room, or known as the gold command room as requested by the DCI. As they walked through the door, they saw this very large light oak oval table that engulfed the room with 30 high back black leather seats round it. Most of the seats were filled by people in suits, only four people with uniforms on, all of them senior officers. No seats were vacant around the table for Reggie and Winchester, but the DCI said "take the seats", pointing to two seats not at the table but to the rear of the room.

The lights dimmed and the blinds remotely came down, the overhead projector came on, projecting on to a white screen at the end of the room, you could see all the seats suddenly swivel, facing the screen. The DCI stood up and started to talk about the situation unravelling surrounding the missing bodies. "Across the metropolitan area we have found out over the past ten years over 60 people who have died, their bodies have just vanished along with all their IDs and personal effects. Until now we have not tied this up due to the computer systems not talking to each borough, but this is now going to change. We have all the commanders in agreement, we are just waiting for British Transport Police."

A knock on the door and two BTP Officers walked in: "Sorry we are late, it's the trains" and the room chuckled. They both sat next to Winchester and Reggie, not at the table.

The DCI continued: "Two of our officers have bought this to my attention and I am stunned to know this is going on under our very noses. The BTP Chief officer is meeting as we speak with the Chief Constable and someone from the security services. What we are going to show you and give you as a handout is marked as restricted."

They went through word for word what Winchester had informed her, and the training manual was also shown.

The lights went back on and everyone was a little fidgety in their seats; the blinds were opened. Winchester and Reggie never got anything given to them, but the DCI, Dolan, looked directly at Winchester and said, "You and PC Reggie need to go to the canteen now and your CI Aston will get you later once we have concluded here."

They both left the room as they knew the brass was going to be discussing security issues well above Reggie and Winchester's rank.

Winchester and Reggie sat in the canteen, with their bacon sandwiches and strong tea, talking.

"What was that all about?" Winchester said.

Reggie said, "You know what, mate, I have no idea at all. I felt very uncomfortable in that room. So much brass and other intelligence services."

The canteen was quiet as most of the shift changes had happened, everyone was out on patrol or dealing with the night's previous custody arrests.

The meeting must have been over as they saw a sudden influx of officers walking into the canteen, picking up trays – this station was known for its good food. Following in behind was CI Aston. She got three teas and walked over, put the teas down. "Right, lads, we need to talk."

"Yes, ma'am."

"The tea looks nice today, it's strong, as I like it," she said. The white mugs made the tea look very strong. Winchester and Reggie really did not want another cup of tea, but they were not going to say no now.

"I bet you two want to know why you were in that meeting first of all." They both nodded. "Well they need to let the others see you to show them all this information is credible. But one thing has come out of the meeting, intelligence has flagged you both as a risk. This is not that you are a risk from attacks, but you are under surveillance, from whom we have no idea yet; it's chatter from the corridors of the black arts as they say. You both will be removed from this station for a few months and will be sent to work out of the big boys' office."

They both looked blank faced.

"Basically, admin at Scotland Yard, helping with intelligence. Also for the next few weeks you both will be under surveillance from MI5 so they can identify who is watching you both. If it's our own intelligence services, then we will find out why; if not, we will find out who and make an assessment of risk." She smiled and her white teeth come into view. This was like the Addams family moment when little Wednesday Addams smiled, it was more frightening.

"Well, we need to get back, lots to do. Drink your tea and Oscar Foxtrot home and enjoy your 9 to 5 while you can. You will both need to respond to all your court and custody duties."

The CI was walking out as the DCC walked in the room and everyone stood up. "Morning, sir."

"CI Aston, can I speak with you for a moment?"

They walked off into the main corridor. Winchester and Reggie just looked at each other.

"How bizarre has this morning been, to find out you are being watched, part of a spy ring, drugs and conspiracies, top brass and now drinking cold strong tea that will make its way through you like a dose of salts!"

As they were just about to get up to leave, the CI came back in the room, looked at both of them. "My office please." Her face was like thunder.

They both made their way to her office; she was about 10 metres in front of them. As they walked into the office she said, "No need to sit down, this will be quick. You are both staying at this station and you will be doing the custody, working with Sergeant Chris Smalley; he runs it like a well-oiled machine, a real stickler for officers to get it right: right reason for arrest, right paperwork, right everything; and if you did not search your prisoner correctly you can expect to be ripped a new A-hole. Many a new probationer has been almost destroyed in front of their prisoners."

Winchester and Reggie looked at each other: my god, we are going to have a lovely time with Chris. Winchester said, "You know him?"

"Yes, we both joined together, he is very good at what he does, once you get a few arrests under your belt you begin to see what he wants, keeps our time to a minimum blocked up outside waiting for ages trying to get your prisoners processed."

"What do you think we will be doing?"

"Fingerprints, Toxic meter, DA Swabs, dealing with the nutters and the ones who want to fight, strip search for drugs."

"Oh nice. It's not every day if we are with him, we are going to work the shifts?"

"Oh yes, we will do court visits as well if it's high profile."

Winchester got home and he was reflecting on the day, his place was home for him, the place to relax; in fact, he was a simple man to please in his mind, he would relax by playing classical music or pop music; his view was if you like it then play it. He did not drink much, a glass of wine was enough, always wanted to be in control of his mind. The sofa was a four-seater and one armchair, TV 40 Inch, cable TV. Never watched soaps but enjoyed watching Dad's Army, Only Fools and Horses, and Porridge. It was funny to watch The Bill trying to show everyone what it was like. But they missed by a mile.

Very 70s in his taste of food, liked pork pies and crackers, pickled onions, beans on toast. His clothes were just as old fashioned – if you saw Winchester, you would not think copper right away.

Winchester once had a long-term girlfriend. She was not from the job or any services and did not want to deal with the shifts and comments she was getting from friends trying to tell her, it's not good to be with a copper; to be honest, her family was a bit of a bunch of Scallywags and land pirates. Having a copper as a possible son-in-law was not a good family's choice. She took everything she could from the flat and went a few years ago now.

Good job the flat was nailed down or they would have loaded that up and taken it. Also, the flat had been left to him by his grandma. Winchester's mother died when he was 17 and his father had left his mum when he was five for another man – yes, another man; he moved to Germany and never tried to contact Winchester or his mother. Winchester's mother had been a Police officer for the Met, she was based out of Brixton and had died of a heart attack at 37 years old – she was chasing down a group of football thugs after the Arsenal and Tottenham match, just collapsed and died, she had a heart defective valve she did not know anything; this was about high blood pressure, the silent killer. Gwen Layton PC 5132 collar number. She took her family name back because her father was a police officer in the city of London.

Winchester was very proud of his mother's reputation in the police; she got a bravery award for dealing with a man with a shotgun, she single-handedly talked him into not blowing his head off.

At the time she also got told off for putting herself in harm's way by her Sergeant. Sergeants in the day were like your second mum, they would not thank you for saying so. Our Sergeant had been a RSM and still says when we go out, "I want you all back here in one piece, be safe", and my god if you did not report in or do what you were supposed to do, you were going to get a good dressing down.

Winchester thought to himself the feeling of protection from your fellow officers was second to none, when you are out there on the streets knowing everyone will drop what they are doing and get to you as fast as possible when you are in trouble, it was so empowering to your confidence and wellbeing, and helps you to be a better officer knowing you are backed up from the rank and files.

Winchester drifted off to sleep on the sofa, to be woken by a feeling of someone is in the apartment, that eerie feeling of pending doom. The TV was on low and he had one table lamp on, but his hair on his hands and head felt on end. Winchester stood up, turned the lights on – it was 0200 in the morning, the small table clock dinged twice. He walked round the apartment: nothing; but he was sure someone was close. He opened the front door to look down the corridor, the light was on in the hallway – that was a sign someone had walked down it within the last 20 minutes, it was on a sensor at night and it would only stay on for 20 minutes from activating. It went out within a few seconds of him opening the door and came back on because he went into sensor range and got picked up by the sensor.

As Winchester went to shut the door, he saw a small lump underneath his front door brown coconut mat. Winchester lifted it back and it had his name on it; it was a padded brown envelope just with PC 71630 only on it; this was very strange. He opened it without thinking it could be a device of some sort, but it was a CD. Winchester now was intrigued but in his mind he also really should get this to the DCI. He should also call Reggie, but he would be in bed with his new love and he thought twice then decided not to call him. Then Winchester thought for a minute, "no, sod him, I will call him, why should he have all the fun and me deal with this alone?" with a grin on his face.

He called Reggie. "Hello?" this confused gruff voice said.
Winchester said, "Mate, it's me."
"I know it's you, no one else would call me at this hour."
"Sorry, mate, but I got another CD left under my front door mat."
"Really, when?"
"I'd say about 40 minutes to an hour ago."

"Bloody hell, mate you woke me up to tell me this? You are buying the teas tomorrow," Reggie said. "You going to watch it?"

"Not sure, that is why I am ringing you."

"I would, because if you lost it say what will you be able to tell them what it was about, also you would look a little silly if it was a Batman CD, or worse, My little pony," Reggie said. "I will come round and see it with you then we can say what we both have seen."

Winchester said, "You sure?"

"Yes, I am on my own tonight, the girlfriend is at her mum's for a few days. Give me an hour, I'll have a shower and head to you."

Reggie arrived with a pack of chocolate biscuits and fresh milk; it was about 4.30am now. "I knew I better bring the milk as I know you will not have any in-date." Reggie was already in uniform under his jacket as he knew they would be heading off to work for their 0630 start in custody.

Winchester put the CD on as they were both looking in anticipation with a tea in one hand and chocolate digestive in the other of course, for dipping. It was the information CD for this company, the head of which was Nikolai Dazary, the head of the Dazary pharmaceutical conglomerate or empire. This CD showed a dark-haired Greek man in his mid-forties, very well spoken. His opening words were, "Yiasoo, Hello and Kalos IRTHATE, Welcome". He was sitting at a head of this long maple tale with 20 leather beige chairs around it, behind him on the wall you could see pictures of buildings and a company name. Big bold letters UK & International Global industries PLC.

Along the bottom of the CD when he spoke other languages were shown a translation they thought, Winchester and Reggie had no idea what the languages were.

"This year we have made profits of 30 billion dollars after tax, this is the annual report and what we are looking to do in the year 2000 to 2001."

Reggie said, "This is just a promo CD."

"Let's carry on watching it."

Then a load of information came on the screen talking about areas of drive and profits and where they saw it and the UK was the biggest market by far. "We are looking to treble our profits in the UK, we have some new viruses we are looking to combat and we have the extra funding from the UK government and the EU. But all works are to only be tested in the UK. We still encourage freelance work but be careful to ensure the freelance work is never traced back to the corporation. If you do you will be excluded and terminated forthwith." When he said this he looked very hard at the camera with a stone face; even Reggie and Winchester moved slightly back from the TV screen.

"Oh yes, he means business, that's for sure," Reggie said.

"It's time we got going, mate, get ready."

The CD ended; it was about 30 minutes long.

"You best give that to the DCI when you get in, mate." But the DCI was not in today, so Winchester left it with the desk Sergeant to put it in her pigeonhole.

The first day started well, custody was backed up due to a fight between the EDL and anti-war protesters in central London; the station had the overflow from the city, 12 to be factual. Most of them EDL head bangers, wanting to beat up the anti-British feeling. All of them had some form of Union Jack on them – if it was not the tattoos, it was a shirt. They all had to be processed and given bail and court date for the public order offences, problem was they had mostly been arrested by the special Constables and they just hand them over and then they have to be allocated to a regular officer, so a lot of the time unless they had committed an assault or criminal damage, they were let off with strong words from the Custody Sergeant. The cells were in a right state: sick, piss and other fluids in the corners, and even in one they left a brown present. Two out of the 12 had been allocated to go to court and the others bailed. Custody Sergeant Smalley was in a bad mood; he needed his coffee, everyone knew that. After about two hours and three coffees, things were getting back to some sort of normal working, if there is such a thing. A few early morning arrests on their way in. Two officers were in the waiting area – this is a room between the outside and the custody. Only one prisoner is allowed in the space at a time, it's also a place if you had anything about you you would search your prisoner for the final time – we are not talking internal but you do not want to get inside and then find something on them, you will be ripped a new one. Experienced officers will know this and they still took the opportunity to have a quick search. On this occasion it was two officers that were from another division having to come to our custody area, due to the demolition the day before they had no room at their station, and as the prisoner was arrested for aggravated burglary of four accounts, he was going to be staying with us. They were waiting for them to be buzzed in; the Sergeant looked at them, he could see the officers looking through the vision panel, he also could see via CCTV into the small holding area which also had panic bars in case of trouble. The officers had removed the handcuffs. This is not unusual because the prisoner cannot exit this location only into the custody area.

Smalley said, "Lads, I don't like the look of this one; he looks agitated, he is moving side to side. I don't know the two officers, when they come in keep close and alert."

He pushed the buzzer from behind the desk and as soon as the prisoner came through the door, he pushed one of the officers against the wall and tried to nut the other and went to grab something by his right ankle. Reggie and Winchester grabbed from behind and slammed him against the wall and they both grappled him to the ground. They managed to get the cuffs on him again; he was fighting them and spitting, kicking out caught Winchester right in the tool box. The other officers were back on top of him as well – for a little lad this person was hard to hold down, not like you see in the films. It can take up to four people to restrain someone. One of the officers had a little cut above his eye so that's his extra charge going on his sheet. But the one thing was the Sergeant had clocked he was going for his right ankle, this lad had on work boots. Reggie took his right boot off and a slim envelope-opening knife fell to the ground. Reggie looked at the knife on the floor for a split second – he would say you could hear a kettle boiling, but it was Sergeant Smalley about to explode. The lucky thing for the two officers was that CI Aston came into the custody reception area and called out, "Sergeant Smalley, need a word now please..." This almost cooled him down for a few minutes but they knew something was going to happen, a dressing down was definitely going to happen and to be fair they did deserve it, could have been a lot worse.

It was an eventful few weeks but really getting boring now it was for officers whom wanted to have paperless job and a relatively easy days. Smalley said he was sick of the sight of them both as he had nothing in common with them.

The DCI had not come back to Winchester on the CD he had left for her; he knew she was in because he had seen her talking to others. It was Monday morning 0700, Reggie and Winchester were cleaning up some stuff from the weekend's mess in the custody cells, when Sergeant Smalley called them both back to his desk. "Well, lads, don't take this personally, but you have finished your little stint here, you are Oscar Foxtrot. See you again when you have nicked someone–" with a grin on his face. "Report to your CI Aston at 0900, her office, go grab a tea; that's an hour away."

Reggie and Winchester were sitting in the canteen drinking the builder's tea, so-called because of how strong it always was. The double blue swing doors burst open, DCI Dolan's team, DS Gary Robbins, DC Martin Byrne, DC Catherine Wineglass, and then Alex Weston went and sat at a corner table and then the DCI walked in. She saw Winchester and Reggie, she spoke to Gary then made her way over to the two lads. "Morning," she said as she sat down.

Winchester could see out of the corner of his eye DS Robbins getting teas and walked over and gave the DCI one and walked back to his table. She said, "Thank you for the CD, that has really put the cat among the pigeons. Now we have been given the funding to put together a task force to look at this, at the moment you have both been assigned to me. You will not be in plain clothes, it would be pointless; you will investigate any thing that is suspicious on the rail network or outside the network. BTP are fully onboard with this, they have offered up two detectives to help; they will be carrying out plain clothes operations on the underground networks. We will have a briefing every two weeks from this day forward, but it could change to every day. Depends on the ongoing situation and what we uncover. Your CI Aston is fully aware; she will see you later today. She will set out what we want. DS Robbins will be your point of contact. The good news for you is for the foreseeable future no nights for you two, it will be early and lates." She stood up and went over to her team and sat down; they were into a very deep conversation about stuff, you could see as they all had their notebooks out, pens ready.

Chapter Seven

Late December 2001, nothing had really happened of note from the last briefing with the team had nothing to report, it was like someone had just turned the light off for the last month, nothing had happened. Mind you, this was said to Winchester by Hellen Blake, this time of year the natural viruses would be all over the place so no need to help it along, look around end of February to September was the active times. This was explained because the trains with the heating being turned on, on the packed trains, it was an incubator for every virus you could imagine.

BTP detectives had been removed from the team; this was due to the workload they had to deal with, this is the time of the year when the pickpockets get more active, drunk people and many other issues on their plate, they do not have the resources the Met have; they will be in loop always and will help out, so the Met team was back to one team.

Winchester was at home, his entry phone sounded; someone was at the door, though sometimes people ring the wrong door.

"Hello?"

"Hello, is that Winchester?"

"Yes."

"I need to speak with you. I am a private investigator and I have some information from a mutual friend, Hellen."

"Come up." Winchester opened his front door as the door to the stairs opened, and this middle aged male walked through, very large man – he was puffing after only coming up two flights of stairs. He was wearing a creased dark brown suit, off-white open collar shirt and black unpolished slip-on loafers.

He put out his hand to shake. "Hello, I am Winchester."

"I know, I am Ben Hooper."

"Come in, would you like a drink? Tea or coffee?"

"Yes, tea, three sugars."

"Sit down, looks like you need it."

Winchester made the tea for both of them and sat down opposite Ben. "So, what can I do for you?"

"I have been given some information from Hellen Blake: you are in danger."

Winchester started to lean towards Ben. "Why am I in danger?"

"The company have noted that you have been the one that has drawn the attention to what has been going on."

Winchester said, "How do they know it's me?"

"They even know that there is a covert team been set up to look at what is going on, headed up by Linda Dolan."

Winchester said, "This is secret."

"No secrets in the Met or the British Transport Police."

Winchester sat back in his chair. "How is Hellen?"

"She is fine. I work with her. I was in the Met for 20 years, detective and undercover drugs officer mostly. Now I run a successful private detective agency. But what I am doing is for Hellen; she has helped me in the past. I will give you my card but be careful, my friend, they will seek to keep you quiet. They are not going to kill you or get you sacked or discredit you, now that is easy to do. Inform your OIC, check everything you do, when you get home look round your place. I have something for you, this is a bug detection device, we will do a quick sweep now then I will leave it with you." He walked round. "Nothing yet. Leave it on all the time. If they come in they will trip it and when you get home you will see a green light that will confirm they have planted a bug. They may plant drugs in your home or in your locker at work; they have people everywhere. Sorry to be the one with the news, call me if you need help. This is big and you are a small fish in a pond full of sharks."

After Ben left, Winchester called Reggie to come over asap.

Reggie asked why.

"I have just had a visit and I need to speak with you asap."

"Okay." That was it, Reggie came round within 30 minutes and Winchester told him what was said. "This will also go for you too, mate, just in case you get targeted as well."

"Did he say my name then?"

"No, just me but, mate, you and I are partners, I would hate for it to mess you up."

Reggie nodded. He said, "We must inform the DCI or CI Aston."

"We will in the morning when we get to the station. What do you think?"

"No, let's do it now. I know where the CI lives."

"No way, mate, she will eat us alive."

"Well we must tell someone. The DCI gave us her phone number and she said we should call her anytime, let's do that now."

Winchester picked up the house phone and called the number. It was about 2230. This male voice came on at the other end of the phone. "Hello?"

"Oh hello, I am PC Winchester, can I speak to the governor please?"

"Hold on." Winchester could hear him call out, "Linda, it's one of your lot on the phone."

"Take a message, I'll get back to them."

The male came back on the phone. "Give me your information; she will call you back," then hung up.

Reggie asked, "Who was the PI that come to see you?"

"Ben Hooper, big lad."

"Old Ben, I wondered what had happened to him, he was a good detective, worked a lot round King's Cross area, drug squad I think. He got stabbed and shot, also run over once; good chap, retired four years ago I think."

The phone rang, and Reggie answered it. "Hello ma'am, it's PC Reggie and Winchester, I am going to put it on load speaker."

"Why are you calling me at this time of night? I guess it's urgent."

Winchester said it was and explained everything about what had happened and what was said.

She said, "I know of Ben Hooper, he's one of the good guys, bit scruffy and overweight but all in all he knows what life is about. Right, come in tomorrow morning first thing as I will need to speak with you both and make a few calls to our friends in the security services to see if they have picked up some chatter."

Winchester got up at 0530 but he was already awake due to his mind playing over and over again what he had been told. He got to the train; it was a cold morning and he could see the cold air coming out of his mouth in a form of misty steam. As he boarded the train six other people got on and sat on different parts of the carriage – not unusual to be honest. As the train progressed into London, the train got more busy. Winchester thought there must be something going on, not this many people normally on the train at this time of the morning. The train was running slow, the driver said, "due to a person taken ill at Bethnal Green station we are running slow."

Winchester thought that's where I am getting off. The train had about 40 people on his carriage; normally he would only have seen four or five people. He was at Mile End station and a good few people got on heading into London, mostly builders and cleaners. Winchester stood up and took hold of the handrail as the train came into Mile End station. Others stood up to do the same to get off. The train pulled up and as the doors opened two men pushed past him to get off, then he was bumped from behind. Winchester thought he felt a little sharp scratch on his thigh.

CHAPTER SEVEN

Winchester woke up in a hospital bed. He started to focus on an officer in uniform standing by his open door; his head was pounding. He could see he was on a drip and on a monitor beeping away. Winchester felt very lethargic and weak. Winchester saw Reggie come into the room with a bacon roll between his teeth and tea in his hand. Reggie said something but was not understandable because he still had the roll in his mouth. Winchester looked at him and tried to say something but he still had a breathing tube in his mouth. Reggie took the roll out of his mouth, and said, "Stay still, I'll get the doctor." He disappeared out the door. The officer outside, whom had a side arm, stood inside the door and said, "Good to see you awake, mate," and put his thumb up.

The doctor and a nurse came in the room. They looked at Winchester and said we are going to remove the tube; we will lay you backward first."

Winchester was so confused. As they pulled the tube out, he choked, and the doctor said, "Take it easy, you need to let your throat get some lubrication before you can talk."

"You are a lucky man," the nurse said.

Winchester was still very confused; Reggie was still not back yet; his roll and tea was on the side. Winchester looked at the clock – it was about 3 pm – wow I been here for a few hours. Then Reggie came through the door. "Mate, you look better; thought we lost you."

Winchester tried to talk but he could not, his throat was not responding. "You want tea, mate?" Reggie said as the nurse came in with a cup of tea in a green cup and saucer. "Take your time, the DCI and DI are on their way in."

The DI came in first. She looked at him and said, "What are you like, always getting in to trouble!"

Winchester still was confused, then DCI Linda Dolan closed the door. She said, "Has anyone spoken to you about anything?" Winchester shook his head. "About three weeks ago, on your way in you collapsed on the platform at Mile End station, full cardiac arrest, the paramedics had just been delayed with another incident, they were still on station; they got to you and managed to get you back, you were, for all intents and purposes, deceased. You've been in a coma for three weeks under police guard. We have discovered some medication in your blood that confirmed you were poisoned. We are sure we know the persons or person that did the deed on you; they are under surveillance, because as soon as I got the call from you both, I got M15 to give you protection so two officers were on the train and saw the persons bump you; but we are after the organisation who ordered the hit on you. They think at this time you are dead, so you cannot go home at this time. It will not take long before they find out you are not, with this information on what drug they use we have exhumed six bodies we think in the past have been possibly suspicious deaths. Not sure if it will help because they have been embalmed.

"You and Reggie have a safe house to go to in Kent. This will be for a few weeks till we can establish why they tried to kill a serving police officer; that is a really reckless action. This has gone to the top of the security services. We also have the head of the organisation, Nikolai Dazary, under all surveillance by the top teams in the country. We know what he is up to, but we have to prove it. We are getting resistance from the Government because they're so interwoven in the NHS and life saving development of cancer drugs. This will make the government look silly."

Winchester was listening with great interest.

"The best way round this is to confirm to everyone we are investigating this company and that way it will make them think it's pointless going after you because we all know now."

Winchester said, "No," then he shook his head; he beckoned Reggie to give him a notepad. He wrote: they will just go underground and you will never find them.

Both the DCI and CI left the room to talk for a few minutes then came back in. "Okay, but we need to keep you both safe. I will call

Ben Hooper and use him as a contact for you. You know his contact Hellen Blake; this name must not be in any communications at all."

Winchester wrote: I don't think that is her real name. I did a PNC – she is not in the system. Unless she has done something she would not be, would she.

The doctors wanted to come back in the room and everyone left but Reggie stayed. The officer on the door changed, and the doctors gave Winchester the once over and removed his drip and the monitoring leads, then said, "A few days' rest and we need to get you out of that bed and remove the catheter." It was painful to say the least. "We also have to give you an enema."

Reggie looked at Winchester and burst out laughing. "Rather you than me, mate. Do you want something other than hospital food?"

"Yes please."

"Great, I will get you a KFC." He shot off. He spoke to the officer outside and asked him if he wanted KFC too. He nodded. The officer on the door was Jamie Mills, 12 years in the job, firearms officer. Winchester beckoned to Jamie to come in the room and sit down and chill out. The TV was on; Winchester could see the football going on, it was an England game, but it was not his thing, he was not really interested. Jamie stood watching the TV, one eye on the door at all times. One of the nurses brought some tea for both of them and the old Rich Tea biscuits on a small green side plate.

Jamie turned to Winchester and said "I don't often ask, but why are we guarding you?"

Winchester said, "To be honest, I don't know. I am at a loss."

"Change of shift soon," Jamie said.

Winchester asked, "How long SO19?"

"Four years now, come from Essex Police, Chelmsford."

"Why you move?"

"I was at the airport, nothing to do but walk round all day, so got into the Met, loved it; my wife doesn't, she is still an Essex officer, firearms too. She's all over Essex."

"Who's replacing you?"

"Pat Snape, he is a very laid back officer; he was Essex once, been in the job 20 years, started as a Special then joined firearms eight years ago, old school, or Sergeant Clarke, big man, he is also our paramedic. He will check in on us later."

The nurse come in as Jamie went out the room. As Pat was being briefed by Jamie, Winchester could hear them talking – "he is one of us, mate. He has no clue why we are here, but he is a P1 priority one. Okay, his name is Winchester. The nurses are great, they get us tea and biscuits. Cool, look out for the sister, she doesn't like us blocking up the walkways."

Pat came into the room and introduced himself, he was on for the next 12 hours. Pat asked, "Are you expecting anyone?"

"Yes, possibly Reggie, he is one of us, he is coming over after shift with some KFC, I hope, though he most probably forgot."

It was about 22:00 and Reggie had not come to see him – that was good he must be getting some sleep. Winchester fell asleep, only to be woken up by a lot of noise and the shouting from PC Snape saying "Armed police, on the ground now, on the ground now, face down, face down, hands spread away from your body now, do it now, cross your feet, cross your feet. Move in, move in."

Winchester got out of bed and looked through the glass vision panel in the door to see a man dressed in black spread-eagled on the floor and two other officers had guns drawn and pointing at him. They cuffed him and lifted him by his elbows and quickly moved him to a side room. Pat came in. "What happened?"

"He was not for you, turns out the next room to here is a big-time drug dealer, he was being watched by Drug squad, he got three bullets in him and looks like they came to finish him off. They contacted me saying they are following him into the hospital, possibly armed. We found no gun but a bloody big samurai. Anyway, they tell me the drug dealer next door is a vegetable, two of the bullets were in the head.

"We just got an update on you, they are moving you to a safe house, where we don't know, we only get told on a need-to-know basis. We are the mushrooms, kept in the dark and fed on shit."

Pat laughed. "Rest up, mate they are moving you at 0600."

"Okay, thanks."

The nurse woke Winchester up at 0500, removed his drip and said "you need a shower".

"Thanks."

"It's just down the corridor on your right."

Winchester got back to his room after his shower to be met by three people, they were all from the relocation team of the M15.

Winchester said, "Right, I am going nowhere until someone tells me what is going on."

"All will be explained to you soon."

Winchester said, "No, I want to know now or I am off home. This is silly, I am a police officer and I need to do my job, not hide away."

The armed protection team had been stood down, then, DCI Dolan walked in the room. She said, "Can I have ten minutes with Winchester please. Winchester, we have reason to believe you were targeted."

"Why me? Not sure."

"Look, we need to just give you a safe place for a few days till we can ascertain the situation. If it was not for the paramedics being on the platform, we would not be having this conversation. The pathologist has found a form of potassium that was very fast acting and would not have been looked for if you had died because it simulates massive heart failure. On examination we found a very small puncture wound in your right buttock, this only could've happened on the train. Did you remember anyone bumping you?"

"Yes I did, in fact it felt like a pinch. I was not sure at the time but don't remember anything after that."

"No, that's because you were on the floor within a few seconds."

"So Hellen was right, they have been killing people."

DCI Dolan said, "Hang on, we have to be sure, but the evidence is pointing that way. If this is the case they are now on our radar and frankly taking the piss trying to kill an officer of her majesty's Constabulary – what were they thinking we are going to do but hunt them down?

"So Winchester, are you going to stay in the safe house for a few days so we can get a handle on this?"

"Yes, okay," Winchester said with a reluctant voice.

This was a tower block in Barking of all places – they will definitely not find me in this place. The lift stank of piss, the walls on the lift had graffiti all over it. Winchester thought if I wanted drugs or a girl it was written all over the lift car walls, the contacts. It was on the 5th floor, 25 Basset House. The place was a two-bedroom flat with a panic room, shower, no bath, small galley kitchen; the furniture was all new, fridge and cupboards stacked with everything so no one need leave the flat. Nice size TV, Winchester thought I may as well make the most of this. As the sudden sound of rubbish crashing down the rubbish chute in the building was right next to the living room wall and so was the lift shaft. The phone on the small table rang. Winchester picked it up. It was an officer from the safety team just saying they would ring in the morning, see if everything is okay. "The door in the safe room opens outwards, your front door has security locking system and the door has a steel sheet in the middle of it from top to bottom. You will get no visits from anyone without a call from us, the code word will be benchmark then we will confirm who they are. We have CCTV outside your door too."

"Thanks," Winchester said.

The bed was like a board, very clean place. In the morning the phone rang about 0830. A voice on the other end just said "Benchmark all good".

"No" – this was the answer to be given back; this would let the person on the other end of the phone know all is well.

Then he started to talk: "You have three visitors today at 11 30, Winchester, two others with the DCI."

Winchester was like a caged animal, pacing around and around looking over Barking railway station from the flat. He lost count how many times the rubbish crashed its way down the bin chute, he was leaning on the window sill, the window was cracked open about six inches, when this object flew past his window smashing on the ground. Winchester looked down at the base of the flats and could see a car with what looked like the remains of a TV on its now smashed and dented roof. He could also see disposable nappies dotted around, some half open, but most like round white balls. The bin men when they come and empty the skips at the base of the bin chutes take their life in their hands as the access to get them was right below the windows, it would be target practice. Thank god, Winchester thought, he did not live here.

The external buzzer from the ground floor entrance lobby buzzed. Winchester pushed the button and asked who it was. Reggie's voice came over the intercom: "It's me, Reggie."

"Come up." He pushed the release button and they got to the door.

"Wow," the DCI said, "that lift smells like an old toilets in a pub."

"I was told the DS was coming."

"He was but he's been called to an incident," the DCI said. "We need to get down to it, we have arrested a man whom we are sure poisoned you; we got him off the new CCTV system on the platform. This will put the cat amongst the pigeons. Winchester, we are looking for you to return to full duties but as a DC with your colleague here." Reggie had a big silly smile on his face. "We will keep you away from this case for the moment, but you will be working very closely on cold cases with BTP; they are wanting to sort this too. You will be working with the Superintendent. They have 34 suspicious deaths still on the books, they are under ten years old. You can go home now; we are sure they will not come after you again, it would be too reckless, it would draw too much attention. They will also think you are off the case, but we are also sure we have someone in the police feeding them information – we are looking into that. If you are asked you are both working on sexual assaults with BTP on the underground, only my team and CI Aston will be aware of what you are really doing. You will report to me. We have set you both up an office in the old property office, you need to sort out the computers and desks also. Clear the room out, its a bit of a mess. It has no windows but the good news is it has light and a heater. Well pack up what you have. See you both soon."

Reggie and Winchester were happy. Reggie said, "To get this assignment someone had to almost kill you. I would have missed you, mate." They both chuckled.

Winchester got home, feeling happy to be in his place but as he got to the door he noticed the tell tale sign he'd put on his front door was showing broken, someone had been in his place. He placed his kit bag on the floor and got out his police 24-inch baton with side handle – this was his preference for Friday and Saturday night fight nights. Turned the lights on: nothing looked disturbed; but what he did was get out the bug detection meter he'd got off the internet after feeling someone had been in his place, it would detect low and high frequencies. He found nothing – or it was a cheap piece of plastic; it was just that. Then a sound of a key in the door and a voice called out, "You're home then." It was Jennie. "I got a few things. I have been here for a few days; no one would tell me what you were doing. I was not worried, but I missed you."

Winchester gave Jennie a long hug and a very long kiss. "Wow," she said, "what's all that about?" and Winchester told her everything that had happened to him. Her face turned to thunder; she was getting very wound up.

"I told my senior operations manager that I thought you may be in trouble, but he brushed it off, bloody twat. Bloody useless, thinks he knows it all, full of himself but a back-stabbing horrible self-opinionated waste of space, fat and sweaty git. Winchester started to laugh. He said, "Never seen you like this before, I gather you don't like him."

"No, I don't."

"Bloody hell."

Jennie said, "I swept the building for bugs; I found three, they are removed. I will give you this one, it is a valuable piece of equipment. Picks up everything."

"They bugged me?"

"Yes I think our lot did, wanting to know what you know. They look like our ones. They have only just been fitted because the last time I was here they were not."

"Did you do a sweep then?"

"Yes, of course."

Winchester just shrugged his shoulders. "Shall we eat."

The following morning Jennie had left to get into work at 0500, she had to talk with another team in some far-off country. Winchester was looking forward to working in his new office with Reggie, not knowing what the old lost property store was like but in his mind it must be big enough. Also he did not now start work till 0900 so he would not be on the really early trains. Reggie had got to work first; he had got the keys from the administration department. It felt strange to have all your CS gas, handcuffs and baton with you being in plain clothes. Winchester went down to the basement that was where he was told the place was. Reggie was at this old metal dark blue door with three locks on it, no signs. "I have been trying to get in this bloody door for about half hour now. It's this last lock it will not unlock."

Winchester pushed the door and it opened. Reggie looked at him with a face that said "don't say a word". Winchester knew better than to say to Reggie anything like that. Just inside the door was the old light switch. Winchester flicked the light switch on and the strip lights flickered and came on; it was a room alright. They both thought it would a bit of an old dive, but no, it had four large oak desks, six leather high back chairs, one meeting table, new table phones, projector screen and meeting table for six but no chairs for that table; it was very well decorated... the room was ten metres by eight metres, no windows; oh and three filing units...

Turns out everyone had forgotten this was done up as an emergency command room for senior officers if a terrorist attack happened to New Scotland Yard. Winchester said, "Mate, this is a turn up for the books, let's keep this place quiet."

"The senior officers will remove this stuff, it's better than what they have now." Reggie picked up the phone and pressed 9 – it gave him an outside line. He rang control to get the number, they gave him the number and said this number has not been used for years. Then a front desk PCSO came to the door. "Hi lads, we have a load of files at the rear door for you that has come from BTP and others from whom I am not sure."

"Okay, let's get them." The good thing was also the rear entrance was in the car park that was on the same level as they were. When they opened the door to the car park, they saw a transit; it was half full of files. A guy standing there with a clipboard: "can you sign for this please".

"Bloody hell, mate, look at that lot."

It took them both four hours to get the files into the office and set them up in persons and cases, then they both went upstairs to the canteen. CI Aston was sitting down with one of the other CIs, Mike Reed, head of traffic. She nodded to Reggie and Winchester, they both got bangers and mash, with chocolate sponge custard, and of course the police tea.

CI Aston came over with files in her hand. She just said, "Sorry about putting you lads in the basement, but as you know we are limited for space. You need any furniture?"

"No, ma'am, we have enough."

"From what I was told it's a room with no natural light, it was used for something other than lost property – is it okay?"

"Yes, ma'am and we have a phone as well."

"That's great, what's the number internally?"

"888."

"Great, that means I will not have to come down to the dungeon."

Reggie and Winchester looked at each other. "We understand, ma'am."

"Oh yes, that's what I wanted to say, they are installing your computers tomorrow. I am off to the monthly meeting with the community leaders, we are making good progress. Together we have taken back eight housing estates from the drug gangs with their help; Islington and Brixton are the benchmark for changes, the MPs and community leaders pulling together make a big difference. You should have all the files now from BTP and the small amount of files we have. I am sure you have enough information. You will have a report for me in ten days' time that I can take to the funding team to keep the funding for you two. I am asking initially for 12 months. So you need to show me something in ten days so I can keep the wolves from the door."

Winchester and Reggie just nodded as she was walking out the canteen door.

Winchester said, "That will mean we are stuck in the room for 12 months."

Reggie said, "No, we will have to go out and carry out investigations. But looks like we will be off the beat for 12 months if ma'am gets the funding," with a grin on his face.

The difference between Reggie and Winchester was time in the job. Reggie over ten years, wanted to be with the detectives but did not want to do the exam; he always wanted to be a custody Sergeant, again did not want to do the exam, because he was dyslexic.

As Winchester has been in the job now for only three years and wants to become a detective, also wanted to do the exam, but he was not ready yet, he still wanted the fast life of the day-to-day. police work with the community.

Reggie and Winchester set up in their office area when there was a knock at the door and the door opened – it was Sergeant Tim Neat. "Morning, lads, just thought I would come down and see you both. Wow," he said, "this is a bit of alright, this is, furniture is good but no natural light. I feel I was in one of the cells. Anyway. Day to day I am running the station admin, station anything really, so if you want anything, contact me, I will try and get it for you. He went out the door and came back in with a brown cardboard box. "Some cups and a kettle for you both, you have to get your own coffee and tea, milk. Pick it up at the canteen and tell them it's on the Admin Account, so I will come down and catch up a few days a week, I will expect a good strong tea, lads."

"Yes, Sergeant."

Then just as fast he left.

"We better get the files in order," Reggie said. "BTP, their filing system is good and easy to work out so I will deal with that lot, and Winchester, deal with the files from the rest of the Met police."

All the room they had yet they set their desks face to face and pushed together, the two other desks were set up just the same at the back of the room; the large meeting table was lifted into the middle of the room, metal filing units against the walls marked BTP 1996 to 2000. Right up to date and the Met police files were station names, from 1990 to 1999, just over a year old. It took them both a week to get all the files in chronological order. This took so long, not because BTP files but the Met – each station seemed to have different systems in place for keeping stuff yet it was not meant to be like that, no wonder things slipped through the nets between stations and forces. It's getting better now but in the 90s it was not great.

Because of this, Reggie came across a report of a man sticking a needle in the back of a man. Witnessed by a doctor on a platform at Liverpool Street station. The met police told the doctor to contact BTP because it was on the station, but BTP did not have anything down for a report for such a situation. When Reggie read on, it was left to the officer taking the information and to get back to Doctor Kildare. "With the report number and a contact number of the BTP officers who he needs to speak with, this looks like an end-of-shift time and when the officer went home it was on his four days off. It got filed as done."

"The person who got jabbed with the needle in his back – what happened to him or her?"

"It did not say."

"Do we have a contact for the doctors?"

"Yes he is a GP in Stratford."

"Let's go and see him, what's the date on it?"

"July 1997, 1030am."

Reggie and Winchester booked out an unmarked car and set off for the GP practice in Stratford, only to find it had made way for a new tower block. This was a bit of a setback, but as they drove away they noticed the new smaller building close by with an NHS sign pointing down a small road. They took a chance and followed it; it came out in front of a single storey building. About 20 metres by ten meters, blue metal windows and sliding electric doors in the front that also were NHS blue.

"We are in luck, I hope," Winchester said.

They parked in the surgery car park only to be met by a receptionist with a face like thunder heading towards them with that 'you can not park here'. As they got out she could see they looked official, so she slowed down to a slower walk. "Can I help you both?"

"Yes." Reggie got out his warrant card. "I am PC Reggie and my colleague is PC Winchester. Do you have a Doctor Kildare working from here?"

"Yes," she said, "this is his practice."

"We are sorry to bother him but do you think we could see him?"

"I think you are in luck, he has just seen his last morning patient. Come with me."

As she led them in through the back door of the surgery, Winchester said to Reggie, "I wonder if he could look at my piles they are giving me gyp today."

Reggie looked at him and rolled his eyes. They sat down in the meeting room and the door opened and the doctor walked through the door. Reggie and Winchester already had the MG11 statement sheets out to take a statement, and their notebooks. The doctor stepped forward and introduced himself and shook Winchester and Reggie's hands. "What can I do for you officers?"

"Back in July 1997 you contacted the police to inform them you had witnessed a person sticking a needle into the back of another person."

"Yes," the doctor said, "that was a long time ago and as no one come back to me I thought it was nothing."

"Did anything happen to that person that got stuck with a needle?"

"Yes, I was trying to tell the officer on the phone at the time, I saw the man who stuck the man with the needle, he just collapsed on the platform. I helped him of course."

"What happened to that man?"

"Well, as far as I could tell he was alright, just very confused, like he was drugged, he was saying something about 'they got me the bastards'. Then the ambulance team turned up so I gave them the information I had and that was that. I called the London hospital to see how he was and they said he discharged himself a few hours after he arrived that day. I tried to access his records at the hospital but because of the changes we were making I couldn't – the computer systems are still not the best, so I left it."

Reggie asked, "What did you remember about the person who stuck him with the needle?"

The doctor replied, "He was I would say about 5' 10", slim, very pale, almost anaemic, dark trench coat, grey haired, he had like a small scar on his left cheek from an old boil I would say – I have lanced many of them in the past. In all my life I have never seen anything like that before. It took me a few months to get it out of my thoughts. Why would anyone do such a thing?"

Reggie said, "That is what we are trying to find out, Doc."

Then a knock on the door. The nurse came in and said, "We have your next appointment in 10 minutes; do you want your cup of tea in your office here?"

The Doctor nodded, looked at Reggie and Winchester and said, "Would you like some tea?"

Winchester said, "No, thank you, we have taken up a lot of your time and we are very thankful for your help. We will of course keep you posted."

Reggie and Winchester left the building and ran across the car park trying not to get too wet from the now bucketing downfall of rain. Reggie had the keys. As they got to the car Winchester said, "You got the keys, open the door, mate, we are getting soaked"

But Reggie could not find the keys, they just stood still while the rain just penetrated their clothes. Winchester said, "Come on, mate, I feel the rain going down my bum crack."

"Found them" in the last pocket of his jacket!

They both looked like drowned rats. As they sat in the car the front screen of the car just misted up. "Let's get back to the station."

Winchester said, "No, we both need to drive to our homes and grab some dry clothes. We will do a round trip." They point to point the Sergeant, who agreed – "put yourselves on break". The rain was relentless; even running from the car park to Winchester's flat he got a bit wet after he changed, but when they got to Reggie's apartment he had a big drive and porch to park underneath, very nice place. His mother had left him the place, or it would look a bit suspicious a police officer with a very expensive apartment like he has. Three bedrooms, a security officer in the reception; two of the apartments were owned by a TV company to put up visitors from overseas. Winchester had only ever been to Reggie's place three or four times. Winchester loved it, it was so welcoming. One room in Reggie's apartment was a library, with two sofas, wooden floor, oak bookshelfs on three walls full of books, coffee table between the sofas on a thick soft rug, no TV but a stack radio system and hidden speakers. His mum had had it fitted out and took out one of the reception rooms. It was so relaxing, the room just was a place to think; it made you feel you had the answers to everything.

Winchester was waiting for Reggie outside while he was getting dressed, he got a point to point from DS Gary Robbins. "Hi mate, could you come to the central hub, we are carrying out CCTV operations; you have been here before; we have got some footage we would like you both to look at."

"Okay, give us 30 minutes."

Reggie walked back to the car.

"We are off to central hub."

"I have been there before?"

"Yes, gold command. We need to park in the underground car park, can you point to point the desk Sergeant and get him to inform them of the reg of this car or we will not get in."

As they drove to the location of the building – it's right behind John Lewis, it looks like just an underground car parking for permit holders only, it's right in the centre of town. Ken Livingstone had just been elected the first elected Mayor of London; he was going to introduce some sort of charges getting into London and the central hub was a real issue because this would put this building in the public eye, as part of public records, and the American embassy was also not happy they would have to pay for the charges too. Oh well, not my problem, Winchester thought. As they drove in the armed security police officer opened the gate and they drove down two levels; you could see all the covert vehicles and police motorcycles and the royal protection cars all parked up, being washed by a Essex fire fighter; he has been cleaning the cars for years, Cristal Clean I think was what was on the side of the van. A bit ironic.

They were met by DS Robbins, or GAZO as he liked to be called. "Come with me, lads, we have some footage from when the doctor gave his information of the incident and description."

"So, the doctor did give a description of the man in the past?"

"Yes."

"As we have only just got it, he said no one took his information."

GAZO stopped and looked at them. "You sure he said that, as this was taken by a BTP officer at the time."

Reggie opened up his notebook and read it out word for word. "What he did say, he called in trying to give information, but no one bothered explaining to him why they were not interested."

"Interesting."

They walked into a room dimly lit with a 20-person oval oak table and black high back leather chairs, at the end of that table on the wall was an 80-inch screen for multiple conferences for members to be on from all over the world. As they walked into it you could hear the room was soundproof as when you spoke no rebound of noise at all; your ears took a little time to adjust. "Close the door," Winchester was asked. GAZO turned on the TV screen; it started to play a DVD of the platform at Liverpool Street station at the time and date given of the incident. The description of the person in DS Robbins' notebook was a male, Asian, about 5,5, grey hoody and black buttons, white trainers.

"So what have you got?"

Reggie gave the description the doctor have given. When they looked at the footage they saw the person right away and now could track him all the way from the platform to leaving and also look at the line to see when he got on.

"Why have we got conflicting descriptions and most of all they both are claimed to be from Dr Kildare. Could you ask to speak to the BTP officer who took the statement. Good job, lads, this will help us track this person.

"Time to go, lads, see you at the next briefing Monday at the Bow station, DCI Dolan's office, 0900 sharp."

Winchester said, "This is getting like an Agatha Christie book."

Reggie looked at Winchester and said, "Yes and you are loving it, aren't you?" They both grinned.

It's Monday morning 0900 they were all in the DCI's office, CI Aston was there too; she was the only one in uniform.

"Good morning, everyone, I will get right to the point. BTP need boots on the ground, they have new operations regarding terrorists, they have to now keep this their main focus. Today I would also like to introduce you to Lloyd and Boyd, they are both from the UK branch of Interpol."

Lloyd was a tall black man, shaven head and beard, very well dressed, like a tailor's mannequin, spoke very softly and to the point, held the room when he started talking. "I've been looking into the activities for this company for some years now and we understand they are up to something and every time we get close our informants just vanish. Until now: due to the real good work of the two officers who uncovered it, we now can start to put together the jigsaw puzzle, we have all the right bits we have to put it together. So my colleague Boyd, who is head of airport operations into the EU, will share with you what we also have. We believe this is not only UK-based, but the UK has the NHS and it's easier to screw us to much unchecked movements of drugs and people."

Boyd was a harder looking man, six foot, held himself like an ex-military man, has worked undercover at one of the major airports. "Interpol has thought for a long time it was a smuggling operation and that is why for five years they have been looking into this, but turned up nothing. They have installed on some of the planes to and from the big destinations like Spain, Greece and France special air pollution detection filters and they will take them off the plane when they have landed back in the UK and send them for testing against the viruses known to be common. Also, they have installed observation CCTV on the planes to monitor movements. As Interpol we can do this, we have the green light from government security services working with us, but we also can keep this on a need-to-know only, for the moment, and now who is in this room. I am sure you know we feel and so do your senior security services, we have information leaks in a lot of places, it's a multi-billion pound operation and they have tentacles everywhere.

"All of you in this room will now be part of the new operations team; this will be code named Central Line.

"There are eight countries taking part, the international information will be channelled through myself and Lloyd. MI5 will be the point of information dissemination for all, meeting of the team will be every two weeks. DCI Linda Dolan will be the UK head of operations; she will have weekly briefings with us too. CI Aston will be operating on the ground coordinating of uniform officers and back up, Sergeant Clarke is the point officer for firearms and back up when and if requested. We have given you all the notes in this folder, on one small note we are allowed to share all information with you as you are with us, we will be also sharing the small office with Winchester and Reggie. I hope it's not too cramped."

Reggie and Winchester knew that no one had still sussed out the office they had and how big it was.

The meeting had ended and everyone went off. Reggie and Winchester said to Lloyd and Boyd "see you downstairs".

"Can we come with you now, we'll get a cup of tea on the way."

"No need, we have a small fridge, kettle and all you need."

Chapter Eight: Operation Central Line

Winchester walked towards their locked office door; it had a digital key lock on it X9999X door code.

Reggie was walking with the other two as they looked around, you could see they were not expecting any grand office, and as they all got to the door Lloyd said, "looks like they gave you the dungeon then," but as Winchester opened the door and switched the light on, Lloyd and Boyd's faces lit up. "This is not what we was expecting at all. Look how big this is, it's great. I was thinking some old cell and little desks. We could fit four more people in here."

"Oh yes," Reggie said, "this is our secret; don't tell anyone or we could lose it or they take the furniture away."

"No, we will keep this to ourselves." Lloyd and Boyd took the two facing each other desks, dusted them off and put their boxes down and said, "our files will be here tomorrow, we have about 60 files, plenty of space."

Winchester said, "This was done up as a gold command area and then once Scotland Yard was finished doing their new fit out this was just got forgotten."

"This is good, do the phones work?"

"Yes, press 9 for an outside line. We have to clean it ourselves at the moment, they have not allowed for cleaners."

"We can keep it clean ourselves," they both said. "We both are staying at this time in the Premier Inn, so we will see you tomorrow."

The morning was an early start, 0700 for briefing in the main conference room. Everyone was at this meeting, the overhead projector shining down onto the screen in big black bold letters 'Operation Central Line'.

"Morning, everyone. Today is the start of the operation and you will only be attached to this, and all your other duties apart from court attendance will no longer apply. All your officers and Sergeants have been informed.

"Reggie and Winchester, you will meet the BTP officers at Finsbury Park station, you are going to get your passes, you are now going to be cleaners on the London Underground on the Central line; they will kit you out and for the next week you will be doing a health and safety briefing about working on and around the LUL stations."

Reggie said, "Do we have to clean out toilets, ma'am?"

The room started to laugh. "No, you are only working on the trains, and yes, you will need to keep the trains clean. Everyone, your new radio code for operation channel 111. You will need to lock it in as after next week only I will be able to authorise any person coming on to that channel, Control will be monitoring it 24/7. Also we are allocating the new Blackberry phones to all of you in this group. This is for day-to-day use; your phones have been authorised to access information. Each one of you have also been issued a security code to your phone, it for your use only, do not change it. I will warn you now, the phones are monitored so be careful what you say. One last thing on the phones: if you hold down number one for five seconds it will call Control and go to open mike – this will be like the orange button on your radios, urgent assistance to you."

The others were given assignments too. Reggie and Winchester had a separate meeting about what they were going to be looking for.

CI Aston was outside their office down in the depths of the station. She was smiling – that was good.

"Morning, ma'am."

"Well, how are you settling in down here?"

"Well, ma'am."

As Winchester opened the door, CI Aston stopped as the lights flickered on; she looked at them and said, "If you two fell in crap you would come up smelling of roses; this place is great. Look at the furniture." She added, "But I would not change my office for the dungeon."

That was good to hear, then Lloyd and Boyd walked in. "Morning, ma'am," they said.

She said, "Nice place you have here."

They said, "Better than most."

"This station was meant to close down a few years ago, but they are keeping it open till the new mayor sorts himself out; we expect to close down in two years. Do we have a direct line down here?"

"Yes, ma'am, it's 888," Reggie said.

"Good, I will not be down again unless I have to."

"We have a load of files coming in, ma'am, we need to sort them out," Lloyd said.

"Good, see you all later," and she left the room.

"Well that's good, I thought she would have taken some of the chairs."

Boyd said to Winchester, "So you both are going to be cleaners on the underground, and I suppose we are going to be your back-up as well."

Reggie and Winchester arrived at Finsbury Park station where they met the British Transport Police Sergeant of this place; his name was Arthur Layton, a big well-built man, 6' 6", hands like a bunch of bananas. Ex-guardsman. He looked at both of them, and grunted Met lads "A". Then in a very deep voice said, "Hang on here, I will take you to the stores, we need to get you uniforms but first I need a cup of tea. I've been in since 0400 early shift."

They walked outside the station to a small Turkish café called Terrace, nice place, makes good tea and toast. They sat down in the café talking about the past and how the BTP and Met did not get on for years, but now seems to be more cooperation between everyone. They walked back to the main store, picked up some fleeces, ID Badges; they had to pose for like a mug shot, then the rest of the day started with an induction delivered by the Sergeant, going into what were all the dangers, doors and passengers, abuses you may get, looking out for stick injuries, ie from shapes, also what was the live track, the yellow line, what to do if someone throws themselves on to the track or falls – well just report it, nothing you can do, don't get on the track and try and save them, get on your radio asap. The driver will see them as he comes out of the tunnel, but not much chance of stopping in time, also look out for suspicious packages.

They both got issued with travel passes. "So you may get pulled by the station manager thinking you work for LU – to keep your cover you will have to help them out, but I am sure you will not have a problem. But please remember one thing, lads, you're not police officers, cleaners is your mindset, report issues to us on the radio, your radio is set to the police channels. We are listening, so is your back-up."

First shift as cleaners was at the Epping station at 0500 the very next morning, armed with clear bin bags and long litter pickers. It was not a nice morning, the rain was heavy bouncing off the waterproof coats they had on as they waited for the driver to open the bloody doors. As they got on to the carriage, two other cleaners appeared. "Hello, who are you?"

Winchester and Reggie said, "We just started and we have been asked to work from this station for a few weeks with yourselves." It was two, say 50 year-old lads: Jacob was from Brixton, strong West Indian accent, Rastafarian, deep voice, really chilled out sort of person; Mike from Dagenham used to work at Ford's, till he lost his right eye in a bare knuckles fight at some place called the

Volunteer pub.

"Well," Jacob said, "we don't mind the help, it's cool. You lads, we'll do the front then to the back we meet in the middle."

They both set off to the front of the train.

Reggie said, "My god, look at the state of this, cans of discarded beer, someone been sick on the floor." They have a specific cleaners for this and the driver had reported it the night before as he walked through the train, so it should have been done. The carriage stank, but very quickly two young women appeared from nowhere and never said a word, got on the train with a bucket, mop and cleaning stuff, went right to the sick, cleared it in seconds, and were gone as fast as they appeared.

Reggie found a nappy with shit in it, and a wallet that had been discarded after a pickpocket had emptied it of its useful contents. They completed their first train, the second train was due out in 20 minutes. As it pulled into the station from the sidings, this was almost clean as the night cleaners had done what they should have done. As they got on the train, two males got on and they looked like cleaners, very well-dressed cleaners. Winchester nudged Reggie: "This them, mate?"

Reggie had a bag full of rubbish, so it did not look suspicious. He dropped the bin bag and the contents went all over the floor, so he could have more observation time of what they were doing.

Winchester said to the two males, "Okay, lads?"

They looked at him. "We are good. You new people then?"

"Yes, we are training at the station for a few months."

They looked hard at Winchester as if they thought they recognised him but then said "good luck" and got off the carriage and went to the next carriage along.

Reggie said, "They are not cleaners – did you see what one of them had on his feet, they are loafers, expensive boots."

The security services had given body cams to Reggie and Winchester, which could be activated by pressing it directly, it had a short battery life, say 30 minutes if on all the time. They had both activated the cameras, they were like small buttons on the jackets. It allowed them to watch without looking, and pick up what they looked like. The train was ready to leave as the cleaners got off, they were both told not to follow them let them go, but the two men both waited for the next train to come in.

They both had baseball caps on, dark blue boiler suits, buttoned right up to the neckline so you could not see what they were wearing underneath, glasses that if you looked carefully were safety glasses, both had on medical grade gloves. This time when they got on the train they seemed to lift a few seats, put something underneath them – talk about in plain sight, but it did look normal as they were cleaners. They got off the train and went down the platform and out the exit. Reggie and Winchester stayed on the train as the doors closed. Making sure no one observed them doing anything but cleaning, as the train left the station, they lifted the seats and saw what looked like an air freshener – if you remove the seats there is a void to the floor, and an air grille leading into the carriage. It suddenly let off a sort of hissing sound as it sprayed on to the grille and into the carriage. Reggie said, "Quick, cover your mouth, we will wait for it to do it again and I will get it on this clean cloth, bag it and they can test it. We best leave it here."

"Why?" Winchester said.

"They will know if it goes missing, someone may be on to them."

"It could be a maintenance man finds it," Winchester said.

"Best not take chances."

They contacted DS Robbins about what had happened, and he said, "I will meet with you at Liverpool Street station, at the coffee shop next to the fruit and veg as you come up the escalators."

They met, Winchester and Reggie debriefed DS Robbins, they gave him the new mini cameras so they could download everything, and took the cloth with the spray on it for testing.

"Good work, lads. What's it like cleaning the trains? Easy job I would think."

"No," Reggie said, "it's disgusting, some people should hang their heads in shame what we found on the train."

Winchester said, "Well, some woman left her knickers on the train, another person left a dirty nappy, sick, loads of empty cans, coffee cups."

"Oh well," the DS said, "only for a short time. Finished for the day now, lads, it's 1300, see you again soon, enjoy the rest of your day."

Both Reggie and Winchester went home, it had been a long day and it was only like 1400, both had to be on station at 0500 again tomorrow; the weather was going to be better according to the weather forecast.

This morning was like every other day as they had been cleaning for a few weeks now, they had not seen the two other LUL cleaners, they were off sick apparently, not sure Reggie being a person who always looks at the negative side of life, is it because in the police after a while you see society for what is. This is no disrespect to everyone, but police in general deal with the bottom feeders. He feels because we are working they know we will clean their shit up as well, see it as a good time to take some sick time and as they get 20 days sick a year why not. Also, both of them have not seen the others.

They both were called into a team meeting this week at station with DCI DOLAN. This will be an update on the spray can found under the seats on the train.

The meeting took place on the Wednesday in the meeting room at Bow. First of all the whole team was in this meeting, the budget was up for review as well to extend for three more months or kill it. First on the agenda was the progress report, the report got right to the point no action can be taken as investigations are still ongoing. But we requested this was granted, then the two CIs left the room.

DS Robbins said, "We have the report back from the labs on the contents of the spray. At first it come back as a standard, cheap flowery air freshener, but when exposed to body temperature it changed to a strong pollen – that will give people with intolerance and low immunity things like running eyes, cough, sore throat, it's perfect, all trains in this weather will most definitely have the heating on, it will act as an incubator, it's a fact on mostly the underground trains colds spread quickly on trains because of the heat and lack of movement of air and of course people rammed together like sardines."

Winchester put his penny's worth in by saying, "We have some concrete evidence, we know this is happening right under our noses, in plain sight."

"Yes, it most definitely looks like it," DS Robbins said, "but we still need more evidence, we have three months to gather everything we need."

Winchester said, "No pressure then."

Winchester and Reggie were in their office with Boyd and Lloyd. They were just reading from files aloud because that way if one of them just said something the other recognised from what they were reading, it would help. They had a white board on the wall with times and dates of people mysteriously falling very ill and they were under 50 years old; this was only confined to underground stations, but the amount of people over 50 falling ill on trains was staggering. Over 400 in one year, average illness-related deaths about 10 to 13. But a spike was this year, 2000, of young heart attacks on the platform and on the train itself. This was seven, they will need investigation. What we need to figure out was are they connected to any of the pharmaceutical companies. This was not on the database, it only worked if you had all the correct information, Date of birth, first name and last, also the home address.

Reggie said, "It's going to be the old way, mate we have to speak to BTP, find out where they were taken and get the names and addresses."

"We have two," Winchester said, "that we been to. So we are looking for five more."

"No," Reggie said, "we are going to have to go back five years, this may have been going on some time; the way they have this slick operation going on, it's too well done for a short term experiment."

Lloyd and Boyd agreed.

For the first time the phone rang in the office, made everyone jump. "It's the front desk, we have a Doctor Kildare to see you."

"Will be right up." Reggie went up and bought the doctor to the office – he looked like a doctor, very upright, well spoken, very soft hands when you shook them.

"What can we do for you, Doctor?"

"I have some information about another person that I was informed about by another doctor on a course I was on at the UCLH Tottenham Court Road. I got his name, Dr Lee Wong, he is a Pathologist at Kings Hospital."

Reggie said, "Grab a seat at the meeting table. Do you want a tea, Doc?"

"Yes please."

Winchester and Reggie had their own tea, milk and coffee in the office.

The Doc sat looking round the room. "This is a big office."

They all chuckled. "This is not the norm. Anyway, Doc, what's this all about?"

"Well do you remember I told you about the person I treated on the platform, I said I thought he was ok? Well from the discussion me and Dr Wong had, actually he died."

"How did you know it was him?"

"Well I didn't till he said the male had two different eye colours. That got me thinking so I asked him more. He said it was strange, his heart was fine, no problems that the post-mortem showed up in reports, but the bloods for testing went missing at the lab twice. Then the body was claimed by the government and taken away. Home land security team, they said they were, never heard of them."

"Have you, Lloyd?" Winchester asked.

"Yes, of course, every country now has its own designated homeland security teams because of the international terrorist."

"But why would they be interested in this, then?"

Boyd said, "It's beginning to make sense to me, we are thinking this is only in London, if Homeland is involved then it's international. We are on another planet to them. They are the real spooks, they are always in the shadows."

"We need to speak with the DCI asap, give her the update in our intelligence."

"If I am right," Boyd said, "they will not renew your funding, they will shut this down."

They thanked the doctor and took him back to the front desk.

The DCI called a meeting for the whole team at 1600 in the incident room on the 3rd floor.

They all sat round the table. DCI Dolan said, "We have two people from Special Branch joining us soon."

A trolley came through the door being pushed by one of the tea staff; it had lots of biscuits, coffee and tea. This was going to be a late one because as Janet the canteen girl left the trolley, the DCI said, "Can we get a refill, say 1900?", she nodded. Janet was an ex-military police officer injured in Northern Ireland; this was part-time job for her, lost her sight in one eye due to a car bomb.

The room was quiet as everyone sat round the table with their notepads and files in-front of them. The DCI said, "Everyone grab a drink and a few biscuits, we need to do some brainstorming."

The two whiteboards were either side of her as she sat at the head of the 20-foot oval maple table. Behind her was a 60-inch screen for the back projector and above that was a pull down projector screen if required.

CI Aston came into the room. She looked behind her then closed the door behind her and sat next to the DCI.

"Right," said the DCI, "let's make our way round the room, let's go for your updated intelligence."

Gary, the DS, started, "Well, ma'am, we have followed up on 30-plus leads around the possible links to this company, we are hitting walls, and when I say walls, I feel like they are one step ahead of us, I feel we are being led in some way but I cannot put my finger on it. But what I can say, I am sure someone in the service is leaking information out, we know it's no one in this room."

The DCI said, "Thanks but keep pressing and following up. But I want you to do one thing for me."

"Yes, ma'am?"

"We have taken on an ex-police inspector as a consultant, Hooper." Gary looked puzzled. "The reason is, I know he is a pain in the ass, but he will get in places and speak to people we can't. He is a good detective, he also has direct contact with Hellen Blake, as we have noted, the name Hellen Blake note of security, please never use the name on your written information the person will be referred to as Queen Bee. Is that clear?"

"Yes, ma'am."

"We cannot run the risk of anyone ever finding out QB's real name, that's if it is really her name, Hellen Blake."

"We must be safe."

Linda Dolan, the DCI, said, "And yes, Gary, I also believe we have people in this station passing information to someone. Unless I give any of you specific direct information, otherwise you will not give critical details away."

"What if a Chief inspector or any senior rank asks any of us?"

"Reference me but don't give them nothing, give them something. You've all been in the job now to know what you would say – we keep the senior officers like mushrooms, in the shade and feed them crap."

Reggie said with a smile on his face, "That include you, ma'am?"

She gave him that look of a headteacher looking over their glasses at you.

The DCI went on to ask did anyone have any other information at this time before the Special Branch team get here.

"Yes, ma'am," Winchester said, "did you get the information we found on the train and what it contained?"

"Yes I did, and this is getting very interesting. I have agreed you two can stay cleaning trains for the next month." The room started to chuckle. "Keep getting the information."

Reggie said, "We have just spoken to Dr Kildare, he gave us a lot of good information on what he saw and what he did at the time."

"Can you move on it?" DS Gary Robbins looked at DC Martin Byrne and DC Wineglass. "You will follow up on the investigations from the Doc, Reggie and Winchester will brief you after this meeting. Okay?"

They both nodded.

Lloyd and Boyd from Interpol said, "We understand this company we are investigating, is based in Cyprus, the Dazary family. The façade to the public, they are a well-run company that is giving to charity and courts a lot of very influential people including governments, but they have 40 subsidiaries run from the Cayman Islands. Profits in the UK 300 billion, worldwide 800 billion dollars. One of the heads of the police widows' charity is member of the Dazary family; we really have to tread very, very carefully."

"In this room I am telling you," the DCI said, "if this leaks to any of your mates in the press I will find out who it is and you will be working for the rest of your career being the bagman for the scrambled eggs upstairs."

Winchester said, "Ma'am, what is the scrambled eggs, the top brass?"

Everyone looked at Winchester, they could not believe he had asked the question.

"The Met reputation is on the line here." The DCI also said, "Is any of you in the freemasons, because if you are you need to remove yourself from the investigation, I do not have anything against you but people will come to you from that angle." The DCI just looked at everyone; the room was still: you could hear the sounds of mugs of tea being put down on the table.

"Oh yes," Linda the DCI said, "everyone from now on makes references to anyone not a police officer involved in this investigation will be given a code name, I will determine what that is, am I clear? And if I hear anyone using the correct names without my specific instructions, you will be off the investigation."

"Yes, ma'am." Everyone nodded in agreement.

The two Special Branch officers knocked on the door to come in, and they did without even being beckoned.

The two special branch lads were in their 30s, very well dressed, dark blue suits, black polished shoes, well groomed.

"This is officer Keith Gunn," who was the smaller of the two, was more approachable-looking than officer Mike Newlands, who was very ginger, hard-faced, looked ex-military. The DCI invited them both to introduce themselves and explain what they are doing and why both investigations would be working closely together.

Keith Gunn was the first to talk. He said, "We have been looking into this company for over five years, it's been a small operation until now. The reason for this is we are dealing with other terror-related organisations, we are just too thin on the ground, all our involvement will be is information exchange. I have bought a file with me to give to your DCI, it's all we have at this time, not a lot but it's good intelligence; if we can help in any way we will. We are reporting directly back to our senior who has a minster very interested in what is going on." His eyebrows moved up and down. "Our budget is tight as is yours. I will hand you over to Mike, whom has some information that you will find very interesting."

When Mike started to talk, his voice did not match his body; it was like a young man's voice and his balls had not dropped. Everyone looked at each other. But one thing was for sure you were not going to tell him that. He must know and like a true professional just brushed it off. As all the people in the room were true professionals and would laugh once he was out of earshot. "We have managed to get a person into this organisation, they are very deep in, they have been in for three years now, and we are starting to get some information out. It's slow as this is a family-run business, it takes years. We will not give you their name, we recruited them from Cambridge University. To be frank,' Mike said, "I am not comfortable giving you this information, I am the point of contact, I am due an update soon. Please, I cannot put enough emphasis on this statement more than please, please do not mention this in any correspondence, they could lose their life."

Keith then said, "I understand you may not trust us and we may not trust your organisation due to your inherently poor reputation for leaks – your nickname is the Titanic you leak so much. Oh yes and by the way, you two–" looking at Winchester and Reggie– "you both look like cleaners on the trains, well done. We can see you through the CCTV. You fit right in. We two also noted what's going on, but we cannot get the CCTV on the trains. Right, we have to go to a briefing." They looked at the DCI and said, "Ma'am, can we have five minutes of your time outside?"

She stood up and said, "Be back soon, have your tea all."

Outside, Keith said, "Ma'am, insider information is that they have stopped doing something on the Central line for three months, our information is they have moved temp to the Piccadilly line, due to the connection to the airport."

The DCI said, "Thanks, we will take that into consideration." They all shook hands and left. The DCI came back in the room, sat down and started to write something down. The DCI then said, "We will resume in five minutes." Linda Dolan was writing something when the phone rang, she answered it: "Thanks for letting me know," she said, "they have left the building."

"Right, well now we know what special branch is up to, they have given me some information that the people doing the cleaning on the Central line so to speak are now doing the Piccadilly line. Winchester and Reggie, stay on Central line. From what I can gather, the information we just got they have known about this for some time, I am not buying this, until we can verify if we can trust them or not, keep it tight between us only. I will feed them titbits, is that understandable?"

Everyone nodded.

"Winchester, the DCI asked, "did you say that AKA QB was once at university?"

"Yes, just as I thought, a fishing expedition, I could be wrong. If you get any senior officers come to you, fob them off. As I said before, point them in my direction and also log it in your notebooks when you had the conversation. It's a safeguard as this way we could trace the timeline of the leak. If we have one."

The meeting went on till very late, it was about getting to know the company's location and head office in Camden; they had this fabulous building with two big black ornamental cats sitting proudly outside the grand entrance; the picture did not do it justice. This was a building 100 metres long, six storeys high.

"This building would have not looked out of place in Egypt in times gone by. From intelligence we have, in their basement secret laboratories. This building has as head of security former Greek special forces, sharp as a surgeon's knife, his name is Peter Rizzo, he runs the internal security network, and his boss is Marina Sava. She only answers to Nicholas Dazary."

Then the DCI said, "Let's take ten minutes for tea and coffee. I need to go to the lavatory, I am bursting for a pee." She was one of the lads, that's for sure. Apparently, she self-built her own house.

Everyone grabbed some tea and digestives, talking amongst themselves before the DCI came back. She said, "That's better, talking to you lot on a full bladder was painful." She grinned. "So, everyone, this is what is going to happen for the next few months. Reggie and Winchester, you are Team 1, you will be continuing to clean the trains." Everyone looked at them with a grin. "Team 2, DC Catherine Wineglass and DC Martin Byrne, you will now be Team 1 back-up – when the suspects leave the station you will follow them. Remember they have not been caught before and there is a very good reason for that – they must be careful, and take your time; if you lose them pick it up another time, you are both fully trained surveillance officers. Team 3, DS Robbins and DC Alex Weston, you will head the ground operations liaison with BTP officers and Interpol Officers Boyd and Lloyd. I will handle the rest. DS Gary Robbins will report directly to me and CI Aston.

"You all have your assignments, oh yes be safe at all times, and remember I will never ask anyone outside this team to give information out, I will never send anyone to you for an update outside this team. Is that crystal clear?"

Everyone said, "Yes, ma'am."

"Oh I forgot, we will be getting a new member of the team soon, I will keep you posted. She can be trusted, DC Megan Burn, she's from Essex Police, I was with her at Hendon; she is a trusted intelligence gathering officer. I will introduce her once she arrives in a few weeks' time."

"Ma'am," DS Robbins piped up, "is it good introducing new people this far down the road?"

"Yes, she will work closely with me, putting together all the information you feed in every day so we have a real-time picture when we all meet again next week same time here.

"Before you leave, it's without saying, welfare checks every day, please, on each other."

"Yes, ma'am," as everyone left the room.

Chapter Nine

I t was 1st December 2003, a very cold day to be starting at 0500 cleaning trains; the frost was thick on the floor and on screens of cars as Winchester and Reggie walked towards Epping underground station, both with the LUL heavy coats on and gloves.

Winchester said, "They look after their employees, this stuff is 100% better than what we have."

Reggie nodded, his face tucked in his scarf, hands in his pockets. They walked into the little changing room on the station and put their coats and other stuff of personal use into this locker, picked up the bin liners and the long litter picker so you don't use your hands.

It had been a few weeks and no activity, but this morning Reggie spotted three people with what looked like a cleaning trolley you get in an office, looked a little out of place. Winchester and Reggie got on the first carriage, saw the three men in black like all-in-one boiler suits, gloves again with clear spray bottles hanging off their belts to clean the hand rails.

Reggie said to one of them, "Hi mate, you good?"

"Yes, we are, we've been sent to help clean the train."

"Oh," Winchester said, "what you using?"

The guy said, "Oh, just your standard home stuff you can get anyplace, we must get on, see you around." He got off the train with the others and moved to the next carriage.

Reggie got on the radio to team 2: "we have contact", two clicks come back on the radio, this was to let them know they understood. Reggie gave the description of them. Winchester and Reggie were trying to keep an eye on what the three men were doing, without raising suspicions, but this morning the train looked like a paper bomb had gone off, the Evening Standard was all over the place, beer cans, takeaway boxes, they had filled up two bags already. The train was due out in about five minutes and Reggie and Winchester had caught up with them. The cleaners were very specific in what bottle they used, one of them had the little notebook writing down what they were doing. Then a passenger got on and most of the people at this time of the morning were police officers or cleaners, but this was a police officer who got on, sat down and looked at Winchester with confusion. "Winchester, is that you?" The three cleaners also looked back at the person who'd got on, you could see he was a police officer, he had the white shirt under his jacket, the black trousers and giveaway boots and a small rucksack. Just as the driver said "we are ready to depart, please leave the train, cleaners one minute," Winchester looked at the officer sitting down: "Sorry, mate, do I know you?" and Winchester winked at him, so he knew right away what to say. "Sorry, you looked like an old mate."

"Wow that was close," Reggie said when they were on the platform.

The cleaners had gone, Team 2 had them in their sights. "We got them, they have a black transit van. Checked on PNC it's registered to Cristal Clean company."

"That's not a surprise," Winchester said to Reggie. "They wouldn't register it to the pharmacy company."

"The train that has just pulled out has been taken out of service at the next station sidings for the boffins to have a look at, they are going to take swabs, this come over the radio point to point."

Winchester replied, "I thought only a few of us know about this?"

"Yes, they do, but this team is from the international control of viral infections, they are totally independent of anyone and we have agreed with them this is a training exercise, we have planted this for them to track and trace to its original chemical make-ups. That is the storyline."

"That makes sense."

Reggie said, "Always anything like this goes down hidden under the cloak of a training exercise and it works."

Then the radio sounded again and Reggie answered, "Yes Gov," to DS Robbins.

"We are following the van, can you both make your way to the sidings at Loughton for us, the station manager and the BTP are waiting to go with you to the train, we are testing carriage 2299, is that right, Winchester?"

"Yes, gov."

"The station manager's name is Rodger." Rodger, Out came over the radio from DC Weston. "The BTP officer is Sergeant Russell Gold. One more thing: the head of the test team is Professor John-Robbins."

Winchester and Reggie arrived by car at Loughton entrance to the sidings; they were met by eight people: Rodger, the professor, Sergeant Gold and five people – three women, all looked like students; and two people including the driver of the train. Quick induction explaining the do's and don'ts around tracks and all given orange hi vis tops and on we went. It was about 0630, trains were getting busier. The three women got to work, opened up their testing boxes; they were black, the same size as a briefcase, it had everything they needed in it, they took out their notebooks, the same sort of notebooks the cleaners had. "See?" Winchester said. "See the notebooks, they are the same."

Reggie nodded.

Reggie and Winchester also had to make notes of what they did. The professor had a small travel metal suitcase, he opened it up and it was full on both sides, little test tubes surrounded in polystyrene, they were all stood up, must have been 60. The tester took a swab, put it in a test tube then the professor took the tube, wrote on the label the location. He took a photo of the location and label as exhibit one carriage 2299. The other woman, Jill, who stood next to him, also wrote down in a notebook, exhibit one, carriage 2299, photo 01. Vertical handrail connector door between carriage right hand side and so on as they made their way through the carriage; it took two hours. The station manager and driver stayed in the carriage talking they were not interested, the BTP Sergeant was really most of the time at the end of the carriage dealing with problems, some sort of demonstration was going to happen today in Central London, his hands were full, he really did not want to be here.

The professor said, "Right, we are done, we can go. I will give my report tomorrow to the DCI. Can you let her know?"

Winchester said, "She will call you later most probably, but I will tell her and thank you."

"Just a moment," one of the women said; this was Wendy. "What's this?" She'd spotted at the top of the open window a small round doughnut-looking green blob. "Looks like the stick on toilet duck." She asked the driver what it was.

He looked unsure. "Don't know, sweetheart."

You could see the women look at him with disdain for saying sweetheart. She got out some surgical gloves and tweezers, opened up this transparent little pot, unscrewed the top and placed it in, put the top back on. It was red to match the paint of the external doors. Then she said, "I know this stuff, this used to be used to put a nice scent around in open doors, it reacts to air slowly releasing the scent over say 12 hours, what's it doing here?"

Winchester said, "Can I ask a question?"

The professor looked at Winchester. "What do you want to know, I will put it in layman's terms for you?"

Winchester looked at him with a hard face. "Bloody cheap shot, mate."

Reggie took it personally and bit: "What you say, Prof?"

The professor saw he had pissed the two officers off, and corrected himself. "No offence, but I will not use the long Latin names for the items."

"Still not good enough but we'll move on," Winchester said. "That item will disperse what it has to disperse and it will vanish?"

"That is about it, officer, perfect weapon, unless you know what you are looking for you would miss it, as the windows are open, the air rushing past will fill their carriage with its contents.

"Your team have been good setting this up, we have enjoyed looking around, very ingenious, it's good that no one has ever thought of this, they could kill hundreds of people or infect them, that's why they do this to outthink them ahead of the game." Little did he know this was a real time situation.

"We are going back to our labs in Manchester, thank you," and they all left.

DS Robbins was following the van; he was on the M2; it was heading deep into Kent.

The following day a team meeting was called, to inform everyone of what had been found on the train by the professor's team. "Updates, reports from everyone."

Winchester was feeling a little tired after working cleaning trains all day – it's a lot harder than people think, the amount of rubbish left on trains was mind blowing. Reggie and Winchester between them cleared 40-plus bin liners, most of it was the newspapers, food and empty takeaway cups, also informing the homeless people that managed to sleep on the train they needed to get off, let the specialist cleaning people come and clean off the seats if they can get there in time to clean off stains left by people, piss stains from some drunk people, sick as well; it's just unbelievable, when you see this, the animal kingdom is cleaner.

Everyone was early in the meeting room. As Winchester was walking down the corridor towards the meeting room, one of the senior officers from the top floor – they are almost never seen below decks so to speak – called out to Winchester, "PC Winchester?"

"Yes, sir?"

"Nice to see you again; last time I saw you was on your pass out."

"Yes, sir."

"How are things?"

"All good, sir, just on my way to a meeting, sir."

"Meeting, what meeting?"

Winchester had to think quick. "Training on surveillance."

"I did not know we did that here, who is running the training?"

"DCI Linda Dolan."

"Off you go, may see you again soon," then the officer was gone.

Winchester could not remember the ACC's name, but he knew he should better inform the DCI and the CI of this encounter. Winchester was the last to walk into the meeting room, and the DCI said, "Nice of you to join us, PC Winchester."

"Sorry, Gov, got intercepted in the corridor by the ACC."

She looked at him hard. "Speak to me after this meeting."

"Yes, Gov."

"Right, let's get on, reports first.

"Covert team, give me the short version of the surveillance of the van you followed."

DS, Gary Robbins laid it out; they had followed it back to some place in Kent, part of the pharmaceutical group of companies, the site was massive. "We could not go in as the security was like an army base."

"We are talking about QPI (Quite Pharmaceutical International)?"

"Yes, Gov."

"Cleaning team, give me the short version as well, I have seen all the reports; this will give everyone an overview.

Winchester said, "Well I never knew how messy people are." That got a little chuckle in the room. "We observed the targets carrying out cleaning, using different bottles. Do you want me to talk about what happened when the trains was taking out for testing?"

"No, I will do that in a minute."

"They did the same things they always did, but we did notice this time there were three of them, not two. One was taking notes."

The DCI said, "Did the Covert team manage to take pictures of them?"

"Yes, Gov, but they are not good enough, due to the location we could not get a clear shot."

"Ok, we got to work on that without raising suspicions. Lloyd and Boyd, any updates from your end?"

"Yes we can confirm that we are now sure this is international."

DCI looked hard at them. "Well we know that, but any update?"

"Sorry, yes," Boyd said, "Our intelligence confirms this is happening on return flights to the UK, we have been in close contact with our team in Lyon, France. The team you used on the train for testing has also carried out tests on three flights to and from the UK. Most of the flights are to popular destinations, Spain, France and Greece. We can confirm on the way out no detection of any contamination, but coming back on the flights can confirm the presence of contaminated air filters and on the flight itself, nothing concrete.

"Our teams closely monitored people from the flights, 60% of the people on the flights confirmed minor colds."

"How did you manage to get that information?"

"We looked at the location of the people and monitored the local pharmacies, as most cold and flu-like symptoms start to build after one to three days. We saw a spike within the days in 60% of the areas of the people from the flights. This is not accurate as we see common colds all the time, but in the summer we do not expect to see the spike, three flights over three weeks has given us good data. We also noted the people who maintain and clean the filters and the cleaning company are subsidiaries of QPI."

"Thank you for that, this is very interesting, but how sure are you this will not get leaked out?"

"We did the same as you did, we informed the team that you used, we were testing the possibility of a terrorist attacking planes in this way, they think it was a training event."

The DCI looked towards the door as a knock sounded. "Come in." It was Professor John-Robbins.

"Come in and thank you for attending our meeting, we will do the introductions later."

"Can I use your computer to put the findings of the report on your screen so it would be easier to explain?"

It took a few minutes to sort, the lights went down.

"First of all I must congratulate your people for doing an exercise that was so realistic and very well thought out, what a worrying situation, if this was real the ramifications could be catastrophic in the wrong hands."

On the screen was a graph. And a picture of a train carriage layout. "Carriage 2299: we took air samples and swabs from upright poles and hand rails, we found pollen, mould particulates and dust mites..."

"Dust mites?" someone said.

"Yes we were very surprised too, but to be honest them little buggers get everywhere, you have dirty old clothes and seats, we found in the seats, blood, let's say bodily fluids from every orifice, but no ear wax."

The room still did not make a sound – I think they were all shocked.

"Then we come across to the two main features your team did that was amazing: under the seats the canister we found was an air freshener at first look, but it was omitting the cold virus, well one of them anyway. Very ingenious, but the one we found between the interlinked doors between the carriages, this was so good–" the professor was smiling and he was excited– "it was a gel like material, it reminded me of the stick on a toilet bowl freshener. As water passes over it, it will evaporate, but this did it with chemically breaking down as the air flowed past it releases the high grass pollen into the carriages, this would give people eye irritation or throat and possibly runny nose.

"That is all we could find. But I must say the plane report was somewhat different. Again in the wrong hands this could be so, so dangerous. The tests on the planes were carried out by another team but we are all the same group. The comments from my colleagues said to pass on their congratulations on thinking of this before any terrorist organisation had thought about this."

Everyone in the room just suddenly looked at each other, with a cold feeling going up their backs.

"We found in the filter system and in the air was the cold virus mostly, as the filter air systems are very good. We found on the floor small patches of concentration of the influenza types, very mild. This would be spot sprayed to release slowly say over three hours and then it would be gone. Again, all the same symptoms. If you say 200 people on a flight 70% would be affected, then whom they then come in to contact with. That is it for what we found, but this could be used like this to just deliver anything, it's frightening. The underground moves millions of people."

"Thank you, professor."

The tea trolley came in the room pushed by the long-term tea woman; she was the other tea person, Theresa, she was one of two trusted tea ladies, she'd been at the station for 15 years, she knew more than anyone the secrets of the station, been in very confidential meetings just handing the tea and biscuits out; no one ever questioned her, she was part of the furniture. Her husband was the ex-Sergeant at this station who had passed away ten years ago. Her security clearance must be high. She was a tall for woman, 5, 9" bleached hair shoulder length, bit of a tank, Dagger, person from Dagenham, you could hear that in her voice, would punch your lights out tough sort. Made fabulous tea. Everyone always said hello.

The professor packed up and left. As he was leaving the DCI said to Gary, "Will you ensure the professor leaves without interception."

"Yes, Gov, back soon."

The DCI said to Reggie, "Close the door please and also the blinds in the door vision panel." She was sure someone was walking past more than once – some senior officers just are nosy and think they should know everything. If it is good try and attach themselves to it to get noticed, but do no real leg work. They could see that the two officers running this, DCI Linda Dolan and CI Aston, were people you just never crossed, they both had reputations of being very direct and suffering no fools.

Everyone had their tea and biscuits with them, white mugs and digestives; the large stainless steel teapot was left on the side, full up for seconds with a bottle of gold top milk, oh yes and sugar lumps.

Theresa slipped out of the room like a ghost, as the DCI stood up and said, "Right, now we know what we are dealing with, this will need to move at a faster pace. We need more resources and funding from upstairs."

"But ma'am," said CI Aston, "this will mean other people will find out what we are doing and we need it to be really covert right now."

"Yes, I agree, but we have no alternative."

CI Aston said, "Who do we know we can trust?

"The ACC, Johnson, he used to be a fire officer, I find him old school and can be trusted; also he is not in the fraternity if you get my drift. We will go see him this afternoon."

"It's a plan."

"So we have now all the evidence we need to carry out a full scale operation on this company. Special branch will be involved from this day forward, but you must still keep the lines of communication through the agreed path I set down. We will instruct you if different – is that clear?"

Everyone nodded.

"Good, new targets, Winchester and Reggie, you are no longer cleaning on the trains, but you both are tracking the missing bodies. Speak to Dr Kildare, get him on board, he will have access to information we would take months to get if we went through the right channels.

"DS Robbins, your team, I need you to carry on surveillance on the people operating from Epping station. Let's find out every little detail and address, background and bank information."

"Yes, ma'am."

"Lloyd and Boyd, we need help from your team on the surveillance on the airports we have identified as the usual routes, I know this could be lots more but we have not got the resources or the money, it's easier to stick to what we know right now."

Winchester said, "Excuse me, ma'am, where are we going with this?"

CI Aston piped in, "Well, PC Winchester, to our knowledge they are suspected of murder, we can expose to the government what they are doing, with regard to the money-making and general assault on the public through spreading viral infections. We need to stop the bastards from doing what they want in this country. They think they are above the law. But remember this, everyone, they tried to kill one of us, PC Winchester, so they will stop at nothing to shut us up."

The DCI then said they "know that PC Winchester had stumbled onto something but they were not sure, keep this in mind. We will meet again next week. I will confirm the time and meeting room. We have an ACC to speak to. Good luck be safe".

Winchester said to Reggie, "Thank god we are off the cleaning, I will never sit on a seat on the underground again, they don't even steam clean them every day, it makes me shudder thinking about it."

"See you tomorrow, mate," Winchester said to Reggie.

As Winchester walked down the road towards the station on a cold damp evening, a voice of a woman called out, "Wait for me, hold on." It was Hellen Blake.

Winchester was caught off guard. "Hello, long time no speak."

"Can we talk?"

"Yes of course, let's go to the greasy spoon, it's safe, only police use it most of the time." She was in a Parka coat, hood was covering most of her face. They walked in and Sid who ran the place just looked at Winchester – "builders' tea, no sugar; and for the young lady?" – "just tea, not so strong". It was time of change of shift so only a few officers were in, all were plain clothes. You could hear the clicks of turned down police radios.

"Any food?"

Winchester said, "I will have a steak and kidney pie, thanks, what about you, Hellen?"

"No, I am fine."

"They do a mean homemade chicken soup, and homemade bread."

"No, but I will have one of the currant buns toasted."

"Coming right up, take a seat," as Sid put two white mugs of tea on the counter top for Winchester to take to the table.

Other officers nodded to Winchester as he sat down. Winchester said, "You see all this seating and tables, they come from one of the old police stations that the soppy government shut down along with its canteen."

Winchester added, "It's good to see you, after the last time we met you was off to the USA."

"Been and I have come back. I found out that you were taken into hospital."

"Yes, they tried to bump me off I think."

"Yes," Helen said, "I was keeping an eye on what was going on and I heard it through the grapevine."

"I am on light duties now for the moment."

"I've got some information for you if you want it?"

"Yes."

"They are on to the investigation, they think it's because they went after you. It's drawn unwanted attention. The person who sanctioned the attack on the police has been removed and been dealt with."

"What, killed?"

"No, he is now working out in Brazil."

"Can I ask you a question?"

"Yes," Hellen said.

"I understand the money they get from this, it must be billions, but why this country?"

"It's the NHS, no one will ever question it, because if they did everyone will scream "you are trying to privatise the NHS"."

"I don't understand," Winchester said with a puzzled face.

"You see there is no joined up thinking from the doctors, pharmacists, hospitals, so it's a win-win."

"I am still baffled."

Hellen looked at him as if he was thick. "If I put it in layman's terms, look at the drug cartels in Colombia, the government leaves them alone, it is safe not questioned; soon as it comes past the borders then the questions are asked. So all operations are kept in safe unchallenged countries through fear."

The penny dropped. Winchester summed it up: "The money they make through the NHS and pharmaceuticals just never gets challenged as everyone just cannot be bothered to find out what the hell is going on with all the money just flooding out of the NHS and over the counter."

"Yes, you got it," Hellen said with her eyes rolling back and a big grin on her face. "But believe it or not, the company makes more money over the counter private sales."

"So, let's get down to the situation."

"What situation?"

Hellen said, "They know we are on to them, they think you are on to them, so they will try and trick everyone to flush out what and if you know anything. From me to you, tell your people to back off for a while or keep everything very close.

"What I can say is this, this goes very high in the government and also one of your senior officers is also being asked to find out if any investigations are ongoing. I don't know the person's name but I know they have links to your particular station. Tomorrow I am heading back to the USA for three months, but please take care of yourself. If I get any other information that is relevant, I will get you a message through Ben Hooper."

"Yes he is now also working with us as well."

She said, "That's good."

They both finished their tea and outside the café went in different directions. Winchester got home and called Reggie, and explained everything to him, and he said "best contact DS Robbins as I think they are on a surveillance operation tonight". Only way to do that was to call control for the DS to call him. After ten minutes Winchester's home phone rang. "Hi Winchester, what's up?"

Winchester told DS Robbins his full conversation with Hellen, and he responded, "Thank god you told me that, we was going to move on the van tonight, could be a trap to flush us out. I will contact the DC but can you contact your CI for me, I will ask for a briefing to be sorted out tomorrow morning, both you and Reggie at the station for 0900."

"Ok." Winchester put the phone down, picked up again and called CI Aston. She was not best pleased to be called at this time of night, but she mellowed off after Winchester had explained everything. It was about 2200 and the door opened and in came Jennie; she was looking very low in her face.

"Hi, you ok?" as she kissed him and put her arms round him. Jennie never even took her coat off or shoes. "I've had a really bad few days, need a hug".

Winchester said, "I will make you a tea and then run you a bath, you look like you need it."

"I do, I have been travelling for two days."

Winchester never asked what she was doing because it was up to Jennie to say. "How long you back for?"

"At the moment I think a week, then I have to go to Hong Kong."

It was about 12 midnight now and Jennie just got into bed and by the time Winchester had brushed his teeth she was asleep – Winchester knew this because Jennie could snore for England. She was lying on her back so Winchester just eased her on her side and he knew he had 15 minutes to get to sleep before she would go back on her back and he would never get to sleep. He did not have the heart to tell her she sounded like a foghorn.

In the morning Jennie was up and made Winchester tea before he was up, then she had the cheek to say to him "you woke me up last night, you were snoring".

Winchester and Reggie were in their office with Lloyd and Boyd talking about the conversation Winchester had had last night, when the phone rang – "we are all needed in the Governor's conference room asap".

Everyone was in the room. DCI Linda Dolan said, "Close the door please."

The CI was sitting next to her in her uniform, not looking best pleased. CI Aston said, "In light of the information we have been given, for the moment all operations on the ground will stop, till we can confirm the facts."

Everyone looked at each other.

"We will explain. PC Winchester has come into some information that suggests we have been rumbled, but this doesn't mean we stop background investigations, it can revisit the booths on the the ground operations in the next few weeks. But first of all, Winchester and Reggie, we feel you are both possibly the weak links in this."

Winchester and Reggie looked perplexed.

"Don't take it the wrong way. They will know you and if you are both not doing your normal duties then suspicions will be raised; also, this is compounded by the fact we may have a person on this station who may have links. Reggie and Winchester, understood, you are not taken off this investigation, but going back on normal patrols and we can use you in the day-to-day investigation, it's very helpful, you both will keep coming to the operational meetings and report to your team as normal. Are we all clear on this?"

"Yes, ma'am."

A knock on the meeting room door. The DCI closed her folder and said "come in". It was the ACC Jamie Mills; he had links to the government and was moving up the ladder, one of the Cambridge University fast track officers, only was on the beat for 24 months. Friends with some big players at Scotland Yard, background check on him showed that his family had links to OPI, this would have not been a problem normally, but in this case he needed to be kept well away from this. The DCI said off the record even though he is a fast tracker, he is one of the good guys. But this could mess him up, even though he was not under suspicion.

"Hello, sir, what can I do for you?"

"We need this meeting room for an important meeting this morning. Do you know when you will be finished?"

"Yes, sir, say 30 minutes."

While we were speaking to the DCI you could see him scanning the room looking at who was here. Then he walked out backwards and left. CI Aston said he was only being nosey, sometimes the nosebleeds upstairs feel left out, hurts their ego. "But again," the CI said, "be on your game."

The DCI said, "Right, we need to get this work done, we all understand what I and the team expects of you all."

"Yes, ma'am."

"And Reggie and Winchester, you are the ears and eyes. Can you both stay back for a moment, me and the CI need to speak to you."

Everyone left the room talking about what they had to do.

CI Aston said, "You both will be only assigned to me. I will be putting you on taking statements, all the locations will be to keep you local. I have agreed with the BTP that you both will attend any incidents of medical or suspicious circumstances on their property. We want you to follow it through to its conclusion, you're uniformed as normal. Under the current situation we need anyone to think you are both on normal duties."

Reggie and Winchester looked at each other, knowing they would be up to their eyeballs in MG11s that other officers could not take at the time. As they both walked back to the office, Winchester said, "This is my fault."

Reggie said, "Yes, it is, but we only have to do five MG11s in a day each."

Winchester said, "How did you work that out"

"That's all they will expect. Don't do anymore. If we can NFA (no further action) them, great. Upstairs will be happy. Get stuff off the books."

Over the speaker from the front desk said, "PC Winchester, you have a visitor at the front desk."

Winchester headed off to the ground floor but on the way the ACC spotted Winchester and made a beeline right for him. "PC Winchester, isn't it?"

"Yes, sir."

"I remember you when you was at training school as a special, I was in the regular squad coming through. Good to see you move on to being a full time officer. So was that some training you was doing in the room today?"

Winchester thinking quickly, said, "Yes, sir, they have been trying to involve us on local issues on the estates we patrol for intelligence. You know, sir, drug dealers and car theft."

"Oh yes, yes, yes," and he said, "got to go," and walked off up the corridor in to the lift as this information was not important enough for the ACC. Winchester point to point Reggie and asked if he could go to the front desk and see what the person wanted.

"Okay, why, what's up?"

"Just need to pop in and see the CI."

"Okay."

Winchester just went back to the meeting room where the CI and the DCI were still sitting in the meeting room. Winchester knocked on the door and they beckoned him in.

"What's up?"

Winchester informed them of the meeting in the corridor with the ACC.

"Good, so we know what to say if and when we see him. Can you inform PC Reggie?"

"Yes, ma'am."

"Off you go then."

Chapter Ten

Winchester and Reggie were on the first few days of taking statements, from "someone broken my wing mirror off my car and I did not see it happen, no CCTV", to shop lifting from local shops getting information. Hoping a call would come in from control – as luck would have it, as they came out of this shop called Candy's, kids have been nicking all the pick and mix – or to be honest they just ate what they wanted in the shop and left. To a full blown punch up in the middle of the road between two men, road rage. One had a baseball bat in his hand, the other the wheel brace from his car. Winchester shouted, "Put the weapons down now." Reggie took out his CS spray ready and folded his arms so they could not see it as they were both trying to deescalate. Both men were slight of build – the baseball bat was almost as big as the person holding it. By now a good few people had stopped in the road and on the footpaths, some beeping their horns. The two men looked at the officers.

"Piss off, coppers, this is personal; he is shagging my wife, my so called best friend."

"Yeah and you are shagging her sister."

They went to go for each other at the same time. Winchester took out his baton, hit the one with the baseball bat on his wrist, making him drop it, and grabbed him and moved him towards his own car; Reggie fired the gas spray at the other, and as Reggie sprayed the gas the male started screaming "my eyes my eyes, I can't see". Reggie just said, "Drop the weapon. Don't touch your eyes – it will pass." What Reggie also did was overshoot a bit, hitting Winchester in the face as well. Winchester was trying to subdue the male and trying to see at the same time, but he could not say to Reggie "I can't see", because the male he had over the bonnet of his car was still not cuffed. Luckily another response car pulled up and two officers, PC Phil Hartley and PC Terry Yeoman, saw the situation and started to laugh and help at the same time, as Terry took over and cuffed the male. Winchester just went "ouch ouch, thanks, mate" while Reggie looked over to see Winchester's eyes streaming and started to laugh as well.

"It's not funny, it's like opening your eyes as soap gets in them or strong onions making your eyes stream and sting like hell, thanks, mate," Winchester said as he was bent over looking at the ground.

"Do you want the nicking, lads, Terry and Phil said. "We could do with going back to the nick."

"Yep, that's cool," Reggie said. "Winchester will be a little preoccupied for a few hours; we will go to the café."

"What we doing them for?"

"Well, they did a lot of dad dancing with the weapons but did not hit anyone, so section 18 public order."

"We agree, that also means the custody Sergeant will not be upset. Nice and easy."

"Cool, see you later."

Reggie went, "Wait a minute, get the keys off them both, move the cars to the side." Also they were going to get a double hit – looking on with his pen at the ready was a traffic warden. They moved the cars and Winchester was sitting in the passenger seat. Reggie had to drive, but Reggie was not passed on any driver qualifications to drive around on blue lights.

They got to the café. The word had gone round about the face wash Reggie had given Winchester with his gas – it happens more often than you think. After an hour it had gone, but Winchester looked like he'd been crying all day. A point to point came to Reggie. "Yes, Gov?"

"You need to attend an incident at Liverpool Street station; one person down, suspected heart attack of a 35 year old man, Central line ambulance just attended, the male is being taken to the Whitechapel hospital. Go directly to the hospital, get his details."

Winchester, who could now see, said to Reggie, "What's the quickest way to the hospital?"

"Straight up Mile End Road."

Off they went on blue lights – "we cannot lose track of the person, control," Reggie asked, "is the person still alive?"

"Affirmative."

"Will you let them know we are ten minutes out?"

The control person came back with puzzled voice, "Why?"

Reggie said, "Stand by, what are we going to say?" Then a point to point came to Reggie from the CI: "Why are you asking to inform the hospital?"

"Sorry, ma'am, we don't want to lose someone again."

"I get that, but don't draw attention to yourselves."

"Yes, ma'am."

"Keep me posted, get back to control and inform them all a misunderstanding."

At the hospital, the ambulance was in the bay outside A&E; it was empty. As luck would have it, the two paramedics were just walking out.

"Hi," Reggie said.

They looked at him. "Hi mate."

To the paramedics, Reggie said without taking a breath, "The person you bought in, any update?"

"Yes, he didn't make it. The doctor pronounced in the back of the ambulance; we've taken him down to the morgue."

"Do you have any information, like a name?"

"Yes, the BTP officers got his name from the travel pass he had."

"You know what?" Ted Lucas said – he was the senior paramedic. "We thought we got him back you know, we gave him adrenaline and shocked him back, but he went back the wrong way twice. He must have a heart defect or something. But that's not for us to speculate, that's for the coroner to find out. Anything else?"

Reggie said, "Yes, his name."

"Oh, sorry," Ted said, "Nicky," – his partner – "you got the name on the sheet?"

"Are we allowed to give that out?"

"Yes of course, they're police officers. She is new to this, just qualified. His name was Andrew Garton, 33 years old."

"Who's the coroner on today?"

"Professor Peter Savile."

"I know him," Reggie said. "He fancies himself as an artist. We need to get on his good side; he is a stickler about his rules and paperwork." Reggie worked for the coroner's office as a police officer years ago, very interesting job but had no prospects and he got fed up dealing with only dead bodies. Good extra pay as an acting Sergeant. They both said thanks to the paramedics and made their way down to the office of the coroner. The area is very restricted, police officers had to ring ahead normally, they get PPE ready for them. Reggie knew the security guard, ex-police officer retired, Rodger Rodger. "Really?" Winchester said, "That's his name?"

"Yep, so whatever joke you have tucked away for comment, don't say a word he has heard them all before and them some."

"Rodger that."

Reggie looked hard at Winchester. "Really?" as Reggie pushed the intercom.

"Yes, who is it?"

"Hi Rodger, it's Reggie."

"Hello, mate, I'll buzz you in." As they pushed the doors open, down this ten-metre, very brightly lit corridor, was a security office.

Rodger was a big man, 6' 6, no hair whatsoever, born hairless, he was a monster. Reggie and Rodger shook hands. "Good to see you, mate, long time, no speak."

"It was two weeks ago down the police social club."

"I know but anyway, who's your partner?"

"PC Winchester."

Rodger put out his right hand that was like the size of a shovel; Winchester also put his somewhat small hand out, thinking it was going to be that crush handshake, but it was not, it was quick, unexpectedly normal.

"So what do you need down here?"

"Well, a person got bought in, a 30-year old male just now."

He looked at his list. "Yes, Andrew Garton, is the possible name."

Winchester said, "Possible name, yes, until he is formally identified his name is not confirmed. Can we speak to the professor?"

"Yes, he is in his office, having a break. We have been inundated this week, 26 new people this week and we are only Wednesday. It's the cold weather, seven unclaimed homeless people. Three murders keep your lot busy.

"If I buzz you in, the professor is the third door on the right."

"I remember," Reggie said. "He put some new artwork on the wall of his office, say it's naïve, it helps."

"Is it any good?" Winchester said.

"That is for you to judge," with a grin on his face. "Oh, sorry, take this." Rodger handed them some overshoes. "Put them on, it's protection."

The place has a certain odour, that once sampled never forgotten – it's the chemicals and the building. Kept at a steady temperature of between 68°F to 75°F in the autopsy room, very eerie if you've never been before, they used to take officers to see dead bodies during the training. This morgue was also allowed to keep bodies for longer for police forensic teams if they had to keep the body longer; this one had fridges that could almost freeze the bodies as most morgues can only keep bodies for a week before they start to decompose.

Reggie knocked on the professor's door. "Hello, professor."

The professor was sitting with his back to the door, looking at his artwork on the wall behind his desk. Next to him was a full-size skeleton and pictures on the walls of the human body. His desk was light grey and his high back leather chair, on his desks were stacks of files. He was wearing his white coat and his name on it care of a small silver name tag. Two steel filing cabinets with locks on it; his computer sitting to the right on his desk.

As Reggie knocked, he spun round and clapped eyes on them. He said right away in this very deep voice, "Oh lord, Sergeant Reggie, how nice to see you again."

"Thanks, professor, but I am now just a PC again, and this is my colleague PC Winchester," Reggie said, but before anything else, love the artwork." Winchester agreed it was good.

"Thank you, just done the last few over the weekend in my home in Wales." The professor lived in London in the week and went home most Fridays to Wales for his wife and dogs.

He looked like a professor, Winchester thought to himself, he was looking over his glasses at them.

"So what have we done to deserve a visit from you, Reggie?"

"Well you see, the body that just came in, an Andrew Garton, suspected heart attack, about 30, we are looking into suspicious deaths and we hoped we could speak to you about this particular person."

"Well, I have not scheduled him in yet, I have two others in-front of him. Dr Hardy is doing the autopsy on the homeless person this afternoon and Dr Skill is doing the drug OD this afternoon, so yes I could do it later say about 1500, if you were to come back say 1700 it would be almost done, I hope, unless anything else comes up. What am I looking for"

"We just want to know if he has been stuck with a needle."

"I will look out for that but I'll keep you posted. Who's the senior officer on this so I can put on the report?"

"DCI Linda Dolan,"

"I know, AKA Columbo." His phone rang and he just stopped talking to both of them and went in to work mode.

"Time to leave," Reggie said to Winchester.

As they walked up the corridor, three men in dark suits were talking to Rodger; they looked very official. They looked at Reggie and Winchester as they walked down the corridor.

"See you later, Rodger," Reggie said as they both passed them. The men were very smart looking, could have been funeral directors or inspectors.

As they came out of the rear entrance they could see their car parked and a note was on the screen: 'sorry for fucking up your car' – as they looked down every tyre was flat. Reggie could see three youths sitting on the wall laughing as they looked round the car. "I bet it was them little gits over there." The good thing was the CCTV looking after the ambulance bay also would capture their car as well. Winchester went in to speak to security and get a look at the CCTV as Reggie called it in for workshops to come and get it.

The security office said the CCTV was not working and has not been for weeks due to cuts and they would have to wait till next budget in April, but one of the paramedic sitting in the ambulance called out to Winchester as he walked passed, "Hi mate, your car tyres, I saw the three kids on the wall putting the note on your screen."

Reggie had disappeared, Winchester tried to point to point him but no luck.

Winchester could see the kids on the wall about 150 metres away and he knew if he went towards them they would be gone like rats up a drainpipe. Then all of a sudden Reggie popped up behind them on the wall and grabbed two of them as one made a run for it. Winchester just set off as fast as he could towards Reggie. The kids, or big kids, were a handful. Winchester grabbed one of the kids as

Reggie held on to the other; the third one was long gone. "Right, you two, you are nicked for criminal damage."

"It wasn't us."

Winchester said, "We got you on CCTV."

"We put the note on the screen and we got ten pounds. Man in a suit gave us the note, did not even notice, copper, your tyres were flat."

Another patrol car come with the workshops' mechanic, following him was a low loader for the car with the flat tyres, also on it was a new car – a BMW estate. They both took the details of the boys and the descriptions of the person that gave them the money for the note, then let them off.

"Who would want us to get a flat tyre, unless they were just stopping us doing something?"

It was now 1500 and they point to pointed CI Aston and explained everything including the men in dark suits.

"So come back, yes sounds like the MI5 lads are on this too. I and the DCI have a meeting later with ACC, we think the cat is out of the bag. DS Robbins is also on his way to you, he is on his radio; point to point him after you are finished with me."

"Yes, ma'am," Winchester said.

DS Robbins turned in to the car park and pulled up alongside their car, wound down his window. "Have you spoke to the CI, looks like the cat is out the bag about our investigation?" DS Robbins was spitting blood, he was not happy. "We bloody don't know how this could have happened. But I do know this, special branch is all over us "now" they want "in" to get it, they went to the Chief Constable. I am sure the meeting room is bugged, Theresa the tea lady said she was coming up to set up the tea in the meeting room and she saw two lads doing something, she was not sure, she told the DCI and she found a bug this afternoon under the table. You could see the anger come across the DCI's face that this is happening in a police station."

"It's them Spooks."

"Who?"

DS Robbins said, "Bloody special branch."

"The good thing is we know they know so can we trust them."

"I hope so," the DS said. "The reason I am here is this: the DCI said to me you both will be in this team but not in this team. This is because you are uniformed officers, they will not think you are part of the investigation. So we are going to keep you out of the meetings, but I will be the person who is your go to person from now on."

As they were talking over the other side of the car park, the three well-dressed men they had passed before down in the morgue were getting into a black Range Rover, blacked out windows.

"Gov, that Range Rover over there, the men in it are the same we saw in the morgue."

"Right, we will get them followed, you find out what they wanted."

So this time they parked the marked car right outside the main entrance – this would send a message to the spooks if they are watching, the police don't know you know it's not covert, keep them guessing.

They made their way down to see Rodger, the security guard. "Back again already, lads?" with a grin on his face.

"Just a quickie, mate, who were the men in suits?"

"They were funeral directors."

"That's all we need to know, mate."

But Rodger said quickly, "My nose tells me differently, I have worked here for years, I have never seen them here before. Could be touting for business but to me they looked security services, mate, I am sure one had a firearm, I caught a glimpse of it I am sure. They said they were in touch with the family of Andrew Garton, but I know that can't be true as they have not been tracked yet."

"Thanks, mate, see you soon. We are going to point to point the CI and ask what she wants us to do."

As Reggie and Winchester sat in the car waiting for a response, another patrol car pulled up, it was the SO19 armed response unit,

Jamie Mills not to be confused with the ACC with the same name. Jamie was by far the fitter individual and his Sergeant Clarke, who was built like a brick shit house, they had an attempted suicide in the back of their car and was bringing him to the hospital for evaluation at the psych ward.

"Hi lads, what you up to?" Clarke said.

Reggie said, "We are waiting for some information and we have to be here till 1700, a few more hours yet."

"Well, that's handy, if I clear it with your CI," Clarke said, "do you want to section this person for us; we need to get out back to an operation, a raid on a traveller site by the Bow arches. You'll get lots of tea and doughnuts while you wait, they are good to us in the ward."

"Ok, we will."

"Great, we owe you one." Clarke called up the Custody Sergeant, who contacted higher up to clear it. "We can assign him to you. We picked him up walking along the rail tracks Bow station, said he didn't remember anything. Lost his memory. No ID."

Winchester got out of the car and walked round to the side of the Range Rover Discovery, opened the door and spoke to the male; he was about 6,2 slim built, short red hair. His clothes were of good quality, shoes were also clean. Someone will know him. He was handcuffed to his front more for his own protection.

Winchester said, "Hi, mate, I am PC Winchester. Come with me, mate, we will get you some help."

He looked very confused, but he nodded. The hospital had a secure entrance for privacy more than security. Winchester and Reggie pushed the buzzer at the section door of the hospital, they got buzzed and as soon as they walked through the door, the nurse who was walking towards them said, "Hello, Tom, you back with us again." The nurse said, "We know Tom, we need to contact his wife and family, he is on medication, he'll be safe with us, we will give him some medication."

He seemed to know where he was going, walked into the cubicle and sat on the bed.

"Thanks, officers."

"We need your name for the notebook and his name and DOB."

"I am sister Death."

Winchester said, "What? Did I catch that right?"

"Yes," as her eyes rolled to the back of her head. "I know, not a good name for my job."

Reggie and Winchester looked at each other: is this a wind-up?".

"Tom should have on him his ID bracelet, it's missing. Tom has short term memory loss, he is okay for a few months then he has an episode. He was in a motorbike accident and damaged part of his brain, he is a nice man. His wife has been contacted."

Reggie and Winchester drank the tea and biscuits they were given then the wife of Tom walked into the ward. Reggie could hear her talking to Tom. "Oh Tom, sorry we lost you today. I am so sorry." She was so upset. Her name was Wendy, she came out to speak to Reggie and Winchester. "We are so sorry, he was with me shopping and he wandered off to the toilet, he then went missing. Where did you find him?"

"He was walking along the rail lines."

OMG, she looked horrified.

Reggie and Winchester went back to their car. As they were walking back they saw the same Range Rover pull up with a black private ambulance to the rear door of the morgue. Quickly Reggie said, "Call DS Robbins," but before Winchester could do anything, DS Robbins point to pointed them. "Stop, don't go to the black Transit Private ambulance, we have it and the Range Rover under surveillance."

"Ok." Reggie looked at Winchester. "Let's go, mate."

The radio buzzed again. "Yes, ma'am?"

The DCI called up: "Once the ambulance has left and the Range Rover leaves, go and speak to the Coroner."

CHAPTER TEN

After about 45 minutes both vehicles pulled out and disappeared. Reggie said, "I will go see the professor."

Winchester said, "I will get the CCTV from the security team here."

"Okay."

The professor was sitting in his office. Reggie knocked on the door.

The professor looked up above his glasses. "Back already? You are too late, your security services have taken the dead body, the one you were very interested in."

"Was it just now?"

"Yes, you probably walked past them.'

Reggie called on the radio using point to point. "Winchester, it was them taking the body."

Winchester said, "I thought it was. The DS has the details and registrations, he will follow up."

Winchester joined Reggie at the professor's office. Winchester asked the professor and questioned him if he had found anything out about the deceased.

"Well not really ,but I can tell you this, unless he had a hidden health problem, his heart and his main organs all were good, so I could not right now determine his cause of death, but I should have the toxicology report back tomorrow, but my feeling is he has ingested something or been drugged somehow. I did look for puncture wounds but could not see anything. Call me tomorrow, I will have the report then."

"Did they ask if you had sent bloods off?" Reggie asked.

"Who?"

"The security services."

"Yes they did and I said no."

"Why did you say no, professor?"

"Because I don't like being talked down to and pushed around. Call me tomorrow, I am busy."

Reggie and Winchester left back to the car.

Winchester said to Reggie, "What are we meant to do now?"

"We report back to the CI. Let's head back to the old greasy spoon." Its first name was the 999 café, but the windows got put through a few times. It was run by Sid and his partner Dolly, she was a typical café owner, if you could picture one in your mind. Little, plump, thick East End accent, hard as nails, red lipstick and red nails and bleached hair tied back. She knew everyone, took no shit from anyone, everyone was called darling.

Winchester and Reggie pulled up in the rear car park; only two other units were in the car park. They walked in through the back and the place was quiet – only six other officers were inside, a few members of the public.

"Hello, lads," Sid said, "tea?"

They both nodded and said hi to the other officers. Dolly came over. "What's you request, darlings?"

Reggie went for the steak pie, Winchester went for the homemade Chicken soup and roll. "Coming up" as the teas plonked down on the table. Two other cars palled into the car park – they were the rest of the team, thinking the same as them: teatime; DS Robbins and DC Weston, DC Byrne and DC Wineglass. All looking fed up to the back teeth. "Tea please, Dolly, all round please."

"Coming up, darlings."

They all sat down round Winchester and Reggie. "We followed the vehicles right down into central London and lost them."

"Bloody hell, did you lose them round Cavendish Square?"

"Yep, I bet they went down to the car park, most probably, but we cannot go there. The DCI is on her way here as well. She wants a meeting of the team. Just for a debrief."

As they just started to drink their tea in came the DCI. "Dolly, tea please."

"Long time no see," Dolly said, "nice to see you again."

"Likewise. Okay tell me what happened today."

Reggie and Winchester went through what had happened and the conversations with the professor; the DS went through the van and cars they followed and where they lost them.

"Okay, this is good, well done, and don't be despondent, we are on top of this. Right, Winchester and Reggie, as of next week you are going undercover at an NHS hospital in South London as porters and odd job workers."

"Why, ma'am?" They both looked very puzzled.

The DCI took a deep breath, as she was not normally questioned, but she also understood Reggie and Winchester were new to this side of operations. "We have been informed from a reliable source this is a hub for research for OPI and two of the people we identified and are under surveillance were followed back to this place and entered the research centre at the hospital with passes. You both will start next Monday morning at 0600 shift work. Four days on, four nights and four days off."

Reggie said, "Great, back to the early mornings."

"You will report back on the comings and goings of the research area. We have another undercover officer from the fraud squad working on the problems at that hospital, he will be your point of contact and line manager in the hospital. His name is Steven Byrne; yes, he is the brother of Martin. He is a DS, he has been undercover for two years." The DCI then said to Reggie and Winchester, "You need to get back out on patrol, I need to speak to the rest of the team at my office 1800, okay everyone."

As she left, Reggie and Winchester both left as well, as a call came over the radio, from a control officer called Winchester's call sign N 716: "We have a report of a person at Liverpool Street station has collapsed and was being treated by paramedics, BTP said he was a young male suffering a possible heart failure."

Reggie said, "Put us on that incident, we are on our way, blue light run it's only ten minutes, we need to be there before the ambulance leaves."

As they pulled up outside the station they could both see the ambulance with the back doors just closing. Reggie got out and waved to the paramedics and walked to the back of the ambulance. The male was sitting up and paramedics were attaching sticky pads to his chest to carry out an ECG.

"All good?" Reggie asked.

The paramedics looked a bit confused. "Yes, officer, but we need to check and get him off to the Royal London."

Reggie called up Winchester and informed him about what was going on.

"Good, you go with them to the hospital I will get the details from here and meet with you later."

"I will update the Governor."

"Which one?" Reggie said, "Better tell CI Aston, she is a real stickler for chain of command."

"I know, I will inform her first." Winchester knew CI Aston would bare her teeth at him if he did not follow protocol. So he point to pointed DS Robbins he would inform the CI and would spread the news. The DS said he would make sure everyone knew and was kept abreast. Winchester met with the BTP Sergeant on the station platform where he was interviewing a female about what had happened. Winchester looked at the female – he was sure he had seen her before, it was her nose, it was bent slightly to the left. She walked away and the Sergeant turned to Winchester.

"Are you the Met lads whom I need to speak with on this sort of thing?" He really did not want to talk to Winchester, the Sergeant – a very larger than life man from the depths of the Yorkshire Dales, very broad accent. Ex-Military police, 6'4 in his 40s, his name Arthur Layton. His hands so big, he had his radio in his hand it looked like a toy. "Right, lad, the young lady tells me she was standing next to him on the Central line train, he just collapsed in-front of everyone.

"He is a young man as well, must have health problems, we normally get this in the summer when the trains are hot and overcrowded. I have put the incident on our system and I will attach your details so you get the information, I operate from the office here at Liverpool Street. Are we all good? I need to get off as we have a few football matches coming up, need to be in the briefing," Sergeant Layton said. He turned like a military person and walked up the platform and off out of sight. As Winchester was leaving the station his mind went back six months ago, it was on the train and he remembered, its was bloody cold, three cleaners were on the train and one was a female, he could not help noticing the female had a slight bend in her nose: that is where I saw her before. His radio was not too good on the platform so he called Reggie on point to point when he got back to the car as Reggie went to the hospital in the ambulance.

"You ok, mate?"

"Yes," Reggie said, "he is having tests."

"I am out in the ambulance bay. See you soon mate, give me 20 minutes; need to talk about who I saw."

Winchester called up the DS again and informed him of what had happened. He responded by saying, "We will get the information from BTP, thanks."

As Winchester pulled up he saw Reggie talking to other officers who were also waiting for people to be seen, two officers from Barking had a prisoner waiting to be seen. Reggie saw Winchester pull in and walked over to him and explained the young lad was in cubicles. "We have about a four-hour waiting time at the moment. That will take us in to overtime, best get clearance form the DS."

DS Robbins replied, "Seems he is being kept in overnight and we can get his details."

Winchester and Reggie walked down to the reception of A&E and Winchester caught sight of the young woman who was at Liverpool Street station, walking quickly out of the main entrance of the hospital.

"Reggie," Winchester said as he tugged his arm, "see, that girl she was at the station just now, why is she here?"

Reggie said, "Quick, let's get to the Cubicles."

As they walked into the main area for Cubicles, the nurse's station had no one at it; they were in one cubicle working on someone, they had two doctors as well and they could hear them say "clear" as they used the defibrillator.

"What cubicle was he in?" Winchester said.

"I don't know but we'll have to wait till someone comes to the nurses' station."

They waited what seemed ten minutes but was only two minutes, till a nurse came out from behind the curtains. "Hello, officers, what can I do for you?"

"We are here to see how the young lad from Liverpool Street station is."

She looked hard at them. "We have just pronounced on him, he died, that was whom we were working on."

Winchester said, "Excuse me for a minute," and walked into the corridor and called up control to get the CI to call him up asap.

The CI called up very quickly – she was with the DCI in a meeting. Winchester explained what he had seen and now the male is dead.

The DCI came over the radio. "It's a crime scene now, keep it that's easy, I will get the SOC team with you as soon as possible. Inform the head nurse. Or Matron, Doctor, everyone to keep away from the cubicle. Get any CCTV of the area from security."

Winchester and Reggie spoke to the doctor who had treated the man. "Did he give you his details?"

"Yes, the nurse took them."

"Did he have any visitors?"

"Yes, his sister came in to see him, she stayed till he went suddenly downhill and we asked her to leave."

Winchester spoke to the nursing sister; she was holding a wee bottle in her gloved right hand. She said: "Walk with me, I need to tip this away."

"What was the young lad's name?"

"David Pandora, that was it I was sure of it, it's on his charts and his date of birth all logged by the ambulance crew."

"Thank you, Sister. Oh, one thing: did his sister say anything?"

"No, she was a little odd."

"In what way?"

"She never spoke to him; he spoke to her, he said something like I was never going to say anything. Then I had others to attend to as Mr Pandora was sitting up and all seemed fine; then he crashed. Why, what's going on?" The Sister suddenly clocked on about all the commotion.

"We need to shut the cubicle for our team; we think she did something."

"Really? What? He had a heart attack."

"Let's hope so, Sister," Winchester said, "let's hope so."

Winchester stood guard outside the cubicle and Reggie was getting statements and the SOCO team arrived; the Coroner was on his way up to the cubicle. The DCI had called the professor and asked him to inspect the body quickly before SOCO started.

"Hello again," the professor said as he walked up to the cubicle and saw Reggie and Winchester, "we keep meeting." He spoke to the doctor before he went in and asked what he had done and what medication was used; the doctor was a little confused as he's thinking this is just a heart attack, not a possible murder. He read off his notes and charts.

"Thank you," the professor said to the doctor and walked into the cubicle and called the Sister for assistance to turn the person over. "Okay," he said, "I need to take some bloods right now please, Sister. And we will get him transported down to the morgue."

Winchester and Reggie could hear this going on and when the professor came out, he said, "I found what I think is a little puncture wound to the back of his neck, but I can't be sure of anything yet till I get him on the table. But we have a problem."

"What's that?"

"I know this man, not sure of his last name but his first name is George."

"That is not what he has given to everyone as his name."

The professor looked puzzled. "He lives in the next avenue to my house, his father is a pharmacist, his mother is a researcher for QPI; we all signed up for the neighbourhood watch, I've been to a few meetings. His poor family, he's an only child. I will give you their address. See you in my office." As he turned away his hand gestured above his head. "I will leave it on my desk as I will be dealing with this poor chap right away."

The SOCO lads, Micky and Jerry, said before they went, "It will be a nightmare to get information off the scene, different bloods and fingerprints, but we will do our best."

Jerry said, "Can you find out who has been in the cubicle?"

Winchester looked at him and rolled his eyes as if to say, wish me luck. He was right: the shift had changed, the cleaners had not been in but about ten people from the hospital team and countless relatives. They were right: four people had been in the cubicle in the last six hours and not been cleaned, but as it was a possible murder scene it had to be work with microscopic precision.

Chapter Eleven

I t was Spring, Monday morning 0900, a meeting of the team was called. The DCI had sent out the request Sunday night; the report was back from the professor on the young man, his real name George Calliope.

Winchester and Reggie sat in the meeting room waiting for all the others to come in. They knew the meeting was due as Theresa the trolley lady was unloading everything on to the meeting table. Winchester went right for the chocolate biscuits, Reggie just looked at him with that all-knowing look. They sat waiting, had a cup of tea; it was half an hour still no one came. Reggie said, "Wait here, I will go find out what's going on."

Winchester, who had contacted Reggie to tell him the meeting was 0900, suddenly remembered the meeting was in the DCI's offices and as he walked out of the meeting room the senior officers were coming down the corridor to the meeting room. Winchester still had two chocolate biscuits in his hand, he walked past with them stuffed in his mouth, hoping no one said good morning. Reggie saw him walking down the corridor. "You bloody idiot, it's in the DCI's office."

They both walked in, and the DCI said, "Nice of you to turn up."

"Sorry, ma'am, we went to the meeting room," Reggie said, "and he had some of the chocolate biscuits."

"Grab yourselves a coffee; we are waiting for the DS, he is picking up some paperwork we need. The deceased's real name is George Calliope, an old Greek family, a lot of influential friends, we are being hounded from above to sort this situation out; they don't know about the investigation so keep it that way."

The DS came into the office and shut the door.

"Did you get what I needed?"

"Yes, ma'am."

The white board in her outer office was covered in people of interest, the investigation board, she put up three pictures of persons of interest. Two men and one woman. "The woman is wanted by Interpol; she has been credited with 16 murders throughout Europe and Far Eastern countries, they are the ones Interpol know of. She is very dangerous. The other two males we know nothing about them apart from they are here in this country, working for the QPI organisation. We have picked her up on the CCTV at the station leaving the same time as George was attacked, and again leaving the hospital after he was found dead. DS Robbins has been and shown the staff who were on that day the picture of the woman – one of the nurses said she said she was the man's sister and was allowed in the cubicle. Winchester, also we have now confirmed she was on the train the day you were attacked, don't think she did it to you as we are sure it was one of the males. We are getting close to making a move on this bunch of Machiavellian assholes."

Everyone laughed, the DCI never loses it. The phone rang in her office, she picked it up; you could see it was the Chief constable, just by the way she was talking to him, he was a sort of old school CC, Peter Savile was his name, been in the job for 25 years from the beat to the top job. Well respected by all, slim man, grey hair, was into his art, his nickname was pointy finger, have no idea why that was.

"The top floor team are all over this, the family are demanding answers, they have connections. The report from the professor was that the stuff they used was a mixture of Flunitrazepam, you know as Rohypnol and Fentanyl. It's very quick and it's a faulty mix that's being used. All arrests will be with SO19, I know some of you can carry arms, but I like them with us on this."

Winchester and the rest of the team passed round the photos of people of interest they were keeping observation on.

"The operation has now taken a step up. We have installed covert CCTV at Epping station. Winchester, you are going back on your own as a cleaner."

Winchester looked a bit surprised.

"Reggie, you will be his back-up, you are going to be in the ticket office, this is so you can be close; we feel if the two of you are on scene again it will look suspicious. DS Robbins, your team will consist of DC Weston, DC Catherine Wineglass. You will follow the female suspect, her code name, S1. The other two males we will pick up them up later. We do not at this time have the trusted resources. We have a new member of the team, ACC Jamie Mills. He found out what we are doing because I need extra funding, I have personally had him checked out; he is okay. He will as always keep away from the meetings. Point of contact is myself and CI Aston. DC Byrne, you're with the Interpol lads Lloyd and Boyd." (Everyone always smiled when the DCI said Boyd and Lloyd; it just rhymes.) "I need you to fly to Greece and meet with the head of microbiology for Interpol, he has some information for us, but do not for one minute think you can inform him of who we suspect, is that clear?"

"Yes, ma'am," Martin said. The other two also nodded in agreement.

"This cannot get out. We know from where they operate from, so we will concentrate on the Company HQ, Mornington Crescent, the building with the two big black cats outside. That is QPI's main office. Luckily for us, only two entrances in and out, so we can cover it easily. Sorry, everyone, this will be long shifts. Operation name is now known as 'underground'. This week is going to be critical to gather information so I can get the money for the full operation.

That is when I can go to the commission and ask for the full funding. It seems silly we have to ask for the money and that will open up the operation to more people, more chance of leaking out."

CI Aston said, "We need to get this really buttoned up first, if we do what she said then when we get the extra funding, if any leaks happen then we will see it happen in-front of us."

"Right," the DCI said, "get about your duties today. We need to start this operation from 0600 Wednesday morning, complete your paperwork, clear everything with your Sergeants and line officers."

Winchester and Reggie had to clear the operation information with Custody Sergeant Smalley, he was always good old school, should have been a firefighter, always wanted to be but could not get in, due to a two-year waiting list in London. He was the person you went to if anyone had a problem, he knew everyone, he also knew where the bodies were buried so to speak; even the CC Peter Savile knew Smalley. As long as you made him a good cup of tea, he was happy. Loved a biscuit; his car was also the cleanest in the car park.

Winchester spoke to Sergeant Smalley – even that fact he had been told by CI Aston, you must confirm it yourself it's the done thing, or you will piss off the person who has your back.

Winchester got home ready to start work on Wednesday as a cleaner again. A knock at the door. He knew it could not be Jennie – she was in USA till Friday. He looked through the peep hole in his front door, it looked like a delivery, he thought to himself, but I was not due any deliveries, though sometimes the old woman who lived opposite gets deliveries and he sometimes takes the items in; she is deaf as a post.

As he opened the door all he remembered was a woman with black hair, very vivid green eyes, she stuck something in Winchester's chest like an EpiPen. Winchester hit his head on the door handle as he crashed to the floor. Winchester, feeling pain from his head as the warm feeling of blood on his face, was incapable of moving, everything was a blur as he was dragged back into his apartment, very heavily sedated and bleeding down his face from the cut to his eye. Then just everything went blank.

Reggie turned up at the Epping station to start in the ticket office and met with Tom Allen, station manager, but no Winchester. This was very strange as Winchester is always on time, but he could be on the train. After a few hours Reggie was getting concerned. He point to point over the radio to speak to DS Robbins, on a welfare check for Winchester, as Winchester's radio would be on a silent mode. But he often checked in. DS Robbins came right back: "we are sending a unit now to his house, no answer on any form of communications".

The closest unit was armed resources team, was Clarkie and Jamie; they both arrived outside Winchester's block of flats, pushed the intercom but no answer. They pushed others and announced they were police need access, they were buzzed in by one flat, flat 9, 1st floor. Jamie banged on the front door – no letterbox to look through.

"Winchester, you okay, mate? Open the door."

On the floor Clarke noticed a blood spatter. "Step back," as Clarke just put his shoulder to the door and pushed it through; the door lock splintered as the door smashed open. Jamie and Clarke said to Reggie, "hang back," as the drew their side arms. Clarke, in his very deep loud voice, bellowed out, "Armed police, don't move."

Winchester was naked, sitting on the dining room chair, hands tied to the chair with zip ties, dried blood down the right side of his face; he was unconscious but breathing. Jamie called back to Reggie, "Come in," as he shot past Reggie heading to the car to get the medical kit and call in an ambulance. They untied Winchester. He was very groggy but not making any sense.

"We need to get him to hospital now," Clarkie said, "help me."

Reggie said, "Let me get a pair of tracksuit bottoms." As Reggie walked in to the bedroom he could see everything was turned upside down, someone had been looking for something.

Jamie came back in with the medical bag and said, "ETA ambulance is ten minutes."

Clarke said, "No, we are not waiting, let's scoop and let's run."

They lifted Winchester and said to Reggie, "Stay here till the rest of the team arrive very soon, we are off to Harlow hospital – from here it's quicker."

They put Winchester in the back seats of the BMW X5 and just went blues and twos screaming as they shot off into the distance. Reggie could hear on the radio Jamie calling ahead to inform the hospital and they were coming in hot, other units said they would block off areas when they knew how close they would be as the Essex police had picked up on this call. Reggie got a point to point from CI Aston: "What's going on?"

"Not sure, ma'am."

"I have sent two other officers to do scene preservation, SOCO are on their way too."

CI Aston said to Reggie, "The armed response team will remain with Winchester, with instructions no one can speak with him or visit him till we understand what's happening."

No sooner had Reggie ended the point to point than the DCI, Linda Dolan, was calling him. Reggie explained all of it to her, as the other officers were at the front door, they knew what they were doing. Reggie put the blue overshoes they gave him, they opened the incident log for logging people in and out of the flat. Reggie said, "Good, lads, I am off."

"Hold on, Reggie, we need some information first, some times and people whom you were able to gain access."

Reggie was desperate to leave, but he knew he had to give the information first. Once he was finished giving his statements – that took about 20 minutes – Reggie jumped into the patrol car, headed off to the hospital.

As Reggie pulled into the main area of the hospital, he saw two armed Essex officers parked up outside the ambulance bay and the unit that Clarke and Jamie were in was in front of the ambulance entrance canopy; the car was empty.

Reggie nodded to the Essex officers and walked into A&E reception to find out where Winchester was. As he was waiting, Jamie Mills came through the doors. Reggie just called him, "What's happening, mate?"

"He's in resuscitation. He stopped breathing on the way here but we got him back. They are working on him. They don't know what is in him."

CI Aston came through the main entrance; she was looking very hard and focused. Two other plain clothes officers also walked through the door, Phil Hartley and John Long. Both murder detectives. They wanted to interview everyone now: Reggie, Clarke and Jamie. The CI said, "They will interview you right now; we need to move quickly – the Chief Constable is all over this."

The doctor, Neil Vint, came out of the resuscitation area and said, "We are not sure what he has taken, –was this a drug overdose?"

"Possibly," the CI said, "but he has been injected against his will that is all we know."

"Winchester's heart rate is only 19 beats a minute; we need to get it up, we have taken bloods and are trying to find out what is in his blood; we will get information back in 30 minutes or so. He has also sustained impact injuries around his testicular area and on his back."

"What has happened?" The CI looked at the doctor.

"We wish we knew."

As the CI was standing grilling the doctor, the CI's radio made the sound of point to point. She said, "excuse me a moment" and walked off a few steps to take the call.

"SOCO team, they have found a syringe, we are getting the lab to test it asap."

Reggie said, "If they have injected him with something, it must be so they could get information, so what would they use?"

They overheard the conversation and the doctor said, "Well, they possibly may have used three that spring to mind, Truth drugs Pentothal, Sodium Thiopental, Scopolamine, they are the ones I would bank on. I was in the military intelligence service for ten years as a doctor." He turned and quickly walked back to the resuscitation room and put a call into the labs to test for any of the drugs he'd mentioned.

"This could explain his very low heart rate, they will have to put him on a ventilator if we cannot get his oxygen levels back up to at least 96%," he said to the other doctor. "I think we need to intubate now if his heart oxygen levels are not addressed now, we could have organ failure and long term damage."

As they were trying to intubate, Winchester's heart went into atrial fibrillation. Dr Neil Vint very calmly said, "bring the defibrillator", then called "clear" to shock Winchester's heart back into normal sinus rhythm, it worked but it was still very slow. But it was now about 25 beats per minute, the other doctor, Steven Chan, who was carrying out a primary survey, said, "Look at the chest, it's moving uneven on the left side." The mobile X-ray machine was now in the room. "Let's get an X-ray of the chest area and get me a portable ultra scan right now."

The phone rang in resuscitation, and the Sister answered it. "It was the lab, they found what you were looking for – it's traces of Sodium Thiopental."

Dr Vint said, "I knew it. Ok, this is good; we need to keep him on IV fluids, but we must remove the blood in his chest, that's what's causing the heart problem. Get me the drain kit, I need to drain the blood from the left side of his chest; we have a haemothorax. Soon as we've done this get him to the ICU. The next 24 hours is going to be hard on him."

In the waiting area were 12 or more police officers, Essex and the Met, four armed officers from Essex, DCI Dolan, CI Aston, Reggie and the rest of the team. Dr Vint came out to speak to them. "Does he have a next of kin?"

"Yes, but they live in the USA and we have tried to contact them."

"How is he, Doc?" the CI asked.

"Well, he will live; the next 24 hours will be hard on him but he is going to be kept under sedation for 24 hours. I am not sure what he will remember because the drug used, Sodium Thiopental, will wipe his short term memory. But he has taken a beating, three broken ribs, five stitches to his eye and other marks that indicate he has been bounced around."

"Doctor, we will have a 24-hour armed officers outside his ward, can you put him in a room not a ward?"

"Yes, we can do that, I will sort out for you."

"Thanks," the DCI said. "Right, everyone, back to the station; we need to get the facts quickly and get the update from Winchester's flat from SOCO. See you all back at my office in an hour."

Reggie asked could he stay with his friend.

The DCI thought for a moment. "Yes, when the doctors let you sit with him. Everyone else, let's get back to the station; we have a lot of work to do so we can get the bastards who've done this."

Back at the station the DCI was speaking on the phone to SOCO lead officer Mike Newlands. He was a bit of an off the wall character. She said "thank you" but when she put the phone down, she had a very puzzled look on her face.

"You okay, ma'am?" DS Robbins asked as the team gathered in her offices; it was a bit crowded.

DC Weston was just walking in last when directly behind him was the ACC Jamie Mills who suddenly appeared at the door.

"Hello, sir," the DCI said.

Everyone looked round at the entrance door. The ACC was in full uniform, heading off to some meeting probably. He said to Linda, "I need an update to take to the Central command meeting, we need to ask for the extra monies for your operation."

Linda replied, "I will have it ready in the next hour for you."

"Well, I will be at the Yard; if I have not got your information in the next two hours I will not be able to request anything; the cuts are hurting every department at the moment, money is at a premium. Them boys at the diplomatic team are always on the want for money and we have a visit from President Bill Clinton soon, that costs a lot of our budget." The ACC turned and just walked out the doorway and left the room.

The DCI said, "Close the door, someone."

"Ma'am?" DS Robbins asked. "What's the operational name we are working under?"

"Underground – is that all clear? It's out in the open now as one of our colleagues has been attacked for the second time; the gloves are off. If they think they can attack us without punitive action they will be really underestimating what we in the police are capable of." The DCI was very angry – you could see it in her face.

"First of all, what is the update on Winchester?"

"No change, ma'am," DC Weston said.

"Is the armed team still at the hospital?"

"Yes, ma'am, they are there till we say otherwise."

"Good, right this is what we know. One: the company that is carrying out all the tests on the tube is QPI; two: the head of this company is Nik Dazary; three: they operate out of the main office here in London, the big building Mornington Crescent, the one with the two big black cats outside the entrance; four: we have identified the suspects that carried out the day-to-day testing on the trains, they work out of the building or factory in Kent. Have we got enough evidence to take all this to court?"

"I don't think so," the CI said, "we need more facts."

Just then the phone in the room rang; it was the front desk. DC Wineglass took the message. "Ma'am, you have a visitor at the front desk, Ben Hooper."

She stood for a moment looking at the white board before turning round and walking out the door, saying as she left, "I will be back in 10 minutes".

Everyone started talking to each other. The CI stood up and said, "Close the door for a moment. Right, I need updates on the following. DS Robbins, do we know the locations of the individuals we have been following?"

"Yes, ma'am."

"Were they anywhere nearby when PC Winchester was attacked?"

"No, ma'am, they were still at the location in Kent. Lloyd and Boyd are still watching them but I do know we did not know the whereabouts of the female in the picture."

"Yes, she is of some interest. Interpol has given us a name, Katrina Austin, she is an ex-KGB operative now works freelance. She is very elusive and is wanted in ten countries. We are sure she was the one on the train and she has been seen on the trains around the times of the deaths, two according to the CCTV, but they are not conclusive because of the quality of the CCTV and she seems to be wearing a hoodie. But we have a clear shot of her on the cleaning at Epping. She would know what Winchester would look like as well if they have found out about the operation."

The DCI came back in the room. She had been speaking to the private eye, Hooper. "I have some information, but first of all I need to assign DC Wineglass and DC Martin Byrne to go and pick up QB, Hellen Blake. She has information and we need to get her into protective custody as soon as possible. I have her address now, Hopper gave it to me, he feels that the company is on to her, he has seen activity around her place and it's not from any of the services. Take the black cab and the cleaners' van from the surveillance pool of vehicles. You will need to speak with the head SO19 team leader; let him know you have spoken to me. I have already requested that they are kept abreast of your location just in case you have any problems. We are not sure what will happen anymore, this took a bad turn when they decided to attack the MET."

They both nodded.

"QB has information for us we will need. Hooper tells me she wants to come in to spill the beans, but she is aware she is under some sort of surveillance. But we really need to move everyone because if this goes sideways it will be taken out of our hands by the secret squirrels."

"What do you mean by that?" DC Weston asked.

"Do you think this has been going on without someone knowing what is going on? It's bloody unlikely, the anti-terrorist organisation would have seen this years ago, they miss nothing. The only ones I would put money on not knowing is us and BPT.

"Hooper also told me a few months ago a newspaper investigator was on to something and that was one of the bodies that went missing after suffering a heart failure a few months ago. His name was Jerry Byrne."

They all turned to look at Martin. "Nothing to do with me."

"Anyway, he turned up in a secure unit in Essex with memory loss; can't remember his name or very much. It was put down to substance abuse. So, Reggie, will you go and interview him? He is in the unit in Barley Lane, Ilford.

"We will all meet back here tomorrow morning at 0700. We have to make our move very soon I am sure of it."

A knock on the door and it was Jan, the other tea lady; she walked in and no one said a word, just thanks for the tea and a warm smile. Plenty of biscuits. No one was moving yet till they had their tea.

Everyone was taking notes off the incident white board of the people they needed to look up and gather information on and locations, the operational name underground was the on the head of the board now. Janet came up to the DCI and handed her her green cup and saucer – standard issue for hospitals and police stations, oh and white mugs. DCI said to Janet, "Thank you, we will be finished soon, come back in say half an hour if you like to clear."

She nodded and walked out of the room, leaving the trolley by the door.

DS Robbins said to the DCI, "Ma'am, the information for the ACC, can we send it now, ma'am or he will be pulling his hair out."

"Yes, I'd almost forgotten." The DCI called the Yard to find out what floor the ACC was on and sent the information to him. Within ten minutes the DCI had a call, she put the phone down and said to the CI, "We are being called up to the Yard, we have to see some people right now."

CI Aston said, "Do you think it's leaked out?"

Linda replied, "It would a bloody miracle if it had not.

"Everyone, listen up; we have to go the Yard and kiss some ass to get the funding, we think, so get on with your assignments and see you tomorrow, keep us posted."

Winchester was showing signs of improvement. Jennie got home to find out what had gone on and made her way to the hospital. When she got to the private room where Winchester was, it had no armed officer or in fact anyone guarding him – that was not what she had been told. She put a call in to speak to the CI and she was told they were out of the station and so was Reggie. She spoke to the nurse who was just coming out of the room: "How is he?"

"Are you a member of the family?"

"Yes, I am his girlfriend."

"Well he is doing much better; we should take him off the ventilator later today as his O2 levels are normal now. But we have him very heavily sedated because of the drugs that are still clearing from his body."

As the nurse went to leave Jennie said, "What happened to the armed guards?"

"They said their shift had ended and another team was on their way."

"How long ago did they leave?"

"About two hours ago."

Jennie checked under her coat, pulled out her Glock 17 from the shoulder holster, checked it was ready and loaded, then placed it back. She walked into the room and she was taken aback when she saw all the drips and ventilator hoses coming out of his mouth. Jennie pulled the chair close and sat next to Winchester and said, "Oh, what a mess you are, if I get my hands on who did this to you they will be sorry." She kissed him on the forehead. She started to look over him and she read his chart: all much better; the drain from his chest was empty so that's good. She pulled back the covers to see the bruises he had, and she could see that he had multiple ones all over his lower body, but she noticed his testicular area was very swollen, about the size of a tennis ball. She knew what that was, they had shocked him. If they had used the drugs they said on the information charts, then he would not remember what had happened to him. Winchester always said he loved Jennie's perfume, but as she sat holding his hand, Winchester squeezed her hand. Jennie immediately pushed the nurse call button. The nurse came in and Jennie said, "He is squeezing my hand."

The nurse called the trauma doctor, who said to Jennie, "Can you leave the room a minute?"

Jennie said, "No, but I will stand here, I am with MI5 for now, I am his security detail."

The doctor looked at her and said, "Well keep out of the way then please." He pulled the curtains and Jennie could hear the choking sounds of the tube coming out of Winchester's mouth.

"Mr Winchester," the nurse said, "we have removed the tube from your throat but we will also reduce your sedation, but you have a lot of injuries so we will keep some of the sedation for the meantime. I will get some ice poles," the nurse said. As the nurse came from behind the curtains, she looked at Jennie and said, "it's good news" with a smile. "Oh yes, I am going to get some ice poles for him, we do not want him to drink, but the ice poles keeps his mouth moist and lips wet. Can you help with that while you are here? Also I will bring you a cup of tea when the doctor has finished."

Jennie had been there for two hours and yet no one came to stand outside. Winchester was beginning to come round very slowly, his eyes would be open for a few seconds, see Jennie and he would smile and drift off again. Jennie used the phone in the room to call the DCI, who was still in the meeting at the Yard. As she put the phone down, Clarkie and Jamie walked into the room in plain clothes. "Hello," they said to Jennie, "who are you?"

Jennie said, "I am his girlfriend, and whom may you both be?"

"We are colleagues of Winchester's. Do you know what happened to the officers on the door?" Clarke asked.

"No, I was told it was a change of shift and I have been here now three hours and they left two hours before I got here."

Jamie said, "That's not right, I am going to make a call." Clarke left the room to make the call but came back in the room after five minutes. He said, "It was a cock up, the Essex lads have a retracted incident at Stansted airport, they got called away and did inform our control but it was not acted on. So we have a unit on its way now, should be here in an hour. How is he?"

"Better, but they've done a number on him."

"Yes, we know. You in the job?" Clarke asked Jennie.

"Yes, once. Winchester has spoken about you both," Jennie said.

"We can hang around if you like," Jamie said. "At least till the ARV gets here."

"I am fine, you go home, it's all good."

As they both left the room Jamie said, "Mate, should we leave her with him with no protection?"

Clarke said, "You kidding? She is MI5 and she is carrying, more than likely, a Glock 17."

"Really?"

"Yes, you could see it underneath her jacket."

"How do we know she is MI5?"

"Remember Reggie saying Winchester's girlfriend was in the service?"

"Yes."

"Well, that's her."

"It could be anyone."

"If she was a bad person she would have done him in before now. Also, two empty cups and a plate of half-eaten sandwiches may be a bit of a stretch of the imagination even for you," and Clarke patted Jamie on the back as they got into the lift. "Let's get home before our wives kill us."

Jennie was sitting talking to Winchester about her work in the USA as the nurse came in.

"Hi," the nurse said, "I am just off." Her name tag said nurse Megan.

"Nurse," Jennie asked, "who's taking over from you and the doctor?"

"Nurse Isabel."

"What she look like?"

"Oh, she is tall with ginger hair and she's from Belfast."

"Thanks. Oh, what about the doctor?"

"Oh that's Doctor Linn, need I say more, he's from Hong Kong." The nurse looked a little puzzled but did her check on Winchester. She turned and said, "They should be taking out the chest drain tonight I was told."

Then two armed officers turned up and walked in the room. "Hello, are you Jennie?"

"Yes."

"We are Officers Graham Allen and Trevor Wilson; we will be inside the room."

"I am just going to go back to the flat to get changed and food and will be back," Jennie said.

"We'll keep an eye on him."

She kissed Winchester on the lips and said, "see you soon," and walked out.

The two officers put the TV on in the room and one sat next to the door and one sat so he could see the door. A nurse came in offering them both tea, which they declined and asked who she was. She did not say her name but said "just sent to ask if you want tea" and left the room. Both officers looked at each other. Trevor, who was sat next to the door, got up and opened the door to see if he could see the nurse. Graham, his colleague, said, "that was strange", then a nurse came in the room.

Both officers said, "What's your name?"

"Sally, I am the staff nurse for the ward, just checking that everything is ok before I clock off."

"Just one thing: we just had a nurse come in and ask if we wanted a cup of tea, never give a name."

"What she look like?"

Trevor said, "She was about 5,9, black hair."

"Don't know her, but I will ask around; unless it's from another ward, but they should not be here."

Graham got on the radio and reported in the incident. They had a list of names of the only people allowed in the room and stick to it was their orders.

Chapter Twelve

Jennie now knew that Winchester was in big trouble. She knew the person that had drugged him and abused him was not finished. Winchester may be able to recognise them. She contacted her head of the covert team in her office and asked for permission to meet with the police over this matter; she put it to her boss that they have an opportunity to catch this assassin that has eluded everyone for years; her nickname was Viper, the Interpol estimate she is responsible for more than 16 high profile assassinations that they know of. This will be an ongoing effort to catch her. This was given the green light. Jennie contacted DCI Linda Dolan and arranged a meeting at the station. The DCI was a bit confused.

Jennie arrived at the station and was taken upstairs to the meeting room where CI Aston and DCI Dolan were waiting.

The DCI went right in with questions as soon as the door was closed. She said, "Tell me what the hell's going on, who are you to this situation?"

"First of all," Jennie said, "I am from MI5 international office and homeland security." That got the attention of the DCI and the CI. "Winchester and I are in a relationship, it's been about six months. He has spoken to me about things that are going on, but I have been away for a few months. But what I can say is this: the person that drugged him we think she is the assassin known as Viper, who is wanted in 15 different countries for high profile assassinations. I don't think that when your team found him she was finished and you must have disturbed her."

"Why do you say that?"

"No one has seen her and lived, and it's a probability Winchester has seen her and she will want that to be not the case."

"His memory of what happened is gone as far as we know."

"Yes, but it may not stay buried for ever. We need to use Winchester as bait."

The CI said, "No way, he's been through enough now."

Jennie said, "We have a plan to catch her, but we need your help and it will be good for your investigations too."

The DCI asked, "What's the plan?"

"We are going to move Winchester to a bigger room, we will erect a full height partition across the room with a two-way mirror and quick access door. Winchester will still have all the drips and fluids monitors, but none of them will be in his body – if she injects anything into the drip it will not go into his body's blood system."

The DCI asked, "What if she shoots him, stabs him or even directly injects him?"

Jennie said, "That would be highly unlikely as she will not want it to be investigated, but it's a risk. We are also putting on the inside of the door handle a radioactive tracking material; we can track this person for 24 hours, but we need to report that Winchester is dead, as it will make her go in to the wind."

"What's the wind?" CI Aston asked.

"Vanish."

The DCI said, "We will go along with this, but I want my team around and I and the CI need to be kept informed, but I will have to get clearance from the ACC."

Jennie said, "No, not the ACC."

"Why?"

"Your ACC is friendly with the head of M16; they are both at the same lodge."

"But the ACC knows about the current investigation."

"Yes, I am not saying he is a leak, but MI6 will muscle in and then we have a real mess. I am involved," Jennie said, "because I care very much for Winchester."

"Ok, but I need to get clearance from someone without screwing everyone's future."

"Well, we could ask for it to be a joint venture with MI5 as an operation."

"ACC will ask me what the joint operation is."

"It's to track down a person of interest in your case. Look," Jennie said, "if this goes well he will get a pat on the back from the top brass; if it goes tits up so to speak he will drop you like a hot potato and say he was kept in the dark: win-win for him." Jennie added, "We will have three armed officers behind the screen, also you could have two more of your team as well. It may take a few days before she tries to finish him off."

"Why are you so sure she will try again?" CI Aston asked.

"We are not 100%, but your officers reported a nurse fitting the description of the Viper, asking if they wanted a cup of tea and once they spoke to another nurse, no one knew of her."

"How did you know that?" the DCI asked.

"We just do."

The DCI looked hard at Jennie. They have suspected for some time now that the security services can listen in on the radios. Jennie left and got the MI5 surveillance team to deal with the hospital and sort the room out as required. The DCI went to see the ACC and ask him for permission to do the joint operation, he was so wrapped up on doing his application form for the Chief Constable vacancy in Scotland, he just nodded and said keep me posted. "Oh," as he looked up from his computer, "it better make me look good," as he grinned and looked back at the screen.

CI Aston had point to point with everyone on the team for an operational briefing at 0700 in the morning. DS Robbins was walking down the corridor as the DCI was walking back to her office from seeing the ACC. "Any news, ma'am, on Winchester?"

"Yes, come into my office, they I have called a meeting in the morning."

"Yes," DS Robbins said, "with all of team; there has there been a development, we need to act now."

The DCI said, "Can you speak to your friends in SO19 and get me Clarke and Mills as protection officers for a few days."

"I can do that, they would be happy with that; they were due to do a week at City Airport. In uniform or plain clothes?"

"In uniform."

That night Jennie was by the side of Winchester all night; her mind was firing on all cylinders she knew the next few days were critical. In her mind she knew that Viper would come for him. Winchester's mind was sharp and one thing he was very good at was remembering details. Winchester was still coming in and out of his coma. The doctor has said he could take weeks to fully come round, they have reduced his medication slowly so that his body will start to cope with the serious trauma his body has been through, plus the head injury sustained when he fell causing concussion and a small bleed on the brain but not life threatening or any long-term effects.

Jennie went to the en-suite toilet in the room just to check her Glock 17 was loaded and ready; she was taking no chances at all. The room was now ready for the changeover. Winchester was moved to a private room that had the new partition erected, the system for feeding Winchester's medication was changed. The real drip was hidden behind the back of the bed and put through a main vein in his leg, the fake drips were tapped to his hand and arm – if then assassin injects they will go for the ones they can see that are not penetrating the skin. Also the heart monitor was on remote control and was not really attached to Winchester, so if they stayed for a few seconds they would see his heart stop or start to stop – this will set the auto alarm off and they would move quickly to get out. Extra thick layers of blankets so you could not see his ballistic vest on him, also they cannot see his chest moving up and down, but they would not stay around too long for confirmation. The observation team were all round the main corridors and would keep everyone posted. All nurses were now MI5 agents, so known to everyone. The trap was set. It's just waiting now.

Jennie said, "This is a dangerous way to bring out the assassin," to the head of the MI5 team, Paul Mitchel.

"We have no choice really, we have a perfect opportunity to get this assassin."

Clarke and Jamie said, "As soon as anyone not known walks in the room they will train their weapons on them and if they pull a weapon they will shoot."

Jennie said, "thanks", as she walked out the door to the ward to sit next to Winchester. She looked at him with his face looking like he'd been ten rounds with Mike Tyson. She did care for him but she also knew that unless they carried out this operation Winchester would be looking over his shoulder for the rest of his life; they must see off the Assassin. The best time was thought the attempt would be is around visiting times or change of shift – this would make it easier to others moving around and not be noticed, with agency staff also turning up to report too.

The Assassin must know this could be a trap, Jennie thought. She thought what would she do, she would cause a diversion first, a fire alarm, incident some place, sit back and observe what happens. One armed officer was placed downstairs in plain sight in uniform, the second one was standing by the nurses' station so he could see the corridor. Just what you would expect, so would the Assassin.

But the lead MI5 agent, Mitchel, had also thought of this too and could see Jennie was too personally involved. But he knew that would work for him as she would be on the lookout for the smallest detail as Jennie has skin in the game.

It was around 2030, the night shift changeover was underway for the 2100 night shift to take over, nurses and doctors gatherings around wards and staff stations, doing the handovers. A loud bang went off in the car park outside the main entrance that was four storeys below Winchester's room window, it was called in as a possible car bomb. The two armed offices were sent to the car park over the radio; the team knew this was possibly the move on Winchester. The CCTV monitoring showed that the corridor was empty, leading to Winchester's room. The two people came out of the stairwell very quickly. This was it. Jamie and Clarkie lifted their semi-automatic weapons. Jennie moved quickly behind the partition; everyone was locked and loaded, the clicks on the radios also noted that the teams had closed in and they would not get out of that room. The two people moved into the room and drew out weapons with silencers; as they did, Jamie and Clarke shouted "armed officer, drop your weapons", and one turned towards them both handgun raised –he was shot twice in the chest and the other took aim at Winchester and was shot six times in the chest and head shots; she was dead before she hit the ground.

The medical team moved in to try and save both the people that had been shot. Winchester had been shot twice in the chest – the second assassin had got two shots off, both hit the vest. As the medical staff rushed in it was hard to stand as the floor was covered in blood. Both assassins were pronounced dead; Winchester was moved to another location in central London. Winchester was still in a coma but some reactions were noticed; however, it could have been the impact of being shot in the vest twice.

Jennie looked at Mitchel and said, "That was most definitely not expected."

"No, it was not; they were not messing about. What did they think this is, the 70s in the USA? Bastards, they deserved to die this way."

A doctor overheard him say that, and said, "We should try and not take life."

But Jennie said, "Doctor, both of them people on the floor have killed more people than you have possibly saved."

The doctor walked out, shaking his head. SOCO was on the scene. Jamie and Clarke had to stand down to be investigated for a shooting. They would be on light duties till this was over. The senior officer DCI Steven Byrne from the Yard and his team would investigate the shooting, interview the officers before they went back to the armoury and their weapons taken and kept as evidence, along with shell casings.

Jennie came into the corridor outside. They could not speak to anyone. Jennie saw Jamie and Sergeant Clarke, she mouthed to them "Thank you" and they nodded back. Winchester was gone already to the safe location, till he was able to get up and about if he ever will.

A shout came up from a woman in the next room to where Winchester was – her flowers were on the floor, a bullet had gone through the wall and hit the vase of flowers. Now they knew the bullets from the officers' weapons did not as they hit the target, it must be one of the assassins.

Jennie said, "They must be vest piercing rounds." She ran out of the room to inform the protection team to check Winchester – he may have been shot and gone through the vest. They called them up on the radio. As luck would have it, as they were wheeling him down in the basement corridor, one of the team spotted blood on the trolley, so the doctors just rushed him into theatre. It was a small nick to his thigh, but he is going to wake up with a real sore chest – those bullets really tested the new vest.

The protection team leader, Carl Ferraro, said, "Well, we will be taking him to the security services secure underground facilities, Cavendish Square, level – 6."

This is the main location for the surveillance operations London division. Jennie would be able to see Winchester there, as she has access to the complex.

Carl said, "This officer is well thought of," then Reggie came walking up the corridor looking very confused. His face was a bit red and angry looking. Reggie is the most laid-back person you will ever come up against; he could not be rattled. But now he was, as his friend and partner was used as bait and had also been shot.

Before he could confront the protection team, DCI Dolan appeared and called out to Reggie. She knew he was angry, she needed to defuse the situation, she knew how he would have reacted.

Reggie said, "Yes, ma'am."

"Let's get a tea, no good getting upset, we will deal with this later, we need to focus on the way forward. We are all in the canteen in the hospital on the 3rd floor, let's see the rest of the team. The good news is he is doing well, it's not hit any major blood vessels or organs. You know what Winchester is like, he will come through this, a lot of moaning that you more than anyone will have to listen to for years to come."

Reggie smiled. "Don't I know it." They both walked off.

The team of nine were sitting round a dining table designed for four people; they had coffee cups and doughnuts on the table. Two seats were vacant for Reggie and the DCI. Doctors and nurses and other staff were sitting all around eating food – this was the staff canteen. A security guard walked over to the group and said, "Excuse me, you do know this is a staff canteen?" But before he finished I think most of the team had pulled out their warrant cards. "Sorry, chaps, just doing my job." He walked away as CI Aston bought to the table all sorts of sandwiches.

The DCI said, "Right, everyone, we now know they are ruthless and don't give a monkey's about whom they take out. So from this day on we will all work closely together, we will set up a welfare system of checking in with each other every four hours till we have this under control. This has also gone way up the tree now, we will be working with the national crime agency, we have a meeting in the office tomorrow morning at 0630 am meeting room 4. Don't be late."

DS Robbins said, "What do we have at this time?"

CI Aston pulled out her notebook. "In a nut shell, we have the location of the two males who seem to be the main people on the underground, we know the location of the HQ of the organisation. We are still gathering information on the missing persons, or missing bodies. We need to find Hellen Blake AKA QB; she has information we need. We will offer her witness protection and a new identity. DC Weston and DC Wineglass, go and speak to Ben Hooper, the private eye, tell him what we need and get QB into protection. You will have to inform him that PC Winchester may have given information out, we cannot be sure, so her life will be in danger. DS Robbins and DC Martin Byrne, you both need to go and see Professor John-Robbins and confirm as much as you can on the results of the toxicity reports he took from the male that was taken before he could finish his autopsy. We need not to move into the final phase of the investigation, I feel the walls are closing in on us, I have had four calls from the Yard today alone, but no one left a message – this tells me it's the top floor."

"Why do we need the National crime team involved?" DC Weston asked.

"Because," the DCI responded, "this goes way above our pay grade, we do not have the resources. Other agencies will come into effect very soon."

Lloyd from Interpol said, "We have been contacted from our HQ in the EU; they are sending some senior investigators over tomorrow, they say it's to help us out but I feel this is looking more like Government intervention."

"I know," CI Aston agreed, but we can only do what we can do.

The DCI interjected, "Do not put your careers on the line, or your futures. We are dealing with very, very powerful people. I am just glad the Americans are not involved."

Everyone chuckled, but DC Wineglass: "I am not being thick but why not the Americans?"

"First of all they will try and take over, they have no clue in this country how to stay quiet and they will be looking to make a film out of it in a few years – you will have Spielberg contacting you, also they overreacted."

Everyone left about 1800, knowing they had to be in the meeting in the morning.

Winchester was starting to come round, very confused; all he could see as everything was blurry was lights and hospital equipment all around him, TV playing in front of him on the wall, his throat was feeling strange as he was still sore from the ventilator; his pain was all over – he could not work out what bit didn't hurt, felt like he had been hit by a car.

The nurse appeared. "Hello, you ok?"

Winchester nodded. The nurse increased his sedation so Winchester would go back to sleep, as he was on maximum pain relief already. The doctor came in and said, "We will remove some of the tubes, he can stand alone now. Nurse, for the next 24 hours I need him to stay like he is, asleep, his body has been through some ordeal."

She said, "Yes, Doctor."

"Oh yes, no visitors without my say-so."

The meeting was in progress at Bow police station, the team were all together. The DCI wanted an update on Winchester.

CI Aston said, "I tried to find out – all I was told was he is comfortable for now and safe."

"Ok, that's good news," DCI Linda Dolan said.

"Right, latest on Hellen Blake, DC Weston."

"I spoke to the PI, Hooper, he has contacted her and said he will get her to us today; she is also feeling they may have found out she is the mole."

"Okay, good, right, after this, pick her up and bring to the station; come in through the custody suite, that is round the back and undercover. Take the marked van, put her in the cage – it will not look out of place if we are being watched. Did we get the professor's toxicology report?"

"Yes, ma'am," DC Byrne said. "It shows he was drugged with a lethal dose of Ketamine and Methamphetamine, commonly known as speed. He also said he did not have the body long enough to confirm whether it was ingested or injected, but he did say he saw a small puncture mark on the left buttock like a needle prick, again he could not document it, because the body was spirited away."

Reggie said, "We still do have the report from Doctor Kildare, Winchester has it on file, again he found a pin prick in the person's back. But again that body went missing before it got to be fully dealt with at the morgue."

The operation board was now full of information.

"Let's all brainstorm this. Let's start from the very beginning. This started when Winchester got suspicious about the cleaning on the underground, it was odd."

Reggie said, "Yes, that's correct."

"The jump of information came from Hellen Blake – she gave him the training DVD and the information on the company, up until then it was just suspicious. That's as far as we know. We have a gap now – what changed over the few months before we in this team got involved?"

Reggie said, "His new girlfriend."

"What about her?" the CI asked.

"She is security services, I think MI5 or MI6, she has been overseas in the USA for a few weeks, she carries a firearm."

"That will not be MI5 on a day-to-day basis, that's more like MI6 or homeland security."

Reggie said, "She was really upset with the protection Winchester at the hospital was getting. She got a team on site within an hour."

The DCI said, "It's clear she is more than an operative."

Lloyd and Boyd said, "We got pulled from a big drug project from the mainland Europe via a small island of Scotland to Greenland.

Our seniors want 24-hour updates – this is not usually done; we are allowed within reason to report as we feel is relevant."

The DCI was sitting very still, looking at the board.

"I think we are being played here, sorry, ma'am," the CI said. "Just look at the facts: they are two steps ahead of us all the time. I know this is off the wall, but every time we feel we are getting closer a smokescreen comes along."

"Yes, ma'am," DS Robbins said, "but why then try and take out one of us, Winchester?"

"I know," she said, "all I can say is Winchester must know something more than he is telling us or they think he knows more."

Reggie said, "I am sure Winchester would have told us, I know him he is blue through and through."

The DCI said quickly I am exploring every possibility. There was a knock on the door and the DCI turned the white board around on its wheels. It was Janet the tea lady. "Come in." The DCI turned the whiteboard back round and carried on. "We are going to divide the room into three, we will brainstorm each section. Once we have done that, we pass it round. We are here for the long haul."

Winchester was starting to come round again. This was being controlled by the medication to keep the pain to a tolerance Winchester could live with. It was becoming detrimental to his well-being to keep him under much longer, the long-term effects on the organs.

Winchester could breathe now without aid but his throat was very, very dry. The nurse put an ice on a stick round his dry lips and said, "Let this wash round your mouth."

Winchester could move his hands but every movement had a pain attached to it – move his arm, his chest hurt; moves his head, his neck hurt. He could feel he had a catheter in as that also hurt. He hated catheters. As the day moved on, he could feel the pain growing in all parts of his body, the only bit that did not hurt was his toes.

The nurse left the room as the doctors came it with a tall, very well-dressed man, looked military – they have the way of standing. The doctor picked up the charts and looked at them, turned to the gentleman and said, "Give him one more day and he will be good to talk to." The man never said a word, just looked at Winchester with a stone face and nodded at Winchester. Turned and left the room then Jennie came in.

Winchester smiled and that hurt his face. She looked at him, grabbing his hand, forgetting he had two broken fingers. She soon got to know as Winchester's eyes went wide. "Sorry, sorry," she said as she kissed him on the lips. Jennie explained to Winchester where he was and that he is under government protection for now. "Tomorrow you are getting visitors from the agency."

Winchester looked hard at her; he could not speak yet. She understood the look. "They want to know what you know to keep you safe."

The nurse came back in the room and pushed the buttons on the bed to lift Winchester to a sitting up position. The nurse also brought in a cup with three ice pops and asked Jennie to help Winchester, to hydrate his mouth and throat.

Jennie asked, "What's happening with all the drips?"

The nurse said, "The drugs are now flushed from his body, we need the strong antibiotics because of infection from the gunshot."

Winchester looked confused; in his mind he did not understand the concept of being shot.

"But we hope to get him on foods and water tonight slowly. Jelly first."

Winchester looked more upset about getting jelly than the gunshot – he hated jelly with a passion from when it was force fed to him as a kid along with dripping sandwiches.

Jennie said, "I need to go now. I will see you tomorrow. You need to rest and enjoy your jelly."

Winchester tried to smile but his face hurt. His eyes were okay to move.

Winchester did not sleep very well as the only way to know the time was the 24-hour clock on the wall, as no windows, so night and day was nothing in this place. The nurse came in again and removed his catheter – it was painful as this metre-long tube came from his penis, but what a relief. The medication drip came out and even the drip was removed.

"We have some porridge for you this morning and some warm tea, do you think you can try some?"

"Yes," Winchester said.

"Good, you also have a visitor in about 30 minutes so we need to get you upright and ship shape."

As Winchester was slowly trying to eat without his face hurting, he looked round the room. It was like a private room in a hospital without windows and a big mirror in the room. Winchester guessed that was a two-way mirror for observation, but why would you have it in a hospital? The door opened and the same tall man walked very upright into the room and did not turn his back to close the door but closed the door still facing Winchester, controlling the room sort of thing. Winchester just thought yes, military or ex-military.

"Hello, Winchester – may I call you Winchester?"

Winchester nodded. "Yes, that's fine."

"My name is Major Ralph Rogers, International and Homeland security. What are we going to do with you, son?" He was in his late 50s, black swept back hair, tall but slender, carried himself with authority.

Winchester looked puzzled.

"You see, Winchester, you have left us with a dilemma. Somehow you have managed to uncover an international and diplomatic situation that has massive implications for a good few heads of state."

Winchester tried to speak but it was hard as his throat was hurting and dry. He said, "Never heard of homeland security."

Major Rogers smiled and said, "We are GCHQ, it's a new name we use; it's an export from the USA. Winchester, I really don't know what to do with you. We can try and erase your mind and most probably will wind up us putting you in an home for the insane, or we could remove you and make you vanish, leave you in some far off place. You are an honest policeman doing your job, I would offer you a position with us, but you are not the sort, too upright sort of chap; we live in the shadows. I want to put a proposal to you and you may need to really consider it. Carry on doing the investigation, but you will need to keep us informed all along the way."

Winchester shook his head. "I work for the Metropolitan police only."

The major smiled. "Right answer, lad, but I do wish to point out we work for the Government and the Queen just as you have sworn an oath to; if we can't turn you I am sure no one else will. We will meet again one day, son and I will follow your career closely, you have an exceptional inquisitive detective's mind."

As the major was walking out of the room, he looked hard at Winchester. "Son, watch your back; you are a marked person at the moment. Don't go home; keep safe. The sort of money involved, you are just an ant to be stepped on to the people involved. I will speak to our American friends to get them to stand down. They also have a lot of time and effort around this whole situation, we are going to let this situation play out. Good luck." He was gone, back into the shadows.

Winchester was still very confused and not sure what had happened – really, did it happen? His mind was shot right now. Winchester fell asleep to be woken by Jennie. "Hello, Winchester." Jennie was mopping his forehead with a cool white flannel. Winchester felt like he was still recovering from being hit by a bus. That was because the medication was being reduced.

"You have a little temperature," the nurse said, "it's to be expected, we need to keep an eye on you for infections. We will keep you for another few days."

Winchester thought to himself how would I know what a few days are, no windows – he was not sure if it was night or day and the clock was not giving much away, it being a standard clock.

Jennie waited till the nurse left the room then kissed Winchester on the lips, the only place that did not hurt.

"When we leave here you will be coming to my flat in London for a few weeks till we can establish your safety. You will be off work for a few weeks, but your DCI also wants you on the case. I have spoken to her. She will visit you tomorrow with me, it's been agreed you will have an hour visit with the DCI and the CI."

Winchester said, "Do they know they can be seen through the glass mirror on the wall?"

"Don't worry, I will be in that room. Someone from the security services must be for your own safety and security, we trust no one. I will inform them as I know you will."

Winchester's pain was becoming a little unbearable, so the nurse was called and upped the strength of the morphine drip; it was also a nice feeling, Winchester thought. He drifted off again. This was becoming tiresome, keeping falling asleep; he knew it was good for recovery, but come on.

DCI Dolan was summoned to see the joint operations policing teams at New Scotland Yard.

The DCI knew that something must have leaked out. The DCI was shown to the 5th floor meeting room; the glass was white – you could not see in or out. It had an oval maple wood table that had 20 chairs around it, small water bottles in the middle, real time live Met units moving round London on the wall, very hi tech. She sat down and a cup of tea was given to her with two small biscuits on a side plate. Then three other cups were laid out on the opposite side of the table. Well, she thought, I know now there are three people coming. The door opened and three men, all very well dressed, said, "Good morning, DCI Dolan, before you ask any questions we will explain everything, so enjoy your tea. We have time to go over things."

As they sat down, she could see they were not police; they were military officers or some sort of upright looking individuals.

"Firstly, introductions, I am Major Ralph Rogers, GCHQ; this is Jerry Byrne, MI6; and last but not least Captain/Doctor Kildare."

The DCI looked confused. "The doctor whom was part of our investigations?"

"The very same one, I am afraid."

Then a young lad walked into the room holding a laptop and was connecting it to some point on the centre of the desk, then walked out again.

The Major said, "We are about to show you what we have on the situation you are investigating. I know you have signed the official secrets act. This is top secret, a little above your pay grade for now, we are going to share it with you."

A picture came up first of the owner "Nik Dazary" of Quite Pharmaceuticals International, QPI.

"This person is off limits to you and your team. You cannot in any way discredit or speak to him, I must make this very clear to you, DCI." The Major looked at her hard. The DCI got the message – she been around too long to know when she was being warned off or lose your job. "This person has friends in many countries, powerful friends–" and the Major looked at the DCI with his head looking slightly down, the old headmaster look. "That is all I have to say on the matter. Now I will be leaving the room, I have other meeting to go to. I will leave you in the capable hands of my two distinguished colleagues; they will take you through some of our information and what we can do to help each other." As the Major stood up, he said, "Your officer Winchester is a good chap, true blue, true blue, keep an eye on him; he will go far. He is recovering well. I saw him myself this morning." And he was gone.

Doctor or Captain Kildare said, "We have been tracking this activity you are investigating for over five years now, we have got to a point where we felt it was not causing a security risk until they started assassinations of others for money. You have given us what we need – the assassin that was shot and still not dead is Katrina Austin; we have wanted her for ten years, ex-KJB."

"We have her," the DCI said, "she was pronounced dead at the scene."

"Correct. We removed the body because she was still alive just in time, but we could not let anyone know." They both give a little grin. "She also worked for the CIA. This has also sent a message to the people that order the hits they are now on our list and they will be dealt with very soon. But you need to close down what was uncovered by your persistent officer Winchester. I will give you this–" the DCI was pushed an A4 brown envelope– "the CD has all the information on you will need to close down this operation. You can only play it once because as it plays it deletes the information and don't try and copy it; it also has a virus on it. Our chaps are very good at what they do.

"The meeting is over, we will not meet again in the near future, but you personally are on our radar."

The DCI said, "Why?"

"Because your reputation is exceptional. Ever want to move up, let us know."

"How would I do that?"

"We will know, we have people everywhere."

The DCI left the meeting with the CD in her hands and got hold of the team to meet in the morning to take notes.

QB was now at a safe house and the PI Hooper was waiting at the Nick for the DCI. As she walked in the main entrance, she said to the desk officer, "Let him in with me."

"It's been a long time, Gov," Hooper said.

"Well it has, should've stayed in the job."

"No, too much politics now. I love my job."

"Well, we need someone to come in and look at cold cases – would you be up for that? You will get an office here and on short term contract."

"Yes. It would be good."

"You will work with Reggie; he wants to come off the beat and become a detective, we have so many murders and rapes to be sorted out now D&A has become so good. This will start in three months, I will get the clearance over then you must complete the security clearance."

The team was in the meeting room. The DCI explained to everyone that the CD will only play once. "I have let the TECH lads look at it; they said it's set up so you can only play once."

"We could film it," one of the others said.

"I know, but I got a feeling they will find out and we all will be walking the beat very soon after."

Hooper was sitting at the back of the room, taking notes as well.

The CD started, it was a training CD for what was required from the teams who would infect the underground, the inbound planes to the UK; more shocking was the London buses – no one had thought of them. The buses were so easy to do for the team, they just got on the bus went upstairs, sprayed as they walked up the stairs and as they walked to the end of the bus; it was only to be the common cold. The buses were starting from outside the capital and made their way on their routes.

DC Weston said, "I use that bus sometimes, I put down the cold I got to just being on a packed bus."

"This is the same CD that Winchester had but it did not talk about buses," the DCI said. "I am sure they do a lot more they are not telling us, but we will get a small win."

"Oh, one more thing: we do not and will not talk to the press or inform anyone outside this team, your jobs will depend on it. Am I clear?"

"Yes, ma'am."

"Right, let's go over the results of the brainstorming we did in the groups and what have we come up with. Also, I need to speak to the CPS to understand what the charges will be. It's going to be completely different to what we are used to, the spooks normally deal with this sort of thing. So what do we have then?" as she pushed the wheeled clean white board in front of everyone.

"Let's start from ground zero, the trains, ie Central line." The DCI drew a square in the centre of the board. "This is what we have. Winchester, yes of course he is also a major part of this, we have identified six different cleaners for the QPI, two females and four males, all in their late 30s-ish. The chemicals used there are all basic, no poisons."

The CI piped up, "That we know of."

"True, but the DCI said it seems to be focusing on over the counter remedies," DS Robbins said, "but some people may have real problems with what they're spreading."

"Agreed."

"QB, she is the whistleblower?"

"Yes, she is in."

"The bodies that have been mislaid conveniently?"

"Yes, that's also here. The people that we suspect have been drugged and killed," the CI said, "but without a body we are really barking up the wrong tree."

"Assassinations and the one on Winchester," DC Wineglass said, "we should follow the money."

Everyone was chatting till one of them said, "The security services, they are all over this; we know they are. We seem to be doing all the leg work. Are they going to come in like the bloody cavalry and take the glory?"

"Not on my watch," the DCI said.

Then there was a knock on the door. It was Jan, the tea lady; she put the stuff on the side and left the room. Everyone said hello as she left. Just as she was walking out the door, the ACC Mills walked into the meeting room.

"CI Aston and DCI Dolan, can I see you both, my office, five minutes. Bring your tea up with your biscuits and I'll have tea, no sugar," with a grin on his face. The ACC left the room as fast as he had come in.

"DS Robbins, you need to carry on with this, we need a plan of action. This will take some time, I would think if we are taking our tea and biscuits."

The CI said, "It may be a lengthy meeting, but I'll leave you a few biscuits," as she grabbed a plate with about 20 digestives on it and put a whole one in her mouth as she walked out the room. The ACC loves a digestive.

DS Robbins started over again. "Let's go through the board again, what are we not seeing, what are we missing?"

DC Weston said I feel we are being led round by the nose, I think we have been second-guessed all along the way, or we have a leak in the room."

The room become a little uncomfortable when that was mentioned. DS Robbins quickly jumped in. "Everyone, he is right to say anything he feels is relevant on his mind, it should have crossed all of our minds at some stage."

Then DC Byrne said, "I thought it was Weston," and the room erupted with laughter. The room become focused after that.

Then DC Wineglass said, "Sergeant, can I have a word outside?"

Everyone just looked at her – what has she got to say that we can't hear in the room?

The DS and Wineglass went outside the room. "What's the problem?"

"I am not sure, but in the far corner of the room, top right hand side as you look in the room, to me it looks like a very small camera, I saw one before when I worked with special branch. I did not see it till I was just looking around while we was having tea. It was not there a few weeks ago, I know I would have seen it."

"Okay, what to do without raising suspicions? I know," the DS said, "let's take this to the canteen. Right, everyone," as he came back into the room, "we are taking this to the canteen. DC Wineglass said she feels a little sick in this confined space."

A few of them tutted and took their mugs and biscuits with them and made their way down to the canteen. When they were all sat round a table, the DS said, "The reason we are here right now is DC Wineglass saw what she thinks is a small camera in the corner of the room, so being safe is the only option. Could I ask you all not to say anything about what we think we saw and don't look at it as it will draw attention to the fact we may know it's there and we are on to whom is watching."

"We can't talk here," Sergeant Martin said, "everyone will be coming down for their breakfast soon; this place will be full of other staff."

"Yes, you are right. I know, let's all meet in Winchester's and Reggie's office in an hour; it's big enough for us all. I will inform the DCI and the CI."

Everyone went off in different directions. As DS Robbins was heading back up the corridor, he saw the DCI and CI coming towards him, looking a little puzzled.

DCI Dolan said, "Sergeant, what are you doing down here?"

"Ma'am, can we talk?" They ducked into an empty meeting room, and DS Robbins explained what had happened and the fact they were meeting in an hour in Winchester's and Reggie's offices.

CI Aston looked at the DCI and said, "This is the missing link, if this is right we now know why they have been one step in-front of us."

The DCI went red in the face; she was about to blow a gasket. "Who the bloody hell has the front to put such a device in my incident room? I will get to the bottom of this. I will call the TECH boys now and get them in there. See you all in an hour."

As the DCI walked out of the room, the DS said, "That is the first time I have ever see the gaffer get rattled."

The CI said, "I have, and when she is like this, god forbid anyone that crosses her." CI Aston just walked away and headed off to her morning briefing with other senior officers.

Chapter Thirteen

Winchester was still in his hospital bed, if you could call it that – he was still not sure what the place was. But one thing was for sure: the staff were very attentive. Every hour on the hour they kept taking his pulse, O2 and temperature. He still felt like he'd been hit by a train. But the biggest shock was the size of his balls – they were like two snooker balls, red and big. Winchester could not remember what had happened to them, but they hurt like hell when he moved. His eyes didn't hurt, no more drips or anything else was in his body, he was taking pain medication orally now. He was getting flashbacks, walking to the door, and as soon as he opened the door a dark shadow did something and he remembered hitting his head – no more than that.

The door opened; it was Jennie. She walked in wearing an all-in-one black trouser suit looking like a powerful person to deal with. She kissed Winchester. "How you feeling?"

"Not sure. Keep getting flashbacks to the night outside my flat door."

Jennie said, "I don't think you will ever remember what went on, the drugs they used on you was to suppress your memory."

"What did they do to me?"

"We are not sure but you were pretty banged up, we think we disturbed them when we came in."

"Do you think they would have killed me?"

"No, they wanted information; if they wanted you dead, they would have taken you away from your place."

"So why did they try and kill me in the hospital?"

"We think it was because they were not sure if you would remember the identity of the assassin, she has been the most wanted for years by almost the whole world."

"That doesn't make sense to me," Winchester said.

"If they would have finished what they wanted they would have drugged you even more so they could be sure you were unable to remember anything. But as they were disturbed it made them very uneasy."

Winchester said, "Jennie, I think my balls are knackered; can you look?"

Jennie smiled. "You old charmer, you, you know how to talk dirty to someone."

They both laughed.

"The doctor has told me it's only temporary, it's fluid build up, nothing else."

"That's okay for you to say," Jennie said, "they tell me another week and you should be able to go home. I will be home with you. Reggie said he will come and see you in a few days."

"Also, Jennie, I had a visitor, Major Ralph Rogers."

"Yes, I know, he is very, very high up in my world."

"I have to ask, Jennie, did you know anything about what's been going on?"

"I wish I did," Jennie said, "I wish I did. This is dark operations well beyond my remit. One thing I will say to you is that I feel you are too deep into this and you have rattled someone, or you wouldn't have got a visit from the Major. I also would like to say walls have ears."

Winchester nodded.

"Right, I am going out into Bond Street, get us some food, what do you want, my treat?"

"I could kill a KFC."

Jennie looked at him with a stern look. "Winchester, we have all the top restaurants around this place and you want me to find a KFC! I am not, on principle."

Winchester said, "I don't know what it is, I'm just craving it with a milk shake."

"They don't do milk shakes, do they?"

"Not sure."

"Okay, whatever you want, you heathen."

"Oh yes, no drumsticks."

"Anything else?" she said with her hands on her hips.

"Peri peri dip please." She was gone before he asked for anything else.

Jennie had never been in a KFC before in her life. She had got herself a chicken wrap from Nando's, that was bad enough, but when she got to the KFC she just grabbed a bargain bucket and cola and was out of there like a shot. It was an experience never to be repeated. They both sat on the bed, eating and generally talking. Winchester was feeling a lot better but still in a lot of pain.

"My god," she said to him, "do you know that I saved your life? You are in indebted to me so you have to do anything I ask."

Winchester said, "Well kill me now then."

The meeting reconvened in Winchester's and Reggie's office. Some of them had never been down into the basement before, and they all said: "wow, this is a gem, look how big it is, but it's great..." "but no windows would do my head in," the DS said.

The DCI said, "Right, so we think we know we are being watched and monitored, but we have some news for you. The secret services have spoken to the top floor, the senior officers, they have known of this situation for some time, but could not understand what they were up to. We have to, from now on, report everything we do. They are going to let us still run with this, but we cannot do the following. Implicate QPI. Is that clear? Again, everything must come through myself and the CI. This has international implications as Lloyd and

Boyd know now they have been informed from their head office. It ties our hands behind our back a bit, but I know we will come up with a solution. Time to get this plan of action moving before everyone goes to ground as this has now become a multi services operation. DS Robbins, get the teams sorted out. I want the cleaners from the training tracked till you know where they live; once we know that we can move. I want CCTV set up better on the rail stations we will identify, speak to our colleagues over at BTP, they will be only too happy to help but they are stretched."

There was a knock on the door. It was the Desk Sergeant Smalley. "Gov," he said, addressing the DCI, "we've a reported death at a station."

"What station?"

"Liverpool Street station, suspected heart attack, it's only just been flagged up to us by BTP."

"Right, DS Robbins, get the team down there asap; do not lose that body. Even if you have to hide it, follow it. Track it."

The team left in three cars. "Liverpool Street station, the body will go to Whitechapel London hospital. So, Weston and Wineglass, you go right to the entrance for the morgue. Me and Martin, we will go to Liverpool Street. Reggie, head off with Lloyd and Boyd to Professor Sir John-Robbins."

"Yes, we did not know he was a sir."

"It was flagged when we did our report; apparently, he never uses his title. Let him know what is going on regarding the body so it does not get lifted again; he will run a full test on the body."

The teams got to their destinations. BTP officers at the scene had put back to their control, said he was a middle aged male just got off the tube and bang went down with a thud, very quickly a nurse on her way to work was on the train tried hard to keep him going; she carried out CPR, she said he looked very pale and she felt he was dead before he hit the ground; she could not be sure, but in her opinion. "Can we speak with her?"

"Yes, she is over there with the other PCSO."

"Hello, my name is DS Robbins and DC Weston of the Metropolitan police. Can we ask you a few questions?"

She looked very flushed.

"Firstly, are you okay?"

She nodded. "I am a nurse; it's not as if I don't deal with this on a daily basis, but in a hospital environment."

"Can I take your name?" Weston was poised with his pen and notebook.

"Jackie Foster, I work at Royal London."

"Did you see the gentleman on the train?"

"Yes, he was standing close to me. I didn't see any sign of him being clammy or pale, it's something I think I would have noticed, but maybe I was thinking of the long day shift ahead to notice."

"Did you notice anyone very close to him?"

"Yes," she said, "now you come to mention it, the train was its normal packed-in-like-sardines, we had a bit of space, yet another man seemed to stand very closely to him, so much so I thought they may have been an item – again you never know on the trains in this day and age. I am on shift in ten minutes; I am going to be late – can I head off now?"

"Just one more question for now – can you give us a description of the male standing close to him?"

"Not really; he was tall because his head was above the overhead handrail above the doors, I would say middle aged, dark hair, that's all I could remember. I really need to go now."

"Yes, of course," DS Robbins said, "we will give you a lift if you like."

"No, thank you, it's quicker to get the train from here."

"Okay, we have your details if we need you again. Thank you, Jackie." She was gone.

The DS said, "Weston, go and speak to the BTP officers, see if we can view the CCTV. It will take us a few days to get a copy; let's look at it right now."

DS Robbins and DC Weston went to the central office with the two officers from the BTP team to view the CCTV. The CCTV had come on a lot over the last few years and the screens and the quality were very good because it needed to be after the terrorist threats. They managed to run back the footage from when the train pulled in, they saw the male step out of the train and just grab his chest, went down like he had been shot. Face first to the ground, They both looked to see if what the nurse had said about the tall male if he also got off the train. No, he did not but what they did see is the nurse follow the male out of the train directly behind him and it looked like she made a sudden jerking movement forward as if she fell into him from behind. That looked very strange indeed; it could be nothing, she may have tripped off the train.

Weston said, "Look, the male makes a little movement with his head to the side she pushed him on, she could have injected him."

"Right, can we get a copy asap please, lads?"

"Yes, but we need a piece of paper, you know that, lads; wish we could do it quicker. We know you have all the powers, but we have to put all our procedures in place."

"Okay, I will get the DCI to get it to your DCI, but can you help us?"

"Already on it, will get it over to you later today for your attention at BOW Nick."

"Thanks, lads, really appreciate it. We need to get to the hospital asap, we need to speak with Nurse Foster again."

"I think it could be nothing," Weston said.

"For some reason I don't think so." DS Robbins looked very stern as if he felt he'd been fed a lie. "Let's get going; the rest of the teams are at the Royal London."

As they both were heading to their car, four well-dressed men were waiting by their car.

"Hello, what can we do for you, gentlemen?"

One of the group produced an identity card. "SIS, name's Steven Byrne; can we have a conversation?" Steven Byrne looked like he'd been working out for years, striking sort of chap, 6,3, well built, well-kept short hair, chiselled face and held himself with confidence, ex-military for sure, more officer type.

"You are heading off to the hospital to talk to Nurse Foster?"

"Yes."

"Please leave her alone; she is one of us, undercover."

The DS nodded and said, "But she is a material witness."

"Yes, but the person you are looking for is on the CCTV. It's the male she spoke to you about; he stayed on the train, he is being tracked and followed by 12 operatives, we will deal with him in due course. DS Robbins, you don't have to take my word for it, but your DCI is getting a call from us as we speak. We are not going to get in the way, but we will inform you of the situation if it clashes with our long-term ongoing investigations."

Weston stood looking on at the others all standing around; not one of the other three said a word – they were all security services, ex-military, shoes very polished, short back and sides, and their suits had not one crease. They were smart, he thought to himself, oh and not one had any fat on them.

Weston and Robbins headed off to the hospital, to meet with the rest of the team and to ensure the dead person was with the professor. Reggie was already at the hospital and was with the professor, the professor still a little upset from what had happened last time, was making sure he was not going to lose this one body before he could carry out the full autopsy. He called in his other two coroners and said he was pushing this one to the front so they will need to cover his morning backlog. They both agreed – he demanded that sort of respect from everyone. He made a call to someone he knew in the government. Reggie could not hear what was being said but he said as he walked out the door, "It's fine, no one in any authority can remove this body till I've finished, so anyone comes to take him you will need to show them the door."

Reggie nodded and got on the radio to let DC Byrne and Wineglass know of what he had been told.

The DS came over the radio. "I want everyone to set up outside the morgue, both entrances, the private pick up to the rear car park, this is where the bodies are removed discreetly by funeral companies, plus the main reception; it has security but I know if anyone flashes a warrant card they will let them in."

Reggie went and sat in the security office with Jeff the big black ex-boxer security guard. He was 6, 5, built like a tank, he was ex-military boxing champion. Reggie has known him and his six brothers, all the same size, for ten years, very relaxed, laid back family; mother was 5,4, father was a Royal Marine in the 80s, sadly passed away. All loved their mum.

Reggie said, "No one can come in today to remove the person with no name."

Jeff grinned and said, "That's cool with me, man, I make the tea."

Reggie smiled and got back on the radio: main reception covered.

While the professor was carrying out his autopsy, the DCI and CI were summoned to the ACC's office again. This time they saw six well suited and booted men with the ACC. "Come in and close the door." Everyone was standing; this was important.

"We believe that there will be a move to remove the body from the morgue today, we have information that they are clearing up before closing down the UK operation. Your officers may be in a bit of danger."

"We have sent six of our team," the DCI interjected, "whom are we dealing with here?"

The lead, Steven Byrne, said, "We are SIS. The team we sent are armed."

The DCI then asked, "What are your intentions?"

"We will remove the body to our location, the same place as your colleague Winchester is in right now."

The CI said, "Why? The autopsy is underway now."

One of them said, "That's quick," as he looked at his boss Steven Byrne.

"It is quick, that was not expected. So we will not move the body then, we will wait for the report."

"But the others will not know that, who are coming."

"No, they won't. Your team – how long before they are at the hospital?"

"They are on site now and are waiting for orders."

"You informed your team on the ground," the DCI said.

"We need a code word."

"Winchester."

"That's good to go."

The professor had finished his autopsy and Reggie got the call to go to his office. "I have finished; it will take me a few hours to write the report, but a quick summary: small injection mark in his left buttock. All organs healthy, no brain problems, so in my opinion whatever was injected seems to be my best bet, but it's gone off to three labs now."

"Three?" Reggie said.

"Yes, three. If anyone thinks they can stop three labs they are better than me." As he grinned, the DCI, DS, CI and Steven Byrne arrived down in the morgue.

Reggie briefed them. "The professor is doing another autopsy right now."

They all stood in the well-lit corridor of the morgue; it has a smell of death, everyone knows it.

"I think we need to let them take the body."

"What?" the DS said to Steven, SIS.

"Think about it; they will not know we have carried out the autopsy yet, we could track them, put a tracker with the body. It will lead us some place."

"I am not comfortable with this," the DS said.

"Why are you not comfortable with this?"

"We lose this body, we are in big trouble. We don't know who he is, do we? Fingerprints come back not on system, we know his ID is fake, the address does not exist."

"How do you know that?" the CI asked.

"I told you we have been tracking him for a few weeks. He lives in a one bed flat in Barking yet he has a bank account that has more than a million dollars in it. We cannot find him on anything, we think he is CIA undercover, we think three of the people that have been killed are from the USA."

"They would tell us."

"No they wouldn't. We found out they are operating in the UK, we would kick them out without clearance with us."

DS Robbins asked Steve Byrne, "Sorry for my ignorance, but what does SIS stand for?"

"It's part of the MI6; we are mostly ex-military or military, secret intelligence service."

Oh that's clear as mud, Robbins smiled.

The tracker was biked over from the SIS office in London, placed in the body. Everyone pulled back to keep an observation now; the Met surveillance team had four motorbikes, two black cabs, two white vans and an Ice cream van to track them if they came.

"We have to be on top of our game," the DCI said, "they will know if they are being followed."

Reggie was sitting at the front desk when he got a call on the radio: "looks like we have company, four males in black combat kit unarmed, looking at them coming towards the hospital".

Reggie said to Jeff, "We will just sit here and see what they want."

Also come over the Radio: "at the rear doors a dark grey transit van with private ambulance on it has pulled up at the rear exit, they are not on the list for today. They are just parked up waiting, two males in the front, they do not look like funeral directors to me".

The first of the four men walked into the reception of the morgue. Jeff from behind his security screen said, "Can I help you, gentlemen?"

The lead male, who was six foot plus, short cropped hair with a US accent, said, "Yes, we are from the secret service."

Reggie sat next to Jeff and just acted dumb, as Jeff said, "I need to see some proof of identification."

He pulled out what looked like an MI5 warrant card.

"Thank you, Officer Keith Gunn, so what can we do for you?"

"We are here to pick up a body of a male that was brought in today from Liverpool Street station."

"Yes, I think that body has just completed its autopsy."

Keith looked hard at Jeff. "It's been done already?"

"Yes."

"That was fast."

"Oh, it's a slow day, Professor John-Robbins did it before he went to court today."

"Just a moment," Keith said as he walked away and spoke to the others, got out his mobile phone and called someone, came back and said, "We need to take the body."

Reggie said, "Sorry, sir, but we will need a court order as the body has not been released yet as the professor has not finished his autopsy, that is later today."

Keith looked at Reggie with eyes that would burn right through him. "You new here, sir?"

"No, I been at the hospital for years, just in another department. I am admin."

"Well, Reggie, this warrant card trumps everyone; this is about national security, so get off your admin chair and show us the way to the person we are trying to pick up."

This was a little aggressive. Jeff said, "Don't talk to us like that", as all four men closed up together as if a fight was going to kick off.

Jeff then stood up and he was like a slow mountain rising up, did not seem to stop growing. Looked down on Keith and his men. Reggie saw in their eyes this mountain of a man was not going to be easy to deal with; in fact, it will be extremely painful.

"Look, I am sorry," Keith said, "we have a job to do."

"So do we," Jeff said.

"Well, I'll take you to the body, but you have to sign for it."

"Yes, yes ok." Keith turned to one of the men. "Tom, stay here and complete the paperwork for the admin man."

Jeff said, "I see out the back on the CCTV the Transit, is that your private ambulance?"

"Yes."

"Ok."

Reggie took his time and made sure that Tom signed the paperwork and put his fingerprints all over the desk and the paper and pen. They were out the back and gone as fast as they arrived.

Reggie said, "Well done, Jeff, great job and thanks." Reggie shook his hand and joind the others on the operation. The tracker was working. The two motorcycles were sent to try and track Keith and his team in their blacked-out Range Rover, but were told to back off if they started to carry out anti surveillance driving tactics to see if they are being followed. They backed off very quickly as Keith's team started doing it almost right away; went round the hospital twice. The private ambulance was heading down the A13 towards Dagenham, Essex, it was moving at some knots according to the tracker.

DS Robbins asked over the radio, "Reggie, did they try and get the records from the Autopsy?"

"No, as we said the professor had not completed yet, he had only completed the rule-outs of heart attack, or stroke and major organs failing. One of them did say has the blood work been done yet. I said no that's this afternoon or tomorrow; they were in a hurry." Reggie added, "We need to report that I am sure they were from the USA, they have that look about them; also two who spoke had that US accent, it was there. I got fingerprints from one of them all over the pen and paper. I have bagged it."

Over the radio came Steve Byrne: "this is good news. Can you get the stuff to me, Reggie, we can track the fingerprints much quicker than your system and we have a bigger database".

Reggie said, "Who is this?"

"Steve Byrne SIS."

The DCI came over the radio: "it's okay, we will collect it from you at the hospital, we are still on site. Everyone stay on channel 19; this is assigned to us for the operation; no one can join it without permission".

DS Robbins came over the radio: "they are giving us the run around; we are backing off; we will track them through the tracker".

Winchester was feeling 100% better. It had been a few days, he was going to be discharged to go to a safe house.

Jennie said, "You are coming back to my place. I live in Baker Street, London, I have an apartment, three bedrooms and security in the main entrance."

Winchester said, "I need stuff from my place."

"I have got what you need from your place."

Winchester looked a little shocked.

"Well it was with me or in north London in a little one bedroom flat, Seven Sisters Road."

"So you seen my underpants drawer."

"Yes, I have to be honest I have seen pants before, but come on, they are budgie smugglers, all of them so out of date."

"But as I said they could have been Y-fronts."

She smiled and said, "If they were then we would have had a problem."

Winchester got into a black tracksuit as all his clothes had been taken away; all he had on, that was almost nothing.

"Get in the wheelchair," the nurse said.

"I can walk," Winchester said.

"No, you are not, do as you are told," the nurse said, "get in the chair; that is an order."

"Yes, ma'am."

Jennie laughed. "I need to be that firm with him."

The walked down this long corridor with steel dark grey doors with numbers on them. Winchester noticed they all had B4 – 12 and B4 – 13, and so on.

Winchester said to the nurse, "What's the B4 stand for?"

"We are basement low level 4, so we are four levels below ground; yes this is the medical wing."

As they got into this lift that said '30 persons only', Winchester saw that in fact six more lower levels on the left, and he thought to himself this is about 100 metres long and at least 50 feet wide, plus all this below a car park in Cavendish Square. As they came out into the underground car park, a blacked out people carrier was parked with its side sliding door open.

"This is for you, you can get off the wheelchair now. Come on, I haven't got all day."

Winchester was helped by Jennie to the car; the nurse was gone in a flash.

The car journey was only 20 minutes. They went down to an underground car park in Jennie's building to a lift that went right up. She was suite 6, the place was so clean, wood floors throughout, leather sofas, fantastic place. The view out of the rear window was the BT Tower and the roof landscape of London. Plus Baker Street itself.

"Your room is this one; it has a super king bed and its own shower room."

Winchester looked at it. "Is this your room as well?"

"It's all my rooms," she said.

"You know what I mean."

"No, I am in this room, it's bigger, because you at the moment with your broken nose and your broken ribs make so much noise when you are asleep, I will probably kill you, but you can use my bath; I will run it for you. It's a two-person bath. I will wash your back later. We will settle down after I will order food in – fancy Chinese?"

Winchester said, "Oh yes, I could kill a Chinese."

"Also, tonight, Winchester, I have to debrief you as this has not happened yet and this is the best way to do it. My bosses said it would be better coming from me, not a total stranger."

"I agree," Winchester said.

The night moved on; it was about 20:00, food all eaten, bath was great. Winchester and Jennie were sitting down on the sofa with white robes on, Winchester having to sit leaning to one side because of his ribs. The TV was off – you could hear the traffic moving up and down Baker Street because Jennie had the sliding doors to the front balcony a little open. They both started to talk about what Winchester remembered from the evening he was attacked in his own home.

Winchester said, "I really don't remember. Oh. I do remember one thing; it was like a perfume smell, really old, I remember it from the late 80s, what was it?"

Jennie said, "Hold that thought for a moment."

She had a new laptop computer; she put in perfumes from the 80s. "That's it: Coty-wild musk," Jennie said. "Think of the smell, focus on it."

"It was a bit hazy," Winchester said, "but, I hit my head but as I opened the door I saw a woman and a very large male, fat but big, my brain said Cima wrestler, could not make out the female's face, they sprayed something in my face that hurt my eyes and I went down in a split second. I remember some pain off and on, they kept asking me questions; I don't remember what questions, but the female was always close, the perfume was always there. Sorry I can't remember anymore."

"Most likely you will never remember as they used strong drugs on you and you started when you were in the hospital to have withdrawal symptoms from the fentanyl."

"You mean I am a drug addict."

Jennie laughed. "You were for a few days, but no, you are fine, just don't get drug tested for a few more weeks yet – and cut your hair!"

"Why cut my hair?"

"Because everything we do regarding drugs is in your blood system and that transmits though the hair as a living organism."

"I will shave my head."

Jennie said, "No, don't be silly, you will be fine. So you need to sleep."

Winchester said, "No, I've had enough sleep for a lifetime. Can we go for a walk?"

"No, till we are sure you are safe we have to keep you under wraps." Jennie saw that Winchester was low. "I know what, I have some old clothes for undercover work; they look dirty but they are not, they are baggy and one of the baggy ones is a hoodie. Let's go but I will drive us to the back of Tower Bridge and we will walk along the embankment. Is that ok for you?"

They went off. Winchester looked like a tramp. "I look like a tramp."

"Yes, that was the look I went for."

Winchester said, "I am amazed how big everything is, tracksuit bottoms even fit. I hope we don't get pulled by the local lads."

Jennie said, "You will, I won't; you would never get me caught in that stuff anymore."

They both left in her car and parked up. As they parked up, she got out of the car and said, "wait here a second", then walked to another car that had just pulled up. The window came down on the other car; Winchester could see the face of a male talking to Jennie. They seemed to be smiling at each other then the car turned round as she walked back to the car.

"Who was that?"

"That's your close protection team, two in the car, they are going for a coffee. They know we are walking; at this time of night it's dark, lots of people, I told them we will be back at the car say 22:00."

Winchester said, "Are you carrying?"

"Yes always, but not when I was at your place."

As they walked over Tower Bridge, Jennie suddenly stopped dead still and said "stop".

"What?" Winchester said.

"I need a toilet right now."

"Starbucks is 100 yards, use it."

She shot in there like a rocket.

She came out holding her stomach.

"What happened?"

"Even my monthly period is not on my side."

She looked at Winchester who was almost hyperventilating. "You okay, Winchester?"

"Bloody hell, you frightened the shit out of me, I thought someone was on to us."

Jennie said, "I am sorry, but it was urgent and my gun dropped on the floor in the cubicle as well – it almost bounced into the pan."

"Well you're not pregnant," Winchester said.

"If I was," she looked at Winchester, "it would be yours."

As they walked past HMS Belfast two police officers walked up to Winchester and asked his name. Jennie saw the funny side of it – they thought he was a vagrant.

"PC Winchester if you need to know."

One of the two officers said, "Yes and my name is Bill and he is Ben."

"Well, Bill and Ben, my collar number is 71630."

"Sorry, mate, but you need to get some more clothes and the slippers don't go with the look." They both laughed, patted Winchester on the shoulder and walked on.

Jennie was killing herself laughing.

Winchester said, "I am glad you find it funny."

They both sat down outside a coffee shop. Jennie went in to get the coffee and a woman and a man walked up to him sitting on the bench.

"Want a coffee, mister?"

"No, I am fine."

The male put his hand in his pocket and pulled out a ten pound note, pushed it towards Winchester.

"Thank you, but I am not homeless, just apparently poor choice in clothes."

Jennie came out of the coffee shop and screamed as she dropped the two takeaway cups and like a Wild West gun slinger so fast pulled her gun out and in a very direct clear voice shouted, "Stand still, don't move, I am an armed officer. Don't move don't move."

The male and female just looked at each other then from behind two males also said, "Stand still, armed officers, don't move. On your knees now."

Winchester was so confused. The male and female looked at each other but they did not look frightened at all, their faces were hard and eyes shifting side to side then four other SO19 officers with automatic weapons appeared. They still stood dead still, you could see in the split seconds they were calculating they life expectancies.

The male dropped to his knees and said, "Okay, okay."

But the female was looking into Winchester's eyes; he knew at that second she was going for it, as if she had said I am going down fighting. Four red lasers were on her upper body, Winchester just knew he had to move very quickly – if she goes for it some of the bullets could go right through her and into him. As she went to the ground she made a move towards her coat. Winchester just dived to the ground and away as best he could. He knew SO19 would try and hit the torso. Shots rang out, she was hit ten times in the upper body; she was gone. The male lay on the ground hands spread out. They stood over him weapons pointing at him. One of the officers that was trained in gunshot wounds started to work on the female, but she was gone, it was a good shoot but all the officers knew they were going to be referred to the policing standards office. Winchester looked at her lying on the floor her eyes open: she was dead, not much blood; she must have died immediately. He was very shaken.

"That's the perfume I could smell," he said to Jennie as she got on the radio.

People were screaming and running off and the two police officers that had earlier spoken to Winchester arrived very quickly.

Jennie went to Winchester, who said, "I told you this was not a good idea."

"I know I know, but we have flushed the people out who wanted you dead now."

"That was a close call. We have a lot of debriefings to do now, we need to get you out of here."

The scene was taped off and the local officers were coming in from everywhere. Two male officers from SIS said to Winchester, "We are going to get you back to Jennie's place, she will need to inform the powers that need to know what has happened. The body will stay here." But the male was cuffed and removed by SO19.

Winchester was still processing what had just happened and the look from the female's face as she knew she was going to die, it was cold as ice look. It is what it is an acceptance; it was her last moments. It was ingrained in him, mind.

As Winchester sat in the back of the car driving through the streets of London, he remembered her face from his perspective. She was the one always questioning him and had injected him over and over again, so some of the memories were coming back.

Winchester got back to Jennie's flat and could not work out was this a set up or was it a random situation, but he remembered that Jennie did not want him to go out at all; she did warn him, so no it was not. A knock on the door; it was Reggie.

"Hello, mate, so good to see you."

Reggie hugged Winchester. "You okay?"

"I think so."

"Good. I have got Chinese on me so let's eat, I am famished."

Winchester was so happy to see his old mate. Reggie filled him in on the operation, then another knock on the door – it was CI Aston, DS Robbins, DC Weston, DC Wineglass and DC Byrne.

"We've come to see you. Sorry the DCI cannot be here as she is at the briefing over the embankment shooting tonight. We got some beer and wine and Indian."

More food! Winchester did not want to say anything as he had just eaten Chinese, but sod it, he will eat more. It was so cool having all the team round the place.

"Your girlfriend has a really cool place, you are punching above yourself."

Everyone just laughed, this coming from DS Robbins who was always going out with models and showbiz people and a sideline in personal protection to TV personalities.

Jennie got home about 12 o'clock, she was knackered and everyone had gone home but the place stunk of Indian and Chinese. She knew everyone had been round because the security guard at the front entrance told her.

She said, "Sounds like you had a good time with your team tonight. Let's hit the sack, but I need a shower first. The paperwork on this is going to be a headache, we had no clue they were going to move on you so quickly. For them to know you were out with me is worrying – they must have been watching me as well."

Chapter Fourteen

D CI Dolan was called into a high profile meeting at the Yard with the CI to explain what had happened as the Chief Constable's office were all over this situation as public members had seen what happened. It's all over the news about the shooting by police and security services on the embankment, the press love a story and it was a quiet week as parliament was closed for a few weeks; MPs are away as is the PM.

Aston and Dolan met in the canteen before the grilling so they got their facts right. This was the normal, when you are talking to the senior managers they are so fast from the real world, it's farcical. They only want to protect their reputation. This time the Home Secretary was also all over this from her holiday home in Wales. They did not want the press all over them. As DCI Linda Dolan and CI Karen Aston walked into the top floor meeting room at the Yard, it was full of people dressed in full uniform or top notch suits. They knew then this was going to be a long day of backsides covering.

Steve Byrne was at the table from SIS. He looked at both of them as they walked in and winked at them, as if to say he has their back.

"Start from the beginning – what the bloody hell has been going on?"

The DCI said, "With all due respect you have the information in-front of you, so I will cut to the chase. This situation goes well above my pay grade."

Everyone in the room looked at each other.

The ACC said, "Keep it to the facts of the night. What happened?"

"We just don't know, it was the MI5 team that was the main spare head on this one. In the report you will see our investigation has been ongoing and they tried to take out a serving Met officer, PC Winchester." The DCI also said, "We have also found out the government has been aware of this situation for some years now and have not informed anyone of this practice on the underground train systems." The DCI also got into them, by saying, "I find it hard to believe that the intelligence services in this building did not know something."

The ACC said, "And you know this how?"

"I can prove it, or are we incompetent?"

One of the Area commanders said, "Can you prove your accusations?"

"No, but it's bloody unlikely someone did not know."

The ACC said, "Right, that's all we need from you both, please leave the room, we have lots to discuss."

The DCI and the CI left the room; the DCI was fuming – "they are trying to stick this on us the ass covering political assholes".

CI Aston said, "Do we keep going on the investigation?"

"Yes, we do till told otherwise. We are almost ready to arrest the people we need to, we have all the evidence."

As they both walked through the entrance to leave Scotland Yard the reception said, "Sorry, you both need to return to the top floor asap, same room you left."

They both went back up in the lift. As they walked into the meeting room, only three people remained: Steve Byrne. Major Ralph Rogers, and a very quiet man in a suit in the corner.

"My name is Major Ralph Rogers, I am head of SIS. The person in the corner is from the Government offices of home security. He is here to convey his wishes and thanks. As of today you will no longer be involved in the investigation of the underground conspiracy or the companies and people involved; this will move into the home office teams and security services. It is of international interest and security between countries. We thank you for all your help and enthusiastic tenacious efforts, it will be placed on the records of all your officers. Winchester, your officer, is now safe and can go back when fit to his duties; we have eliminated the threat to him."

The DCI said, "This is bullshit, you know we could close this down very quickly."

Steve Byrne said, "Yes you could and that would have ramifications on the government. If you persist you will lose your jobs – it is not worth it for no gain."

"But the bastards tried to take out a Met officer."

"We know and we are sorry, we should have been quicker to react to the situation. We have been following this for the past five years."

The CI said, "I feel we will need to complete this."

Then the person in the corner stood up and said, "Let me make this very clear to you. If you get in the way your career is over, both of you. You can stand on your soap box and crow as much as you like, it will only end in tears. You are both very good officers and will go far, I am sure, but leave this to us. Do I make myself clear, do I?"

They both looked at each other.

"But I am not a total asshole. In your investigations you would have come across a major drug cartel, you will take them down with your team."

The DCI said, "No, we have not."

"You have been following some people from the train station; they are also trafficking drugs from the coast. We will give you the information, that will cover the costs of your team's efforts over the last few months.

"I am leaving now, the Major will fill you in on all the details of what has been going on over the past five years. Oh yes, just as a point we would like to see PC Reggie and PC Winchester promoted to DC as soon as possible, we are very impressed with their work. To uncover what has been in plain sight but so well covered has just been simply astonishing."

The shadow government person left the room and was gone.

The DCI said, "Who was that?"

"Never mind, let's put it this way," Steve Byrne said, "you really don't want to see him again, you really don't. If you value your future and officers around you.

"The major and I will meet with your team next Thursday at your meeting room at 07:30. We will give you everything you will need to know then your whole operation is moved on to us and the other security services. Also, we will give you the information on the drug dealers you can take down."

The DCI said, "Can we confirm that everyone involved on the policing team will not be affected in future years?"

The Major piped up, "On the contrary, it will do very well for your futures, my expectations of yourself and CI Aston getting up the chain of command are very positive, you have both shown leadership and discretion, qualities that are hard to come by, to many old boy networks these days."

"We need to go now," Steve said to the Major.

"Yes, Captain."

They left the room. ACC Mills walked into the room as they left and exchanged nods. ACC Mills closed the door as he walked in. "Please sit down, we have to talk."

The CI and DCI were still confused and processing what had just happened; they both sat down at the long maple meeting table, and the ACC sat at the end of the table.

"So I have some information for you, but it is very secret right now, till all parties are told officially."

They looked at him with intense looks.

"DCI Dolan you will be promoted to ACC head of intelligence when I leave next month; I have got my promotion to Chief Constable of Wales. CI Aston, you are also moving up to DCI and will be taking the place of the current DCI."

DCI Dolan said, "Is this to keep us onboard with the situation we have uncovered?"

"No, this was decided six months ago, that is why I have been around evaluating both of you. I applied for my job last year and got it, but it has to stay very hush hush. One other thing: PC Winchester and Reggie will be offered promotion to DC if they want them, but I think from my discussions with Reggie he took his Sergeants exam two years ago and no vacancy, well we have one here as of next month as one of the Sergeants is coming with me as a CI and he is from Wales too.

"Again that is for you to disseminate to your team. Talking about your team, they will get commended for their work on the Operation Underground case. I am sure the new case you are now looking into or will be looking at, will make this station very proud. We will have one up on the boys at the Yard. It would be good if you put that one to bed before I go, good for me too. I'd like to thank you both for being very professional. Oh just one thing, the CCTV in your meeting room was not in operation, never has been; it was put there as a way of stopping people from not being professional if they thought they were being monitored. It was placed there five years ago; it was forgotten about."

The DCI and CI looked at each other with contentment for what they had just been told.

"I am sure that was not there two months ago," the DCI said, "as I had the room swept because of information leaking out about operations."

"That's what I am being told by the intelligence team, but soon, Linda, you will find out yourself as you will be head of that team. So are we all in agreement now? The information is for your ears only. You can discuss with your team but please wait till next week when it will be public knowledge I am the new Chief Constable of Wales."

"Good luck, sir," CI Aston said.

"Thank you, both. I need to go home – me and the wife are going out to celebrate the good news. She will be very happy; all Gwendoline, my wife's, family live in Wales."

Off he went with a big smile on his face and a swagger like the cat who got the cream.

"Bloody hell, ma'am," Aston said, "that was not what I was expecting. Did you?"

"No I was not, but I am happy for the promotion, it's been well overdue and you, well done, you will be inheriting a good team."

"Did you feel like we are being bought off?"

"No, not at all," the DCI said, "if that was the case they could just transfer us to some godforsaken place. We need to get the team together and inform them all about the meeting next Thursday, I will look at the intelligence report on my desk for the drug traffickers and assign the team to what is required. I will copy you in on everything as I know you need to be kept in the loop, as I am sure you will be taking over soon. I will send you my personal appraisals of the individuals in the team for you to look after; we are short by three other officers, sorry two as PC Winchester will be on your team no as well."

"Are we sure," CI Aston enquired, "that PC Reggie wants to be a Sergeant?"

"Well that is my understanding, we could use a Sergeant as you will be losing DS Robbins to your post."

"But ma'am, as the ACC you could give me a Sergeant and a CI."

"I don't think we have the budget."

"Yes we do, save on the DC times two."

"Can you manage with the team being that small?"

"Well, it's not that small, is it, with all the wealth of knowledge."

"Yes, let's do that, but what I will do is get a new DC for you as well. I think Jamie Mills from SO19 has done ten years in armed response, wants to come back to being a DC, I also think it's because Sergeant Clarkie is leaving, done his 25 years, going to be a paramedic part-time. From a tactical side Jamie will be a real asset. He is studying for his Sergeants exam so say you will keep him say two years," said CI Aston.

"Well good, let's get back to our day jobs, shall we," DCI Dolan said. "Oh no."

"What, ma'am?"

"I have to get a new uniform, I have not had my one on for ten years."

"Better order one then, ma'am, lot more shiny stuff on it soon then, as I," CI Aston said, "will go into my wardrobe for some time now."

Both parted and headed off to their offices.

Winchester was getting up, feeling a little better but was still processing what had happened with the shooting and knew the Police complaints team would be round to interview him this morning. Jennie had gone at 0530 as she had to put together her reports of what had happened a few nights ago for her senior operations officer. She did not get a shot off as the SO19 lads did. It was a good shoot from a procedure outcome, but not if you had to shoot.

It was about ten am the bell went on the intercom; it was the three internal affairs officers: two men and one female. Winchester was dressed, coffee on and set up round the kitchen table that would easily sit ten people. Winchester opened the door and beckoned them in.

"Go right through to the kitchen."

"Nice place you have here, expensive."

Winchester just let that one go over his head, never said a word. They sat down at the table, books and notebooks out with pens and a tape recorder with a small microphone.

"Do you want any coffee or tea, even water?"

All said, "No thanks."

Winchester said, "Well I have one but you are all welcome."

The lead officer was Inspector Chris Burt, grey haired man with a little grey moustache; the other two officers just took notes, DC Keith Crow, DC Joan Crosby.

"This is an informal discussion for now as we need to establish what happened last night, but I wish to point out, you are a serving police officer, so I will caution you."

Winchester said he understood; they started the tape. Winchester just told them what had happened step by step. He was done in an hour. They did not ask much right then as they knew Winchester was looking a little shook up still from what had happened and they knew what he had been through.

"Thanks, we will pick this up again later at the station, it was only to get the investigation going as fast as possible."

They left as they had come, with not a lot of niceties. The phone rang. Winchester was not sure whether to answer it or not so he left it and it rang again and the third time he answered it; it was Jennie.

"You okay? I was getting worried about you. Why did you not pick up the phone?"

"Was not sure if I could."

"Well of course you can. I have given my number to you. The CI she is calling you later this afternoon, just to let you know."

"Thanks."

"Love you, see you tonight."

Winchester said, "Love you too."

It just came out then silence on both ends of the phone as they both just twigged what they had said. Then slowly put the phones down.

As soon as Winchester put the phone down it rang, it was CI Aston.

"Hello, Winchester, how are you feeling? I was informed what happened a few nights ago. Are you holding up? You have been through a tough few weeks."

"Yes, ma'am, little sore."

"I need you to come in so we can talk about your health and other stuff, I bet you are fed up being home already, well good." That was before Winchester said a word. "See you at ten am tomorrow morning, I have some desk work on a new case for you."

"New case?" Winchester interjected. "What about the one we are dealing with?"

"It's moved on now so all will be expanded on in the morning. Let's speak more when you are in. Oh yes, we will pick you up; you are for the next few weeks still under close protection."

"Why? They got everyone."

"We just need to make sure, we can't go losing you now after what you have been through, it would not look good for me," she chuckled.

Winchester has never heard the CI laugh, only smile with her big white teeth.

Jennie got home about 1830 and was very quiet, Winchester was sitting looking out of the apartment windows at the fabulous view.

"Hi," she said.

Winchester looked round and smiled. Jennie walked over and put her hands round his waist. "Did you mean what you said on the phone?"

"Did you?" Winchester asked.

"Yes, I did."

Winchester turned and said, "From the day I met you."

Jennie kissed him, then said, "Took me a few months but I seem to have got there."

They both laughed.

"Well, takeaway tonight then."

"That's great. I got the call from Aston, back to work tomorrow."

"That's good, it's for the best. You need me to take you?"

"They are sending a car."

"Yes I would, you are still classed as possible target, but from the intelligence we have you are not."

"Why was I?"

"Winchester, order the takeaway, I will shower and we'll sit and go through what I know."

They both sat on the sofa looking at each other.

"What I can tell you, the person we shot in the hospital was one of a pair."

Winchester looked confused.

"For years we could not understand why we could not catch the assassin and take them out. When SO19 took out the attempt on you the other evening, it was luck the operation had not been stood down. As soon as I came out with the coffees, I thought I was seeing a dead person come back to life, from the interrogation of the male that night, this was a personal assassination because the female assassin's sister was killed trying to take you out in the hospital. It was not sanctioned by anyone, they were instructed to clean the house and get the hell out of the country."

"So we are sure now it's over?"

"We have to make sure so give it a few weeks."

"It feels very surreal I was a target for an international assassin or assassins."

"It became apparent you knew too much, they could not determine what you knew, so they got you in your flat. Tried to drug you, see if they could not get it out of you at all. They were not going to kill you until they knew you had not passed your information on."

"I still don't understand, why wait till the hospital?"

"I said before they did not expect to get found so quickly at your place and as the assassin did not know if they had erased your memory enough to not identify her, she had to take you out; they both banked on anonymity."

Winchester said, "That's all clear as mud. Thank god it's over."

"Well," Jennie said, "you and your team are off this now, it's with us and SIS."

"Why's that?"

"Because it's an international investigation by the Government, you cannot tell anyone till your meeting next at the station with your commanders, promise me," Jennie said. "I was not meant to inform you."

"Okay, what about Reggie?"

"He also cannot be told."

"He's my best friend."

"No, Winchester, just no."

"Promise, yes okay."

In the morning Winchester was dropped off outside BOW Nick, as two uniformed officers walked out.

"Hi Winchester, getting taxis now are we. Good to see you back, mate."

"Thanks." As Winchester walked in the front desk officer let him in. Headed off to his office and saw Reggie sitting on his own.

"Hello, mate," Winchester said. Reggie got up and gave him a hug. "Wow, mate, thanks, needed that."

"We have to go upstairs to CI Aston's office. As soon as you get in we have some paperwork to look at, new case."

They both went up to the CI's office as Reggie had rang up to say Winchester was in and they would be ten minutes. On her small round meeting desk for six was a tray of tea and biscuits. She was sitting behind her desk; she smiled as they walked in – the happy teeth they both thought.

"Take a seat at the table, tea and biscuits; we need to talk. Can you close the door please.

"Well, I have some news for you both. First of all, you are both off the Underground operation. The reasons I cannot go into right now, but all will become clear Thursday; we are taking over a big case of drug trafficking shipments from Afghanistan comes through the East India Dock. So I will give you the access clearance for the files and computers; you will also be getting a heap of files to study."

As they drank their tea, CI Aston said, "Also, I need to give you some information that must not leave this room. At the end of the month, I am being promoted to DCI. Now a question: Winchester, are you still looking to become a Detective Constable?"

Before she had finished asking the question Winchester said yes with a grin on his face.

"Reggie, you have a choice: desk Sergeant or DS with me?"

Reggie looked at Winchester and said, "I am going to be in charge of him?"

"Yes."

Then he said, "Well that is a yes from me then," as Reggie patted Winchester on his sore shoulder, "yes I will," as he started to laugh.

"Great, but this is hush hush."

"Yes, ma'am."

"Will I be on your team as well?" Winchester said.

"Well yes I thought that was clear. Now both of you go to the main desk; the files have arrived. Take them to your office and get started. Also you will be still working with Lloyd and Boyd on this one as it is international, keep the team together for this job."

As they were leaving, the rest of the team came up the corridor looking a little surprised to see Winchester.

"Hi Winchester, you all good, mate, great to see you back. We're going into meeting with the CI, anything we should be worried about?"

Reggie said, "Not as far as we know," and winked at DS Robbins, Wineglass, Weston, Byrne and DS Gary Robbins, then went into the office and closed the door.

It was about an hour's work, and Reggie and Winchester had just got the last of the 60-plus files stacked on the meeting table in their office when the team came in all looking pensive.

The DS soon-to-be the new CI Robbins was saying to the team, "Look, this is bigger than us, it's a trade-off: we get this drug case that is almost ready to close down."

"Hello lads," as they walked in, "my god, is that the files?" Weston said.

"Yes, lot of homework; it's going to take a few days to put this together. DS Robbins will be the lead on this I am thinking."

Winchester said, "Yes you got that right, but we will alternately report to the DCI and the CI."

As he finished speaking, DC Wineglass said, "Tell them the good news, Gov."

"Okay, just keep this to yourselves, I will be the new CI."

DC Byrne said, "You be able to still get in your uniform? Few pounds have been put on..." as everyone started laughing.

"You are so funny. I get a new uniform. Let's get on."

Then Lloyd and Boyd walked in. "What's the occasion?"

"We are the team," Robbins said, "to deal with this big drug case."

"Yes, we have just been told about it. Really fed up we could not finish the Underground case."

The room went quiet. Everyone knew how much effort had gone into it; it's hard to let it go.

"All will be revealed Thursday morning. We have four weeks to get this sorted so everyone including the Governor's getting credit and CI Aston," Winchester said, "and the ACC I would have thought."

"Of course."

Over the next few days before reporting to the DCI and CI, the team worked on the files to get an understanding of the surveillance operations and tracking information so the team could take over from the MI5 boys and HM Customs, who will work with the team as well.

It was Thursday, the day of the meeting between SIS and the team. So everything will be explained. It was 0900, everyone was in the DCI's meeting room, the overhead projector was set up. Steven Byrne was standing at the head of the oval meeting table and everyone was facing the white screen.

Steve said, "We are just waiting for the ACC and the Major. Before we start, everyone have tea or coffee?"

Reggie said, "The biscuits are soft, must be from yesterday."

That broke the ice, few chuckles, then the door opened and the Major and ACC walked in.

"Right," Steve said, "we will get started."

The Major said, "Wait a few minutes, we have a guest, he is on his way from the toilet."

A knock on the door and in walked a big man, say 6'4", suit, short hair, very smart. You could tell by his suit before he said a word he was an American. "Good morning," he said in a deep southern accent, "Mike McClendon, FBI, based here in the UK."

Everyone nodded with confused eyes and faces. He took a seat to the side with the ACC and the major.

Steve Byrne said, "First of all before we get in to details, I would like to say this team has done a really fantastic job on getting the investigations to its current levels. It's been simply eye opening and nothing we could have ever imagined.

"I will start from the beginning. We have been investigating QPI for the last five years, we knew they were doing something, we thought it was using drugs that were not allowed to be used in the UK, ie under licence. Getting cheap drugs from third world countries, making them at 10% of the costs and selling it to the NHS and others for 1000% profits. Our colleagues in the USA, the FBI and CIA, have lost five operatives to this company, it first was looked at beginning of the 90s, the transit police in New York reported an unusually high flu and sickness on the system, it was clear this was something manmade. But as quickly as it started, it stopped. It got the interest of the FBI, the FBI reached out to other cities with underground systems to see if they have a similar situation, we answered no, we could not see it and we had no complaints from BTP. Or the MET.

"Three of the deceased people you have dealt with, were undercover operations Agents from the USA, one CIA, two ATF agents. The bodies at the hospitals that were spirited away by the CIA, UK government sanctioned." Steve look round the room, saw faces looking a little perplexed.

"I understand this is a lot to take in," the Major said. "We will answer your questions later." The Major nodded to Steve to continue on with the information overload.

"What I will get into now is the other agents you have been coming up against, Hellen Blake MI6, she is an informant for the Government, she befriended PC Winchester because he was starting to stumble into a dangerous situation and was trying to move him away from the attentions of the QPI internal security teams. The private eye Hooper works for MI5 and again was trying to directly put PC Winchester off the scent. But as we know, Winchester seems to be like a blood hound, just without the big ears—" a few chuckled in the room— "Doctor Kildare, military SIS doctor, finally the nurse you met at the last incident well, she was an QPI operative, we're sure she's the person that made sure the last agent found on the platform of Liverpool Street was deceased. She is now being tracked, she has left the country heading to Greece as we speak. Not much more I can go into without showing you the DVD we managed to smuggle out from QPI at great risk to the operation and undercover team. What I am about to show you is an instruction and information sort of operational manual. I will add something first." He looked directly at Winchester. "In fact can I have two minutes with you outside the room afterwards, Winchester."

Winchester nodded though he was not sure why.

"Good, I'll get on, shall I. Turn the lights down please."

Wineglass did, the DVD started, it went through safety notes about PPE, what was needed before they used the different canisters that had numbers on them, there were 40-plus different references to the canisters. Then Steve Byrne started to commentate on what was going on... "so we have here a chart come up, Winter, Spring, Summer, Autumn.

"Below each reference you see is noted next to the month is what to use, what canisters and code numbers we assume is different viruses." Then the DVD showed a typical train carriage for the Central line, with arrows pointing to parts of the train, Winter W,12546 use to clean all handrails pointing in the carriage.

A small arrow pointed to the grille behind the seats in the carriage, lift off and place small canister the size of small mug, Winter, W C B99089 slow release 72 hours and remove. The list went on for winter, making reference to the train will reach incubation temperatures when the train is full of people allowing the bacteria to develop very quickly.

"We have worked out the prefixed letter is the seasonal changes, so the W is winter and SP is spring etc. We have come to the conclusion this is purely for money, it's clear now it's a billion pound enterprise for QPI. Some of the viruses they use are very low in strength, this is deliberate because it will spread much quicker. We noted hayfever is used a lot in the spring and summer; this just on the modelling makes about ten billion over the counter sales of medication. What also is very worrying if a terrorist organisation ever got hold of this, we would have a real problem on our hands. We can confirm that the government sanctioned ten years ago a test that will remain in this room, in the summer to put a trace virus on the Central line that affected two million people with a small sneezing fit, two million people got affected just from one day's use on the Central line. This was done in the light of other possible attacks on the transit trains in New York. It was also carried out in other countries which had an underground network.

"Any questions before we get to the rest of it? Lights back on please."

CI Aston asked, "Why has this gone on so long?"

The Major jumped in. "We knew they were up to something but we were not sure what they were doing, sometimes doing something in plain sight is missed. It was the observation of your officers that got our attention. We also had a communication for the FBI informing us they had lost contact with a few people and we needed to act to help.

"Through Interpol and yourself we have concluded they have been doing this for about eight years for money. The money we are talking now is hundreds of billions and they will not just write this off easily. That is why the undercover agents have been eliminated, we think."

DCI Dolan asked, "Why have you not taken this company down?"

The Major said, "That company is a worldwide global company, it has given money to third world countries, it currently is helping one country to stave off the world's bank default."

"Who is that?" Reggie asked.

"That is well above everyone's pay grade in this room."

Steve Byrne said, "We are now taking over this operation as you well know, but what I can say is thank you all for your understanding and I know this is frustrating for you not to see this through, but believe me when I say we will stop this."

The DCI asked, "What about the head of QPI, Nicholas Dazary?"

"He is a very, very powerful man and has friends in the G7 countries, he is almost untouchable. He is a very intelligent man and no roads lead back to him; him and Bill Gates are the same level, need I say more?"

Lloyd spoke up. "What about the planes?"

"Good question. We are not sure what they do, what we can gather, it has to be airborne, we cannot be 100%, the filter systems on planes are really good. It's still a mystery to us. What about you, Winchester?" Steve asked.

Winchester looked surprised. "Who, me, why would I know?"

"Just checking," Steve chuckled; so did the rest of the room. "What we are sure about is it's not used on overland trains, our scientists have looked at the swabs you had done when you pulled the train in a few months ago; they work for us."

Everyone looked at each other.

DCI Dolan said, "Next you'll be telling us the tea lady Janet works for you too."

He looked hard at her and said, "You never know. It seems the viruses they use are suited to the underground systems, very compact, not much movement of air and the heat generated by humans on a crowed train is a perfect incubator.

"The viruses they use are airborne and can be spread through touch. Nothing we would say was deadly, all mild. Enough to spread like a wildfire.

"Overland trains they have air flow and are by their very nature getting airflow from the outside and they don't get that warm.

"So in conclusion, we have uncovered a very dangerous, Machiavellian and unscrupulous Operation right under our noses and the biggest worry we did not see it in plain line of sight. Again, I thank your team for bringing this to our attention."

The DCI said, "We didn't."

"You did," Steve said, "as soon as you went to the hospital and our operatives become involved; we are everywhere you know; we have to integrate into all walks of society, terrorists are more active than they have ever been. SIS has been dealing with the IRA and other organisations for years.

"Any questions?"

Reggie said, "What happens now?"

"Well we are going to debrief your team over the next few days and take all the files; we will take a long-term view with this situation and will work closely with Interpol and the USA. We will not require any more assistance," the Major said very sternly.

Winchester said, "Why do I feel we are being fobbed off with a drugs trafficking ring?"

The CI was very quick to jump in and said, "Winchester, they are doing this out of respect for our hard work; this happens all the time." She shut down Winchester very quickly and everyone knew this would be a big thing for this station and division to get this big drug bust.

"Your CI is right," the Major said. "I understand your frustrations, all the time and effort and personal investment, it's politically a real situation that can only be dealt with by the security services. One miss-step and reputations and careers will be over. Now if this has explained everything, we need to move."

Steve said, "Winchester, can I speak with you after everyone has left? Before you all leave, I'd just like to say one more thing: this is not the end of the matter, but it has to go up to the Home Office and the Home Secretary, they will deal with it in a way that is above all of the people in this room's security clearance. It is not what you want to hear. But on this, I will say if this comes out or is in the press or any leak, the only people in this room will be held culpable. If we find anyone leaking it you will be spending a long time away from your families and friends – do I make myself very clear?"

The room was quiet; this is the second time this has been said and it drove it home. It was said very calmly, very matter of fact. Everyone was left in no doubt.

"We look forward to working with some of you again in the future, I am sure," Steve said. "We are finished."

Winchester walked over to Steve as the Major shook the hands of everyone who left the room and then walked out with the CI and DCI in some sort of private conversation. Steve put his hand out and shook Winchester's hand. Standing at the door was DS Robbins waiting to speak to Steve Byrne.

"Just to let you know, Jennie is not part of this investigation. She took herself off after the first time she met you, she said you were someone special and she felt that something bonded between you the first time you met. I think you needed to know that, she was not just with you to keep a watching brief. That is why she went away for a few months. Let us get a handle on the situation. Jennie is my friend, a great girl, you're a lucky man. Oh, DS Robbins or should I say Gary." They both hugged.

"So good to see you my old friend," Gary said.

Winchester looked confused.

Gary said, "We go back a long way, we are best friends, we were inseparable as we grew up, lived together, did everything together. Missed you, mate."

Steve said, "We must always keep in touch."

"We do," Gary said, "but only twice a year, well you know, away on operations most of the time."

"You married, Gary?"

"No bloody way! Are you?"

Steve said, "Gary, you know me, that's never going to happen. Want to go out tonight, mate?"

"Yep, let's go out," as they put their arms over each other's shoulders and walked out of the meeting room talking. They look so happy, Winchester thought, just looked like brothers.

Winchester and the team had a new case to look into and Reggie was going to be a Sergeant and Winchester a DC effective from now. The new DCI Aston was changing things for the better along with the new ACC Dolan, and CI Robbins was still the bossy boots he always was.

Jennie and Winchester were living together in London. It was a few months later when a news story came on the TV and Radio – three people were arrested trying to put poison canisters on an underground train. The minister for transport was interviewed and said, "In light of this worrying situation, we are stepping up security, it is a very safe way of travelling – that is why the British transport police was very quick to intercept the suspect. To put the public's mind at rest we have agreed with the unions from now, on each train, there will be fitted CCTV on every carriage. The drivers will be inspecting the trains before they takeover each turn round or first thing in the morning and closed down at night. As always, please be vigilant."

Winchester saw this on the news saying someone has been captured for what they have been doing, a fall guy that is for sure. The team made the biggest drugs bust in the Met for 20 years, it was a 30 million pound haul, came in up the Thames in a rubbish barge pulled by a tug. Fifteen arrests, major drug ring shut down, all over the press, everyone on the top floor patting each other on the back; the ACC Jamie Mills went off with a big deal under his belt; the DCI was getting her promotion to ACC effective immediately, as did CI Aston to DCI.

Winchester was still not 100% convinced the story of the virus spreading on the underground was over, he still felt it was a big cover up by the security services because of the embarrassment to the Government. He was sitting on Jennie's balcony drinking a cup of coffee.

Winchester said to Jennie, "I feel that I did not get the job done."

She looked at him and said, "You are going to need to get used to it, when you deal with very powerful people with very powerful friends, sometimes you just have to let it go. The security services will keep this in their locker and will use the information to an advantage."

They both watched the sun going down over the city.

Jennie said, "You were right: Janet the tea lady, she is MI5, always has been but you must never tell anyone."

Winchester smiled. He was right again.

www.ingramcontent.com/pod-product-compliance
Lightning Source LLC
Chambersburg PA
CBHW050016180626
46810CB00002B/438